SLAVE OF THE VOODOO SPELL

Madelaine La Branche watched from behind the vines as a beautiful woman, her skin like onyx, leaped into the semi-circle of Negroes gathered around the fire. Madelaine knew it was Vedette, the voodoo queen, as the woman weaved to the beat of the drums.

Vedette reached into a large box inscribed with strange symbols, bringing out a writhing mass of coils—a huge snake that entwined itself around her lithe body, moving to the primal rhythm.

Suddenly, a giant Negro, his naked skin glistening in the firelight, leaped in front of the vines that concealed Madelaine. He extended his hand to her, his gleaming eyes holding her as if she were a bird, and he the snake. Without willing it, the young white girl's hand met his, and he pulled her out into the semi-circle.

How black he is, Madelaine thought as she began to sway uncontrollably. Her long hair came loose, tumbling down her back, and she tore at the buttons of her gown. She stepped out of her dress and undulated beside the giant Black, feeling the heat of his naked flesh as she abandoned herself to the all-consuming spell of the voodoo beat . . .

The Making of America Series

THE
CREOLES

Lee Davis
Willoughby

A DELL/BRYANS BOOK

Published by
Dell Publishing Co., Inc.
1 Dag Hammarskjold Plaza
New York, New York 10017

Dell ® TM 681510, Dell Publishing Co., Inc.

ISBN: 0-440-01526-X

Printed in the United States of America

First printing—June 1982

Chapter 1

ALL streets leading to the square were thronged with processions and onlookers. Tanguy La Branche, staring down from a crowded Cabildo balcony, was taken back seven years to Paris and the rioting mobs in the city streets. He shook his head to dispel the memory. This was New Orleans, not Paris and, despite the thin drizzle, the Creoles were celebrating.

Below, to the left of the Place d'Armes, the Louisiana Regiment and the New Orleans militia stood at attention. To the right, the Spanish Cavalry Squadron sat stiffly on their mounts. The Spanish flag hung wet and limp but nothing dampened the spirit of the crowds about the square.

The wooden gallows thrusting up near the flagpole seemed out of place, an unpleasant reminder that the Place d'Armes had less joyous usages. The sight of it made Guy remember that this November 30, 1803, wasn't exactly the festive occasion that most thought.

He felt a hand tug at his sleeve.

"Guy, we can't see," his sister Madelaine complained.

Taking advantage of his authority as an aide of *Prefet* de Laussat, Guy cleared a space at the balcony's iron railing for Madelaine and her friend Annette-Louise Courchaine. No one objected, the men smiling at the two pretty fifteen-year-olds in their high-waisted gowns and colorful shawls and bonnets.

A thunder of cannon from the *Argo,* the French brig-of-war anchored in the Mississippi River just beyond the Place d'Armes, saluted the arrival of *Prefet* de Laussat and the Spanish officials as their processions halted in front of the Cabildo, the government building.

When he'd been sent home to *Nouvelle-Orleans* from France, Guy's eyes, dazzled by *la belle* Paris, saw the small, stockaded town of his birth as a country village instead of the city he'd always believed it to be. New Orleans had perhaps four thousand houses and certainly no more than ten thousand inhabitants, half white, the rest either free colored or Negro slaves. But New Orleans was his home and he loved it.

Annette-Louise turned her head to glance at him. As he met her gaze, she blushed and looked quickly away. He smiled, wondering if she realized he still thought of her as a little girl despite her ripening figure. Hadn't she and Madelaine plagued him ever since they were toddlers, getting underfoot, trying to follow him and his friends everywhere?

"They're coming into the Cabildo," Madelaine said. "What happens next, Guy?"

"Governor Salcedo and *Prefet* de Laussat will sign the documents issued by Napoleon and agreed to by King Charles of Spain, the papers that transfer the colony of Louisiana back to France after forty-one years of Spanish rule. Think—we'll be able to call ourselves French in truth."

"We're Creoles," Madelaine said, "not French."

"Yes, but a Spaniard born in the Louisiana colony can also call himself a Creole," Guy said, "while he can never be a Frenchman."

"I think maybe being a Creole is enough," Madelaine said.

6

Guy shrugged. She'd never been to France, she didn't understand.

After a time, the *prefet* and the governor, followed by the *marquis* de Casa-Calvo, the Spanish commissioner, said to be the man who'd really ruled the colony, appeared on a tiny balcony to Guy's right. The crowd below cheered.

As the troops presented arms and the *Argo* saluted with cannon volleys, the Spanish flag came down and the French tricolor rose to the top of the staff. Guy threw up his arms and shouted in triumph, his cry echoed by hundreds of Creoles, the shouts continuing as the Spanish troops withdrew from the square.

"This is a proud day for Louisiana," *Prefet* de Laussat said, beginning his speech.

Proud, yes, Guy told himself, but in truth, a mockery. He recalled what the *prefet* told him when he'd been appointed as aide.

"Tanguy, you already speak Spanish in addition to our language. I must insist you also learn English."

"May I ask why, *prefet*?"

De Laussat had sighed. "I have the curse of being able to choose the best course for the benefit of the most, even though it goes against my own instincts. I don't expect you to understand why I ask this of you. Do it."

Guy had complied, inadvertantly teaching English to Madelaine when he asked her to help him memorize words.

He smiled at her now, though her attention was on de Laussat. Intelligence as well as beauty shone in her sable eyes. If only she could be a bit less willful, a trifle less determined to have her own way. Creole women should be accommodating.

He forced his mind back to the speech, one he'd heard many times as the *prefet* tried it out on his aides. Guy was the youngest of them, only nineteen.

"Money can never be ignored," his friend Rafe Devol had said pointedly.

7

Guy knew the truth of this. His father had left him La Belle, the sugar plantation with its manor house and vast acreage below New Orleans as well as the yet undeveloped land on Lake Pontchartrain and the townhouse on the rue de Royal. Certainly Pierre de Laussat took this into consideration when choosing his aides, although Guy hoped there'd also been other reasons for his appointment.

After the speeches were over, Guy saw Annette-Louise safely to the Courchaine townhouse, then walked with Madelaine the four *islets*, the four blocks, to the rue de Royal. The ditches along the dirt streets ran with water and mud splashed up onto the *banquette*, the sidewalk, from passing horses.

"My slippers will be quite ruined," Madelaine protested, poking a satin-covered toe from beneath her gown.

"If you expect me to carry you, you'll have a long wait, dear sister," he said. "I happen to know you have dozens of other slippers while I'm your one and only brother. Wear out the shoes, not me."

She slanted a look at him. "Do you imply I'm too plump? I'll have you know that just yesterday a gentleman admired my figure most fervently."

Guy frowned at her and she laughed, showing a dimple in her left cheek.

"I hope it wasn't Philippe Roulleaux," he said. "I saw him talking to Annette-Louise and it certainly seemed to me you were enjoying the encounter."

"Can I help it if my best friend and your worst enemy are attracted to one another?"

"Nicolas has the honor of being my worst enemy, not his younger brother Philippe. But Philippe is also a Roulleaux and don't you forget it. Any Roulleaux is a foe of a La Branche."

Madelaine stopped walking and faced him, hands on her hips. "The stars will fall from the sky before a La Branche will forgive a Roulleaux," she intoned mockingly. *"Pouf!"*

"Those words are not a joking matter," he told her, tak-

8

ing her arm and urging her along. "How can you forget papa was killed by a Roulleaux?"

"In a duel!" she cried. "Papa challenged him over a trifle. All because of some ancient fight more than a hundred years ago. Great-great-great grandfather Yvon may have had his reason for saying what he did about falling stars, but why do we have to keep on with it?"

"When has a Roulleaux offered to forgive one of us?" he demanded.

"Someone must be first—why not a La Branche? There's only the two of us left, you and me. How many Roulleauxes? Nicolas and Philippe. It's time to forgive and forget before there are none left on either side."

"You're safe enough from duels, Madelaine."

She clutched at his arm. "How can I bear it if you challenge Nicolas and are killed?"

A wry smile touched Guy's lips. "Maybe I wouldn't die. I could be lucky."

"I don't want you to kill Nicolas or Philippe either. I've had enough of death. *Maman* and our baby sister and papa . . ."

He looked at her exquisite heart-shaped face, framed by her black curls, and felt his heart contract. He couldn't bear to think that anything unpleasant would ever happen to Madelaine. She was so pretty, so trusting and so dangerously headstrong. At fifteen, she might not recognize the pitfalls that lay in wait for young women.

"Are you so interested in the welfare of the Roulleauxes because of your encounter with young Philippe?" he asked.

"You twist what I say," she said angrily. "Is it so wrong to worry about my brother?"

Guy smiled at her, relieved. "Any day now Gabriel Davion will offer for you and you'll have a husband to keep you busy so you won't have time to fuss over me."

She tossed her curls. "What makes you think I'll accept Gabriel?"

Guy shook his head. Poor Gabriel would have his hands

9

full turning Madelaine into a proper Creole wife. How empty La Belle would seem with her gone. He'd not yet found a woman he cared to marry but, of course he'd have to think about taking a bride one of these days.

The Roulleaux curse on his La Branche ancestor slid into his head. "Seven times have you stabbed me, Yvon La Branche. Before I die, I ask Almighty God above and the Devil below, whichever of them will heed my prayer, to wither your line before seven generations take their place in the sun."

Yes, he'd have to consider marrying, if only to produce an heir to spite that ancient Roulleaux.

By late afternoon the rain had diminished. Guy saw Madelaine, resplendent in gold velvet, to the Courchaine townhouse. She was to be chaperoned by Annette-Louise's mother at the evening ball given by Governor Salcedo in honor of de Laussat.

Guy continued on to the governor's house. The men, as usual, would gamble before the women arrived and also after the dancing. He touched the ruby ring on his left hand, his lucky ring. He never gambled without it, neither at cards nor dicing.

His father had introduced the dice game of Hazard to New Orleans. Craps, the bedamned *Americains* called it, after the name they called the Creoles, *crapauds,* frogs.

As he neared the corner of Toulouse and Levee, a carriage drew up at the governor's gate and Luis Cirillo, long and lean, climbed out, assisted his wife, plump as a stuffed sausage, to descend, then turned to help a young woman to the ground.

Guy caught his breath.

Mon Dieu, who was she? Spanish, no mistaking that haughty look, but beautiful, a rarity, a blonde *senorita,* her eyes blue as sapphires. Guy bowed to the Cirillos and watched them and the *senorita* walk ahead of him through the gate and into the courtyard. He followed slowly.

A hand clapped him on the back and Guy turned to see his friend Gabriel Davion grinning at him.

"Guy, you look bereft of your senses. I never thought I'd live to see the day a woman struck you dumb. Can it be the *senorita* has added you to her string of conquests without even a glance in your direction?"

"Who is she?" Guy demanded. "Why haven't I met her before?"

"Ah, while you've been amusing yourself trotting about after the *prefet*, the rest of us have gotten a head start. Although, *helas*, Nicolas Roulleaux leads the pack for she smiles at him oftener than at anyone else. Her name is Senalda Gabaldon, the niece of *Senora* Cirillo and she's on a visit from Spain."

Gabriel took Guy's arm and urged him across the courtyard. "You won't see her again until the ladies join us, so come console yourself with the turn of the cards."

"Dice, I think," Guy said. "But a bit later."

Once inside the house, Gabriel left him to go to one of the eight gaming tables. Guy looked for *Prefet* de Laussat, passing two long dinner tables set with silver and crystal. He spotted de Laussat with a group of Creoles but, before he reached him, Guy was intercepted by Andre Lafreniere, a plump man with thinning hair who'd been a friend of his father's.

"I wish your papa had lived to see this day," Andre said. "He never took to the Spanish. 'Long-nosed, stiff,' he called them."

Guy wondered what Andre would say if he told him the most beautiful *senorita* in the world had just captured his heart. But it was true his father had hated the *marquis* de Casa-Calvo. Hadn't the *marquis* helped Bloody O'Reilly put down the New Orlean's rebellion against Spain before Guy was born? In 1768 it had been, and one of Andre Lafreniere's distant cousins, a ring-leader, had faced the firing squad for challenging the Spaniards.

"Is it true, as they say," Andre asked, "we shall be Frenchmen for only a brief time?"

"I fear the rumors are right," Guy said. He'd been

warned by de Laussat not to talk about what would happen in the next month, but he couldn't lie to Andre.

Andre sighed. "At least the Spanish are gentlemen, they have manners. Whatever will we do with the *Kaintocks?* Louts, every one. Drunken brawlers."

Guy didn't want to be drawn into a conversation about this touchy matter after being warned away from it by the *prefet.*

"Why not join me in a game?" he asked Andre, inclining his head toward the nearest dice table. He'd gamble a little, since the *prefet* seemed too occupied to be interrupted at the moment.

"I prefer cards, thanks all the same." Andre slapped Guy on the shoulder. "I trust you'll be luckier than your papa with the dice." He dug an elbow into Guy's ribs. "Still, you might do better to take after him with the ladies—a *success fou*, eh?"

"I can't claim papa's luck there," Guy said, smiling. "At least not yet."

As he sauntered toward the gaming table, Guy glanced once more at de Laussat, still talking to the group of men.

"I count on you to give the proper toast," the *prefet* had said earlier. "We'll speak of it at the party."

Now didn't appear to be the best time. Guy reached the dice table and looked over the shoulder of one of the players. A Spaniard had a large stack of gold coins piled in front of him. The other players, mostly Creoles, weren't doing as well.

Guy touched the arm of the Creole in front of him, a man he knew slightly. "*Monsieur,*" he said politely, "pardon, but is there room for one more?"

Guy won a little, lost a little, then won heavily until the Spaniard was far behind and quit the table. A man slipped into the empty space. Guy glanced at him and stiffened.

Nicolas Roulleaux.

They usually avoided gambling at the same table. Why had Nicolas chosen this one? An accident? Or was the choice deliberate?

There was a brief silence as the other gamblers looked from Guy to Nicolas, then began to talk in loud voices.

Nicolas' friend, Marc de la Harpe, came up to look over Nicolas' shoulder and, a moment later, Guy sensed someone behind him, looked back and saw Gabriel. Like seconds for a duel, he thought.

When Nicolas' uncle had met Guy's father near the Bayou St. John for their fight with the *colichemarde*, the rapier, Guy's father had died on the field while Roulleaux lived but a day, a lung punctured. How would it be when he, Guy, faced Nicolas?

Guy practiced every day with fencing foils, his teacher a master fencer named Francois La Branche, a free man of color sired on a mulatto woman by Guy's father. Black or no, Francois was the finest swordsman in the city. Guy had never bested Francois though he felt he came closer each day.

If he faced Nicolas there'd be no nonsense about first blood. A duel to the death was the only possibility between a La Branche and a Roulleaux.

"I feel lucky tonight," Nicolas announced.

Guy smiled thinly.

"Lucky enough to challenge the toss of the dice," Nicolas went on, "and lucky enough to win the most beautiful woman in New Orleans."

"*Senorita* Gabaldon?" Marc asked.

"None other." Nicolas threw down a handful of gold coins. "She's already promised me the first dance. Weep while you watch us for I shan't relinquish her."

Guy forced himself to remain silent though the arrogant curl of Nicolas' lip infuriated him.

From the first throw of the dice, Nicolas lost. Lost and lost again while Guy's winnings piled higher. Guy began to feel nothing was out of his reach. When Nicolas lost yet once again, Guy stared at him until Nicolas met his gaze.

"You may have your dance," Guy said. "You may monopolize *Senorita* Gabaldon for the evening. But not after.

13

Before Mardi Gras, Senalda Gabaldon will be my bride, the mistress of La Belle."

There was a dead silence at the table. Voices and laughter came from others in the room to Guy's ears as though from another country. Nicolas' hazel eyes gleamed with anger as he drew himself up stiffly. The moments stretched out as the two men faced each other. Then Nicolas took a deep breath and visibly relaxed, forcing a laugh. He gestured at the gold on the table in front of Guy.

"Every man knows the saying. Lucky at dice, unlucky at love. I don't believe you'll marry her, before or after Mardi Gras."

All eyes swung to Guy. A quiver of fury swept through him. *Dieu,* how he hated this man. Nothing but a challenge could satisfy him now. He started to speak but his words were lost in the roar of cannon. Everyone started.

"The guns!" Gabriel shouted. "We must drink the toasts."

Abandoning the gaming tables, the men hurried to the dining room where candles gleamed in the silver chandeliers overhead. Wine sparkled in crystal decanters and stemmed glasses. Gold braid glinted on military uniforms.

Luis Cirillo raised his glass of white champagne. "To the First Consul of France, Napoleon Bonaparte," he said. "To the French Republic."

The two land batteries and the *Argo's* cannon boomed through a twenty-one gun salvo while the men drank, standing.

After all the glasses were empty, Pierre de Laussat picked up a goblet of rose champagne. "To King Charles of Spain," he said. All drank again while the guns roared.

De Laussat's eyes fastened on his young aide and Guy frowned. What toast did the prefet expect of him? De Laussat inclined his head toward the wine on the table. Guy took a deep breath, realizing the toast must be to what was to come.

Guy reached for a glass of white champagne and raised

it. "To President Thomas Jefferson," he cried. "To the United States of America."

There was a moment's silence. He saw de Laussat's approval, Andre Lafreniere's sardonic glance, Gabriel's raised eyebrows and the mocking smile of Nicolas Roulleaux. Then everyone lifted their glasses and drank as the cannon continued their salute.

Nicolas grabbed a glass. "To the fair and lovely ladies of all countries," he said.

With wild shouts of approval, the men drank, glasses raised in complete agreement.

For the moment.

Chapter 2

THE day was clear, the weather mild after the rain. Guy sauntered along the *banquette,* the plank sidewalk, past delicately colored two-story houses of blue and peach and pale green stuccoed-over brick. Across the street a Negro woman, a slave, emerged from one of the tall glass doors onto the lower gallery.

The contrast of dark skin with her red *tignon,* the madras handkerchief tied over her head, was pleasing to the eye. The Spanish hadn't succeeded in humbling the Creoles of color with Governor Miro's ordinance twenty-five years before that forced *tignons* onto the heads of Louisiana women of color, free or slave. None had dared to appear in public without a *tignon* since then, but female ingenuity had made *tignons* ornaments to enhance the beauty of the women.

The slave sloshed water from a bucket across the wooden floor, once, twice. Through the iron scrolls of the carriage gate, Guy caught a glimpse of a banana tree rising in a courtyard. A small yellow bird flew through the space between the tip of the gates and the archway above and soared into the washed blue of the sky.

Blue as the Spanish eyes of Senalda Gabaldon. Guy's

steps slowed as he remembered dancing with her last night, for one dance only. Ah, how beautiful she was, but how aloof. She wished to return to what she called the "civility of Madrid." He'd have his work cut out convincing her she should stay in New Orleans and marry him. Before Mardi Gras. Not merely because he'd openly announced his intentions, but because he wanted Senalda for a wife. After seeing her, only she would do. He hadn't seriously considered marriage before meeting her.

"Un bon placage vaut mieux qu'un mauvais mariage." A good *placage* is better than a bad marriage. He muttered the words under his breath. Wasn't it possible for both to be good?

He was no different that most of the Creole men he knew, taking a free woman of color as a *placee,* in place of a wife.

Francois, the fencing master, was born of such a union between Guy's father and a mulatto named Genevieve Olivier. She'd died of yellow fever the same year the disease killed Guy's mother and his baby sister.

Francois was seven years older than Guy, a black half-brother, freed as a matter of course by his father. He bore the La Branche name and was certainly as talented as any La Branche with the sword—as well as with the mulatto women, or so it was rumored. But, of course, no black could ever inherit a white father's property. Francois had no claim on La Belle.

Surely Senalda would be happy at La Belle, Guy thought. He'd make her as happy as she'd make him by consenting to the marriage.

As he neared St. Louis Cathedral, next to the Cabildo at the Place d'Armes, Guy looked to his left, seeing the masts of the ships in the river, French, Spanish and American, stretch out like a forest afloat, as many ships as he'd ever seen anchored there at one time. He turned right onto Orleans, passed the gardens behind the church and walked toward the rue des Ramparts, his pace quickening. He'd not see Aimee for nearly a week with the press of his duties as aide to the *prefet*.

Ah, Aimee, with her skin the color of heavy cream and as smooth and tasty. She had the ripest breasts, the roundest hips of any quadroon in the city. Guy smiled as he remembered how he'd won her from the very arms of Nicolas Roulleaux at one of this year's Quadroon Balls. Aimee had been far and away the belle of the ball.

Gentle Aimee, eager to please him in all ways. Was he to give her up when he married? Not all men deserted their *placees* when they married. He'd at least see Aimee was provided for. If Senalda was his, he wouldn't need a *placee*. Would he? Some men said otherwise.

His father hadn't given up Genevieve for there'd been other children besides Francois, one a girl the same age as Madelaine. All except Francois were now dead of Bronze John, the yellow fever.

The afternoon was too fine to spend worrying about the future. It would take care of itself, would all work out. Meanwhile, he'd enjoy Aimee.

At the rue des Ramparts, Guy turned to his left toward a row of one-storied white cottages built directly on the ground. Aimee's was at the far end, somewhat apart from its neighbors. He'd bought it for her. As he hurried his steps, he saw her on the porch, waving. She ran to meet him and Guy caught her in his embrace.

"Oh, I've missed you so," she whispered.

He picked her up, carried her into the house, strode directly to the bedroom and laid her atop a spread of ecru lace covering the mahogany four-poster.

"*Un minute, s'il vous plait*," she begged, sliding off the bed and taking off the lace cover, folding it carefully. Her hands began to unbutton his waistcoat.

"No," he said. "Take your clothes off. I want to see you as I undress."

With the charming grace of a kitten she swayed and bent as she slipped off her gown and her chemise. The light brown nipples of her breasts came erect as he gazed at her, his coat and shirt in his hands.

She was lovely, a pale yellow Venus, and she was his. Guy tore at the buttons of his breeches, ripping one off in his haste. It rolled onto the floor as he yanked his breeches down, stepped out of them and reached for Aimee.

She came into his arms with a little cry and then he could think of nothing but his need, feeling her silky skin, the softness of her breasts. He lifted her onto the bed and lay beside her, wanting to savor his excitement, but when he touched her he couldn't wait.

Her sex was smooth and warm as he entered her and she clung to him, fueling his desire so that it rose out of control, mounting, mounting, until he exploded in a spasm of release.

A few moments later he lay beside her again, facing her, lazily watching the rise and fall of her round breasts. His fingers moved to a nipple and he caressed it gently.

"What have you done while you were missing me?" he asked.

He thought she tensed. "I—I've done nothing," she said.

Guy raised himself on one elbow to look at her. She stared up at him, her yellow cat's eyes wide.

"Nothing at all?" he said.

Tears spilled over and ran down her cheeks. "Oh, why do you ask?" she cried. "You know I'm yours and no other's."

"Sweet Aimee, I wasn't accusing you."

She began to sob brokenly. Guy gathered her into his arms, stroking her back. "Hush," he murmured. "Hush."

She pressed against him, her tears damp on his chest. As he caressed her, his hands moved down her back and along her hips until at last she sighed and wiped at her eyes. He trailed his hand along her thigh, between her thighs and she quivered and clung to him.

His mouth found her breasts, first one, then the other. Aimee moaned, closing her eyes. He kissed her eyelids,

19

tasting the salt of her tears, then ran his tongue over her lips until they parted.

"My love, my heart," she whispered.

When he mounted her he did so gently, easing inside with a slow rhythm that increased only when she arched to him, her hands insistent on his back. Then he let himself go, pounding into her faster and faster, hearing her small cries of pleasure before his own passion climaxed.

Aimee slid from the bed a few minutes later.

"Don't go," he said.

"But I must find the button you lost and sew it back onto your breeches." She slipped her arms into a peach-colored robe whose thin batiste revealed the contours of her shapely body.

He watched with amused affection as she threaded a needle and bent to her task with solemn concentration. She was dear and wonderful and he would take care of her always.

Aimee looked nothing like her mother, Vedette Rusert, f.w.c., free woman of color, who'd once been the *placee* of a Creole planter from upriver. Vedette was tall and thin and her skin was darker. He'd only seen her once.

"Aimee, does your mother still dance the voodoo?" he asked.

She looked at him in surprise. "She's the *voodooienne,* the voodoo queen—she must dance."

"Doesn't it frighten you?"

"A little. I don't like to go to the voodoo. Since I have my house here with you, I never go. My sister Estelle . . ." She paused.

"I've met Estelle," he said. Taller, older, darker, more like their mother. Estelle had never been presented at a Quadroon Ball, no Creole would chose her as a *placee.* She was the wrong type. "What about her?"

"Estelle understands voodoo. She's not afraid of the snake like I am. She goes." Aimee bit off the thread and smoothed the breeches across her lap. "There."

He yawned and sat up. "I'm hungry," he said.

Aimee rose and placed his breeches on the chair. "I've made okra gumbo with shrimp and *pain patate,* sweet potato cake."

"Have you wine?"

Aimee bit her lip. "Only *biere douce,* sweet beer, I'm afraid."

Guy liked the Creole beer made from the skins and eyes of pineapples fermented with sugar, rice and water. He smiled at her. "My favorite meal."

Aimee served him, taking nothing herself while he ate, although he urged her to sit with him. "I'm not hungry, that's all," she told him.

"Can you please stay for the night?" she asked hesitantly as she set coffee before him.

He took a sip and sighed appreciatively. She'd made the coffee exactly as he liked it. *Noir comme le Diable, forte comme la mort, doux comme l'amour, chaud comme l'enfer.* Black as the devil, strong as death, sweet as love, hot as hell.

"I can't stay," he said. "I'd like to, but I can't. There's a party tonight, one every night this week to celebrate the Spanish transfer, and the *prefet* expects me to attend them all."

She crossed her arms over her breasts as if cold, though the room was warm enough. He reached out to touch her. "I wish I could be with you tonight," he said. Still she didn't smile or change her posture.

"What's the matter, Aimee? Are you all right?"

She dropped her arms, only to clutch her fingers nervously together. "I'm fine. I'm very well. Nothing is wrong."

"Sit, then, and have coffee with me."

Aimee poured herself a half cup and perched on the edge of a chair next to him. She touched the cup to her lips. The sun slanting through the slatted blind on the window gleamed in the black hair curling to her waist. She turned her head and he noticed the lovely curve of her throat. Desire flickered in him again.

If only he'd ridden instead of walking. There wasn't time. Guy got up from the table. Aimee rose, too, taking his arm and pressing her body against his side as she walked with him to the front door.

"Tomorrow?" she said hopefully.

He lifted her chin and looked into her eyes. Something troubled her. Was it his week's absence? "I'll come tomorrow," he promised.

As he walked away from the cottage he saw a dark-skinned woman dressed in white, her *tignon* white as well, and as she passed, he recognized her as Estelle, Aimee's sister. He turned and called her name.

She stopped, looked back at him, then turned to face him. She said nothing, her large eyes as dark and unrevealing as bayou water.

"Estelle, I want to ask you about Aimee," he said. "She's upset. Do you know why?"

"You'd have to ask her, *Monsieur* La Branche. Only Aimee can say."

"If you know, tell me," he demanded.

"There's nothing to tell you."

He stared at her, certain now there was a great deal wrong and also certain Estelle wouldn't reveal a thing. She looked sullen, almost defiant. He quelled an urge to grab her shoulders and shake the truth from her. It wouldn't do to lay hands on Estelle in the street, and besides, he had little time to spare. Already the gaming tables at the party would be . . .

He heard a shriek and looked over Estelle's head to see Aimee running from the house toward them.

Estelle turned just as Aimee flung herself at her sister. "No, you mustn't tell him," Aimee cried. "You promised you wouldn't. Not him or *maman*. You promised."

Estelle put an arm about Aimee and urged her back toward the cottage. "Be still," she said. "Don't be a spectacle for others to watch." She didn't glance at Guy.

He stood for a moment watching them. By damn, he'd discover once and for all what this was about, he vowed, striding after the two women. Aimee wept wildly and he took her other arm, helping Estelle lead her inside. He shut the door.

"You may as well tell me," he said to Estelle, his voice cutting through Aimee's wailing.

Estelle sat beside Aimee on a settee upholstered in gold velvet and held her sister in her arms. She looked at Guy over Aimee's head.

"No," Aimee sobbed. "Please, no."

"I must speak now, *cherie,*" Estelle told her. "It's too late to ask for silence." She took a deep breath. "I want you to understand, first of all, that Aimee isn't to blame. She's not like me, not a fighter and she was helpless."

"I know what Aimee is like," Guy said impatiently. "Just explain what's wrong."

"He came here two nights ago, Aimee told me. She thought it was you and so opened the door. He pushed past her into the house. Aimee was so frightened she couldn't cry or even move. And who'd have listened if she had screamed for help?"

"Who was he?" Guy spoke through clenched teeth, glaring down at the two women.

"He took Aimee against her will," Estelle said angrily, tightening her hold on her sister. "She's afraid you'll blame her and leave her. She says she'd die if you left her, and she well might. So she didn't tell you. Aimee has feelings for you . . ."

"Damn Aimee's feelings," Guy shouted. "Who is this man?"

"*Monsieur* Roulleaux," Estelle said. "*Monsieur* Nicolas Roulleaux."

In the blueness of early evening Guy paced back and forth on the *banquette* across the street from the Roulleaux townhouse. Seized with fury as he was, he still wouldn't lower himself to ask for entrance into the house. Nicolas would be out sooner or later—he could wait.

Guy took deep breaths, trying to calm himself. His *defi*, his challenge to Nicolas, must be proper even though he longed to batter the bastard with his fists, to grind him into the mud of the street with his boots.

The small door to the courtyard opened, a man came out. Guy drew himself up and stalked across the street. "Nicolas Roulleaux!" he called.

The man turned. "I'm Philippe," he said.

Guy stopped abruptly. The brothers looked much alike, and in the fading light he'd mistaken the slighter Philippe for Nicolas. They both had the same brown curls, the same hazel eyes. Roulleaux eyes.

"I seek your brother, not you," he said. "Where is he?"

"Who seeks me?" Nicolas' voice came from behind Guy. He whirled, saw Nicolas standing in the courtyard door.

Guy strode back to him, raised his hand and slapped Nicolas across the cheek, a light blow but hard enough to jerk Nicolas' head to the side. Guy gritted his teeth to keep the furious words back. A *defi* must remain courteous.

"To the death." Guy's voice was low and intense. "No apology accepted. You know the cause, it need not be stated."

Nicolas smiled mockingly. "If you think you've grown expert enough to challenge a master," he said, "we shall meet. My choice is the *colichemarde*, the rapier."

"My second will be Gabriel Davion," Guy told him.

"Marc de la Harpe will be mine. *Sous les chenes*, under the oaks?"

"I prefer to meet on the Fortin plantation, in the old place," Guy said. He didn't add that La Branches had met Roulleauxes there before. Nicolas knew this as well as he did.

After the duel, he knew, the question would be asked a hundred times and more in the coffee houses.

"Which of them lived?"

Guy vowed the answer wouldn't be, "Nicolas Roulleaux."

Chapter 3

ALTHOUGH the sun had risen, tendrils of mist still wavered like ghost moss in the branches of the cypress trees edging St. John's Bayou. Frogs croaked in unison and from among the reeds came the high-pitched whistling call of a red-winged blackbird.

Guy shifted from one foot to the other, his rapier unsheathed and ready.

"You're good," Francois had assured him earlier. "Only I, myself, could take you for sure now. Don't lose your head, go after him like a cane snake, only don't give warning like the rattler does."

I'll take Nicolas, Guy assured himself. Take that bastard. He could feel the beat of his heart, rapid, impatient for the duel to begin. He started when Gabriel spoke to him.

"Are you ready?"

"Yes."

"I'll inform your opponent's second." Gabriel left Guy's side and walked to where Nicolas stood talking to Marc.

The seconds conferred briefly. Only the four men were on the field beside the bayou, since both Nicolas and Guy had refused to have a doctor stand by.

Guy moved into position, Nicolas did the same. They faced one another, unsmiling.

"*En garde!*" Marc cried.

Swift as a Chitimacha Indian arrow, Nicolas' rapier cut through the air. Guy avoided the thrust adroitly, feinting to the right, then lunging so that Nicolas turned slightly to face him. Guy twisted and came at him from the left, his blade catching and slitting Nicolas' right sleeve.

Guy changed his ground, circling Nicolas. Nicolas closed in, pressing Guy warmly. Still Guy circled, feinted, circled again. The rapiers flashed in the sunlight as first one man, then the other, parried murderous thrusts.

The tip of Guy's rapier pricked Nicolas' right arm. Blood stained the torn shirt sleeve. Had this been a first blood duel, Guy could now step back, his honor satisfied and the duel would end. But he was out for his enemy's heart's blood, nothing less would do.

Guy smiled tightly as he sidestepped a rush from Nicolas, his confidence growing, feeling he'd become the better swordsman. He began maneuvering to keep Nicolas to the right so he could finish him with a well-directed *coup de pointe a droite*. He circled, making Nicolas follow him. He was almost ready . . .

A woman darted between the men so suddenly that Guy almost ran his rapier into her.

Madelaine!

"Stop," she cried, "oh, please stop."

As Guy stared at her in shock and disbelief, she screamed and he felt the hot bite of Nicolas' rapier as it slid into his right shoulder.

"Cease!" Gabriel cried. "The fight is over. Interference on the field. He walked between the duellists, Marc by his side.

Blood ran down Guy's arm and onto his hand. He felt his sword handle grow sticky and transferred the weapon to his left hand. "No," he said, trying to fend Madelaine off as she clutched at him. "No, get away. How dare you come onto a duelling field?"

27

"We, as seconds, agree to declare this duel a draw due to interference," Marc said. He reached out his hand for Nicolas' sword.

Gabriel held out his hand and Guy reluctantly surrendered the rapier. Guy turned to Madelaine. "What possessed you to interfere?" he snapped.

She was crying, tears running down her face as she struggled to pull a lace-edged handkerchief from the pocket of her pelisse. "You're bleeding," she sobbed, bringing the dainty square of cloth up to dab at the bloody hole in Guy's shoulder. "You're hurt."

"Thanks to you," he said grimly, pulling away from her. "Go home."

Gabriel pressed folded white cotton cloth against Guy's wound and Guy allowed him to bind it tightly.

"I couldn't stay home once I heard," Madelaine said.

"I'd like to know who told you."

"No duel is ever a secret," she said. "What does it matter where I heard it? What matters is you. What if you'd been killed? I couldn't bear that, Guy."

"I was in no danger of being killed."

"Nicolas, then. If you killed him in no time Philippe would challenge you over some trifle because of this crazy feud that should have died out years ago. Then he'd die. Or you would. I want it stopped." She put her hands over her face and wept.

"You sister is tender-hearted," Nicolas said.

Guy turned his head quickly to see Nicolas standing a few feet away. "You did draw first blood," Nicolas went on. "If you'll accept an apology for my behavior, I'll admit I was drunk and shouldn't have indulged myself. It was ill-advised."

Guy's shoulder throbbed painfully, oozing blood reddened the white bandage. He was in no shape to fight a duel now or in the near future. The wound might take months to heal. Hatred pulsed through him with every heartbeat. If only Madelaine had minded her own business, Nicolas would be laying dead at his feet this very moment.

He took a deep breath and let it out slowly, knowing he had little choice. "Apology accepted," he managed to say, the words choking him.

Nicolas turned on his heel and walked away. Guy stared after him. Nothing would ever wipe the insult from his mind, certainly not an apology. Yet by the duelling code, the incident was closed.

"I'm sorry about your shoulder," Madelaine said. "I hope you won't have to miss many of the parties."

"The parties be damned," he said. "I'll wear a sling."

Nicolas and I will meet again someday at sword's point, he told himself as he let Gabriel help him onto his horse. When that day comes I'll have my vengeance.

Without lighting a lamp, Madelaine crept quietly across the parlor and into the corridor. She inched the outside door open. It was likely that no matter how careful she was, Odalie would know she'd left, but Odalie, who'd raised her since she was five, could be trusted to keep her mouth shut.

Guy was asleep in his room, his shoulder no longer bleeding. He'd not waken, for Dr. Goodreau had given him laudanum. Guy was still angry with her for interfering with the duel this morning but he'd be far more upset if he discovered what she was doing at this moment.

Life was once so simple. Rather dull, maybe, looking back but she hadn't thought it dull at the time. It was only in comparison with now that it seemed dull. For now, ah, she was in love. Love was wonderful, thrilling, more exciting than anything else in the world, but it wouldn't let her rest, it drove her forward with a coachman's whip. She had to disobey Guy.

Madelaine tiptoed across the courtyard and slipped through the small door set in one of the leaves of the tall double gate. She drew her shawl of soft white wool closer against the chill of the December night and stared into the darkness, prepared to duck quickly back inside if she heard a carriage coming. She heard instead the whuffle of a horse and then her name called softly.

"Madelaine."

She saw him, a dim figure in the starlight, coming across the street. She hurried to meet him.

"Philippe," she breathed.

He held her close for a moment, then led her back to where his carriage waited, helped her inside. As soon as he was seated beside her she flung herself into his arms. He kissed her, his lips so warm against hers that a fire spread down into her loins. She pressed herself against him and heard him groan.

"Ah, Madelaine, I love you so."

"We must do something soon. Guy . . ."

"Imagine your brother's fury were I to come to him tomorrow saying, 'So sorry about my brother running a rapier into your shoulder, may I have Madelaine's hand in marriage'?"

She smiled, then sighed. "If you hadn't told me about the duel, Guy would have killed Nicolas."

She felt Philippe stiffen. "My brother isn't a novice swordman to be so easily disposed of," he said. "The duel might well have ended with Guy dead on the field."

Madelaine drew away. "I was there. I tell you Guy had the edge."

"Wasn't I watching, too, well concealed in the trees?"

"I didn't see you."

"I saw everything." Philippe grasped her hands. "I thought for a moment they both would run you through. You took a terrible risk dashing between them as you did."

She relaxed against him and he stroked her hair.

"I will have you, Madelaine. We'll marry. Even if I must challenge your brother to make you my wife."

"No! You must never do that. I won't be the cause of a

30

duel between the two men I love best in the world. We must find another way."

As they kissed, his hand touched her breast, sending shivers of desire through her body. "Oh, Philippe," she murmured, "my sweet, dear love." She knew she must stay a maiden and yet she was aflame with wanting him to make her his and no other's forever, in the way of men and women.

"I missed you at the ball tonight," he said.

She pulled away a little. "I imagine you danced with all the prettiest girls."

"Annette-Louise mostly. She missed you, too."

Madelaine pressed her lips together. "I'll wager she did. Ha!"

"But she's your friend."

"Not when you dance with her." Madelaine struck his chest lightly with her fist. "I hate not being there to see you and yet I hate being at a ball and not being able to dance with you."

"Once you wouldn't have danced with me even if we were the last two people on earth," he said.

"Just think, if you hadn't rescued me last summer," she told him. "I'd still believe a Roulleaux carried some strange and dangerous evil."

"You were frightened enough of me then," he said. "You didn't know which was worse—your mare mired in quicksand or the devil himself come to help."

Madelaine laughed. "Who could stay afraid of a man completely covered with mud? You were a sight."

"As I recall, you weren't exactly spotless yourself," he said. "I fell in love with you right then and there when you dared me to jump in the bayou with you to wash the mud off our clothes. I've never met anyone like you in my life, Madelaine. I'll never give you up. Only death will separate us."

She shivered. "Don't say that. Too many Roulleauxes and La Branches have died already."

"And all over a cow in the beginning, wasn't it?"

31

"A sheep, Guy told me."

"Roulleaux tradition says it was a cow." He laughed. "See, we shall never agree. What a stormy marriage we have to look forward to."

"No, no, it will be marvelous. Wonderful." She nestled close to him.

He bent his head to kiss her, then held. Carriage wheels rattled on the rutted dirt, the clop of horses' hooves. Neither spoke until the carriage was past and the sounds fading away.

"Be damned to this skulking about!" Philippe exclaimed. "I'll wait until your brother's arm heals, no longer, then I'll go to him and ask for you."

She clutched at his shoulder. "No, no, there'll be a duel, no, you mustn't ask Guy. Promise me."

"Do you think I can't fight him? Is that your worry?"

She drew away. "What kind of marriage would we have if you killed him? I love my brother. He can't help the way he feels. Doesn't your brother feel the same? If Guy should kill you . . ." She flung herself at him. "Oh, I'd die."

"I can't promise," he said, "but I'll try to think of another way."

She melted into his embrace. Long moments later she pulled back with a sigh. "I must go in. But one question. I want to know, Philippe, do you have a—a *placee?*"

"Madelaine!" His voice was shocked. "Women don't ask such things."

"Well, do you? I know most men have them. Guy does."

"As it happens, I don't. But you must never ask me again."

"You sound just like Guy sometimes. Why should I pretend to be blind and deaf and dumb?"

He put his hands on her shoulders and gave her a little shake. "You're incorrigible and I love you very much." He kissed her quickly and then she scrambled out of the carriage.

When Madelaine crept up the stairs to her bedroom, she found Odalie sitting, waiting.

"I thought you were asleep," Madelaine said.

"How can I be sleeping? Who be in this room if *Monsieur* Guy take a notion to ask about you?" Odalie had risen as soon as she saw Madelaine and now she faced her, hands on her hips. "You be getting yourself in big trouble, easing out to meet up with a no-good."

"Oh, don't scold, Odalie, I haven't done anything wrong." As she looked into the slave's black face, tears swam in her eyes. "It's just that I love him so."

"Do be love that gets all women in trouble," Odalie said, putting her arms around Madelaine. "Don't fret, girl, not a man be worth it."

"*He* is, oh, he is, Odalie." Madelaine pulled away from her and sat on the bed.

"Then why don't he come see you proper?"

"There are reasons he can't."

"You don't be taking up with a married man?" Odalie's voice was shocked.

Madelaine stared at her, then laughed. "*Mon Dieu,* what a question to ask me. Of course not."

"I should hope you don't do that. Ladies don't be *placees.*"

Madelaine glanced away. "I think Guy fought that duel over his *placee,*" she said, trying to keep her voice casual in the hope Odalie wouldn't tell her to hush. "Do you know who she is?"

There was a few seconds silence before Odalie answered. "Not to say know. Her *maman* be a woman you don't want to be knowing. She be *voodooienne.*"

"A voodoo queen? Really?" Madelaine stood up. "What's her name?"

"Her *maman's* name be Vedette Rusert."

"Do you go to the voodoo dances, Odalie?"

"Don't have them no more, that be the law."

"*Pouf,* you don't expect me to believe that. Not when I

33

can hear the voodoo drums at night sometimes. No one pays any attention to that law."

"You don't be asking me about voodoo, girl. You don't be having nothing to do with voodoo. *Pere* Antoine say you go straight to hell for that."

"I don't care what the priest says. I'll wager you've been there and danced yourself."

Odalie frowned.

"Is it true the voodoo queen can make love potions?"

"You hear foolish talk. Time you be thinking about a husband and keeping your own house, like that, not this creeping out to meet no-goods and listening to voodoo talk."

"But can they? Does Vedette sell love powders?"

"You don't be needing such things. Mirror tell you how pretty you be."

"Does she sell them?"

"There be nothing a voodoo queen can't do, she want to," Odalie said. "Now hush such talk. You best get to bed."

Madelaine walked to her dressing table and sat on the blue satin bench before the mirror, gazing at the reflection of her flushed face, her tumbled hair. She picked up a brush and Odalie took it from her hand and began brushing Madelaine's long, silky black hair.

Does Philippe really, truly love me? Madelaine asked herself. Does all that laughing and flirting with Annette-Louise at the dances mean nothing? Annette-Louise is very pretty. Everyone but me would be happy to see them marry.

Still, Philippe says he loves only me.

Does he?

If I had a love potion, if I gave Philippe a love potion, then I'd be certain.

"One more question and then I promise I'll be quiet and go to sleep," Madelaine said. "Tell me where Vedette lives."

Chapter 4

On December 20, Guy, his right arm in a white silk sling, followed *Prefet* de Laussat in a parade toward the Cabildo. The sun shone and the feel of festivity was in the air despite Creole uneasiness about this transfer. Pretty girls waved from balconies and the *banquettes* seemed even more crowded than last month. Creoles stood shoulder to shoulder with free men and women of color, slaves and *Kaintocks,* the roughly dressed *Americain* boatmen from up the river.

In the *grande salle* of the Cabildo, the *prefet* took the center seat and his staff grouped to either side of him, waiting. Invited guests crowded the room. Guy, to de Laussat's right, knew what was to come, for the little play had been well rehearsed. Nonetheless, when the runner dashed inside and hurried to the commandant, Guy's pulse speeded.

"*Americain* troops at the city gates, demanding entry," the runner gasped.

The commandant bowed to *Prefet* de Laussat. "I've been informed *Americain* troops demand entry to New Orleans," he said ceremoniously.

De Laussat nodded. "Permit entrance," he ordered.

Guy edged close to a balcony when the hum from the massed crowd in the square below told him the *Americains* were near. He looked out and saw, coming into the Place d'Armes, the *Americain* governor-to-be, William Charles Cole Claiborne, wearing a bright ceremonial sash and General James Wilkinson, Commander-in-Chief of the United States Army, in his dress uniform. Behind them marched lean and bronzed soldiers armed with long-barreled rifles. Squirrel rifles, the *Americains* called them. The Mississippi militia followed.

The troops deployed in a long skirmish line, backs to the river, and Claiborne and Wilkinson entered the Cabildo. Guy hurried back into place as the two men approached de Laussat. Once again articles of transfer were read—in French, then English, this time, instead of Spanish. De Laussat bowed and offered the center chair to Governor Claiborne.

After de Laussat released the Louisianians from their oath of allegiance to the French Republic, everyone descended to the square. A flourish of drums rat-a-tatted and the French flag began to flutter down the staff. Guy's throat tightened as he watched an officer step forward, take the flag and wind it about his body. Accompanied by an honor guard of Creoles, the flag-draped soldier marched past saluting *Americain* troops.

A hush fell as the Stars and Stripes began to rise. Part way up it fouled the halliards. Exaltation filled Guy. The *Americain* flag was ashamed to take the place of the tricolor. Didn't the United States owe her freedom to Lafayette and France, after all?

The problem was solved and the flag reached the top where a brisk breeze from the river snapped it out smartly. The *Americains* waved their hats and cheered but the Creoles stood silently. Something had been taken from them, there was a change, and things would never be quite the same.

Guy calculated quickly. President Jefferson had bought Louisiana from Napoleon for fifteen million *Americain* dollars. Fifty thousand people for fifteen million dollars. That made every Louisianian worth three hundred dollars. He shrugged. The land and the port at the mouth of the Mississippi River was what the *Americains* wanted, not the Creoles and Cajuns.

He attended the *prefet's* luncheon at three o'clock. A toast to the United States in Madeira. One to Spain in Malaga. Another in rose champagne to France. All to the roar of the guns. More toasts to government officials, to good feelings, to cotton and sugar. Guy, even with his good head for wine, felt the effect of the liquor and told himself it was because of the blood he'd lost.

His wound didn't give too much trouble as long as he wore the sling but he was awkward with his left hand. It helped little to see Nicolas swagger about as though he'd won the duel.

Tea was served at seven, gambling and dancing followed. Guy skirted the card and dice tables, looking for Senalda.

"Oh, *mon pauvre Monsieur* La Branche," she said when he found her. Her French was heavily accented but he thought it charming. "Are you in pain?"

Senalda was dressed in pink, the color of a hibiscus bloom. Her gown had a high waist, just under her breasts, and the silken material fell in graceful folds to the floor. At her throat hung a pendant of rose amethyst. Her blue eyes were full of concern as she looked at him.

"It's nothing," he said.

"My heart aches to think how you've suffered." She touched her breast with her fingertips and lowered her eyes, blushing.

It belatedly occurred to Guy that she thought the duel had been fought on her account. He swallowed. He could hardly tell her otherwise. He'd be a fool, though, not to take advantage of her error.

"Since my dancing is unavoidably clumsy at the moment," he said, "can I persuade you to sit out a round or two with me? We might promenade in the courtyard."

She smiled, showing even white teeth. Her lips were delectable—the same pink as her gown. He longed to taste them.

He offered her his left arm and they descended the stairs into the courtyard. A marble statue of St. John brooded over a lily pool in a far corner and he steered her in that direction. Paper lanterns on the branches of a magnolia tree cast a soft glow.

"Perhaps I should have put on my cape," Senalda said, letting him lead her past other strollers toward the deeper shadows.

Something plopped into the water as they came up to the pool.

"Ooh!" she exclaimed, pressing close to his side.

"A frog," Guy assured her. "We've disturbed his serenade." He put his arm about her waist and she resisted only slightly. "You won't be cold next to me," he said. "I'll keep you warm." He touched his lips to her hair, breathing in the scent of gardenias.

"I hope you'll stay in New Orleans," he murmured. "You brighten the city with your beauty."

"Ah," she said, "sometimes New Orleans reminds me of Madrid. Other times . . ."

"I'll make you forget those other times," he said, moving his lips to her temple. She half turned toward him and he kissed her mouth.

Her lips were soft and sweet. They quivered beneath his and desire flared. He had to have her as his wife.

Senalda pulled away. "I must go back inside," she said.

"So soon?"

Her laughter was like the tinkle of crystals on a chandelier when a river breeze blew. "Oh, but we've been here too long already." She slipped from his grasp and he cursed his useless arm. A one-handed embrace was a poor imitation of the real thing.

At the party the following evening, de Laussat made a point of steering Guy to a circle of men that included Governor Claiborne, then leaving him there.

"How do you do, Governor?" Guy asked, pronouncing the English words carefully, hoping his accent wasn't too atrocious. He'd found Spanish much easier to learn.

The governor brightened when he heard Guy's words. "You know English, *monsieur*?"

Guy bowed. "Tanguy La Branche, Governor. I speak a little English, yes. I'm still learning."

"I admire your industry."

"*Prefet* de Laussat encouraged me."

"I thought I recognized you. One of his aides, I believe." The governor examined Guy quite frankly.

Guy looked back at him with interest. This was the closest he'd been to Governor Claiborne. They were much the same size. The *Americain* was older—near thirty, Guy thought—and wore his brown hair short. Though he wasn't fat, there was a hint of beginning plumpness under his chin. His eyes were shrewd.

"You're a New Orleans resident?" Claiborne asked.

"I was born here," Guy said proudly.

The governor nodded. "I look forward to seeing more of you," he said.

Later, de Laussat took Guy aside. "Has he offered you a post?" he asked.

"*Non*."

"He will. Either with himself or perhaps he'll arrange for a place on General Wilkinson's staff. I could see he was impressed with you. Work with the *Americains*. You have a flair for politics and Louisiana will need you. Fight for what she needs, don't merely fight against the *Americains* as so many of your friends are doing."

Guy stared at the *prefet*.

"You know I'll be returning to France in a few months," de Laussat said, clapping Guy on the left shoulder. "I can't stay to help Louisiana make the change, but you'll be here. I haven't pushed you, for all would be suspicious, then. The Creoles. The *Americains*. With no reason to be, but men are like that—seeing deviousness where none is intended and missing the obvious threat. Work from the inside, Guy, don't stand on the outside, complaining. And good luck."

Guy drifted through the courtyard, let himself out onto the *banquette* and walked aimlessly, his thoughts a blend of disbelief and excitement.

Did he want to be on the *Americain's* staff? Being de Laussat's aide had been rewarding but Claiborne wasn't French. He'd had a favorable impression of the governor but still—work for an *Americain*? He was a Creole, after all.

Non, wait, since yesterday he was also an *Americain*, like it or not. Many Creoles would condemn whatever Claiborne did, right or wrong. He was no more eager to be a United States citizen than they, but the fact remained that they all were.

It wouldn't do any harm to work with the governor. Perhaps it would do some good, as de Laussat seemed to think. He admired the *prefet*, had learned something of diplomacy from him. Certainly his advice was worth considering.

Very well, if Claiborne approached him with an offer—and that was still to be seen—he'd take him up on it.

Guy took a deep breath, looked around and found he was nearing the rue des Ramparts. He stopped abruptly. Without realizing where he was going he'd headed toward Aimee's cottage. He turned on his heel to go back to the ball. He didn't want to see Aimee again.

As he approached the house where the party was going on, he could hear laughter, music and the agreeable noise of merry-making. He stood for a moment outside the gates, listening, feeling a strange sense of being set apart, of actually being an outsider.

A ridiculous notion. Guy shifted his shoulders uneasily, feeling pain stab through his right arm. He'd known those inside all his life. There were few strangers except for the *Americains*. He belonged if anyone did.

He pushed open the small gate, crossed the lighted courtyard and went into the house, eager to banish his uncomfortable feeling, to take a drink, to plunge into the party mood. Glass in hand, he looked for Senalda and saw her dancing. With Nicolas.

Rage tensed his muscles. He took a step toward the couple, then stopped. This damnedable sling. The wound had seemed trivial once Dr. Goodreau had stopped the bleeding, but it was slow to heal. The doctor had suggested leeches, but Guy had refused. Certainly he was incapable of challenging Nicolas at the moment.

Deliberately, Guy turned from the dancing, his eyes scanning the gaming tables. He headed for one, then stopped. He had little heart for the dice tonight, he felt drained of vigor. Slowly he turned his back on the tables and walked away, again finding his way to the courtyard.

The night was so chilly few couples braved the cold. He sat on an iron bench beneath a large fig tree, staring down at the flagstones between his feet. I'll be the St. John of this courtyard, he told himself wryly. The notion failed to amuse him.

The year was ending, another would soon begin. He felt like old Father Time himself tonight. Where were his friends, Gabriel, Rafe, Andre, that they didn't rally round and help him shake his dark mood?

"Have you forgotten me so soon?" a woman's voice asked softly. Senalda's voice.

Guy looked up, got hastily to his feet.

"*Non*," she said. "Don't rise. I'm teasing, for I know the pain in your shoulder is what drives you from the party."

He said nothing, tongue-tied by the sight of her before him like a visitation in a dream with her gown of white, embroidered with the palest pink, the enticing rose lips, the blonde curls falling to white shoulders.

She sat on the bench and nodded her head to indicate he should sit beside her. Guy reseated himself.

"I could never forget you," he said, leaning toward her. "I'd like to sweep you onto my horse and ride off where none would find us, to keep you to myself for the rest of time."

41

Senalda smiled and lowered her lashes. "Is it only your arm that prevents you?" she murmured.

Guy's eyes widened at this encouragement. He leaned closer, ignoring the slice of pain down into his chest.

"I want you to be mine," he said. "Say you'll marry me, say you'll live with me and make La Belle as radiant as any *casa* in Madrid."

She swayed toward him, then straightened. "You must know I can't give you a hasty answer," she said so softly he could scarcely hear her words, "but if anything would compel me to stay in New Orleans . . ." She left the sentence unfinished.

Guy's heartbeat quickened. As good as a yes. He reached to embrace her, but the throb of agony in his shoulder stopped him. She edged away with a cry.

"Your wound—it's bleeding."

Guy glanced down at his right shoulder and saw the stain on the sling of white silk. The pain increased until sweat broke out on his brow. Senalda bit her lip, her eyes frightened.

With an effort, Guy stood up and bowed. "I'm sorry to distress you," he said, feeling his head whirl, his legs tremble. "Please pardon me."

He walked away from her, determined to get out of her sight before he showed any sign of weakness. *Mon Dieu,* why did this have to happen at such a moment?

Once outside the small gate, he leaned against the wall, taking deep breaths. He must get home, get to bed, have the doctor summoned. The rapier wound was putrifying and making him sick. He'd have one of the slaves here send round for his carriage.

No, he wouldn't go back inside. It was less than a mile to his townhouse. He could make it on foot. He would make it. Guy pushed away from the wall. His head spun as he set off and he had a dim awareness that his thoughts weren't logical.

"Feverish," he muttered. "Must get home."

The *banquette* stretched out endlessly, then dirt, mud,

underfoot. There shouldn't be mud on the way to—where? Where was he headed down these endless streets? He was dreaming, a nightmare . . .

Someone screamed his name and he was falling, falling.

"Guy!" she called again. "Guy!"

With great effort he forced his eyes open and found himself looking into the yellow cat's eyes of Aimee, then everything went dark.

When he came to himself, the first thing he noticed was a pungent but not unpleasant smell. Guy stared about at a familiar room, he lay in a four-poster bed, the one he'd bought for Aimee. He was in the cottage bedroom, he was at Aimee's. And the smell—he felt his right shoulder, his fingers encountering a soggy mass of leaves plastered over the wound.

"Aimee!" he shouted, sitting up.

She ran into the room.

"You're better, *merci de Dieu*," she cried.

"What's this?" He touched the poultice bound onto his shoulder.

"Healing herbs from *maman*. She said they'd draw out the evil and heal the wound."

"Voodoo," he said with distaste. He flexed his arm, testing the shoulder. Very little pain. Cautiously he shifted the shoulder. Definitely improved.

"Much evil flowed green and yellow from your shoulder," Aimee told him. "Now it's all gone."

"Voodoo or not, your *maman's* herbs seemed to have cured me overnight," he said in apology. "You must thank her for me."

"Oh, but you've been here three days," Aimee said.

"*Dieu!*"

"Your sister sent a slave to inquire and I told the woman you were sick but recovering."

Guy eased himself onto the edge of the bed, feet on the floor. He only vaguely recalled leaving the party, feeling sick. Surely he'd meant to go home, yet he'd come here.

And luckily, for this herb poultice was less repulsive than Goodreau's leeches.

"I worried that you'd never come to me again," Aimee said, sitting beside him. Timidly she touched his face, brushed his hair back from his forehead.

He looked into her eyes, large and fearful, and remembered Nicolas, the duel.

He moved his head and Aimee's fingers fell away. She clasped her hands in her lap, gazing down at them. He sighed, watching her. Estelle was right—Aimee wasn't a fighter. For all her cat's grace she was only a harmless kitten, afraid to use even her tiny claws.

No match at all for any man who tried to force her. He gritted his teeth. As Nicolas *had* forced her, there was no doubt in his mind that had been the way of it. Aimee came willingly only to him, to Tanguy La Branche.

How could he hold her to blame? And yet he did.

"Aimee?"

She looked up hopefully.

"Aimee, I know you couldn't help what happened," he said. "What I have to tell you has nothing to do with that. I plan to marry in a month or so."

She put her hands over her face and began to sob, rocking back and forth with grief.

He put his arm around her shoulders. "You've always known I'd marry one day," he said. "Don't cry."

She raised a tear-stained face. "I knew you'd marry but I hoped . . ." her voice broke but she swallowed and went on. "I hoped you'd come to me sometimes even afterward. Now you won't. Because of what happened. And I—I love you so."

His heart twisted in his chest. He loved her, too, in his way. How could he hurt her? "I'll see you again," he promised. "Now, smile at me and be done with tears."

Her quivering lips trembled into an attempt at a smile and he pressed her head to his chest. She flung her arms about him, her soft full breasts close against him. Guy felt his loins quicken with desire.

Aimee pulled away. "I, too, have news," she said. She stood up and put her hands, one over the other, on her stomach. "I carry your child."

A bolt of joy and pride shot through Guy. A child. He'd sired a child! He smiled up at Aimee, a smile that slowly faded.

The baby might well be Nicolas'.

Chapter 5

MADELAINE bristled with impatience as she waited for Guy to return to the townhouse. This was February and in only a few weeks more the season would be over and they'd be back at La Belle and she wouldn't be able to attend the public balls, not that many were held in the heat of summer. She twirled in a circle, arms out to an imaginary partner. How she did love to dance!

If only she and Philippe could be together in public, could dance in front of everyone, acknowledging their love.

She tapped her foot restlessly. Why didn't Guy come home? He never let her go anywhere without him in the evenings and he was so often late these days. No one could understand why he'd taken a post as aide to General Wilkinson.

"What, Madelaine, your brother works for the *Americains?*" her friends asked, eyebrows raised.

She had no answers for them or for herself. All Guy would say was that he wanted to do it, that *Americains* were human beings not ogres.

Some of the *Americain* dances were so funny—jigging up and down as they did. Still, she thought she'd like to try the reel sometime, though with a Creole, not an *Americain*.

With Philippe she dreamed of the quadrille, being held in his arms as they executed the movements of the dance. She circled again, smiling.

"Oh, *mademoiselle*, may I have the pleasure?"

Madelaine whirled to find her brother grinning at her.

"You were lost in a world of your own with your imaginary partner," Guy said. "Who was he? Gabriel?"

"I—no—that is, I imagined I was dancing with a French prince," she said.

His eyes took on the glaze she'd come to associate with his infatuation for *Senorita* Gabaldon. "I, myself, dream of dancing with a Spanish princess," he said.

"Will she be there tonight?"

"At the public ball? No." Guy frowned. "Senalda can't abide the *Americains*."

"How does she like your new position then?"

He shrugged. "What I do must be my concern."

Madelaine suppressed a smile. Senalda could be quite outspoken and she must have told Guy in no uncertain terms what she thought of his being General Wilkinson's aide.

"At least you can dance again," she said, "now that your shoulder's healed."

Guy flexed his right arm, relaxed it, flexed it again. "Come to think of it," he said, "I don't see Gabriel calling on you of late."

"Oh, Guy, will you stop trying to marry us off? I've known Gabriel so long that I think of him as a brother. I'm certain he still sees me as the little nuisance who trailed after the two of you, spoiling your fun."

"You're much prettier now," Guy told her. "Plus certain other differences. Gabriel's noticed the change, there's no doubt of that."

She made a face at him. "Do get dressed," she urged, "or we'll never get to the ball."

As Guy escorted her into the ballroom, Madelaine

47

looked quickly about for Philippe but didn't see him. The orchestra was playing a quadrille, with the dancers circling and dipping through the patterns. She was pleased with her gown, a brilliant green satin with gold embroidery at the edge of the bodice and shirt, and a gold ribbon about the high waistline. It was made in quite the latest Paris fashion. Guy had let her wear a small emerald pendant set in gold that had belonged to their mother, and Madelaine knew it complimented her gown perfectly.

Along both sides of the long room, girls sat with their mothers in loges against the wall, reached by stairs. *Bredouilles*, they were called, wallflowers, as they waited to be asked to dance. She rarely sat up there, for when Guy had first allowed her to come with him he had made certain his friends asked her to dance. Now most of the men were eager to dance with her.

"*Dieu*," she heard Guy mutter, "those men are armed."

Madelaine looked behind him at a large group of Creoles who had followed them into the hall. She picked out Henri Leroque, Antoine Beaumont and others she recognized. She tightened her hold on her brother's arm. "Why?" she asked.

"Trouble." He guided her farther into the room, away from them.

Madelaine saw a few *Americains* forming for a quadrille on the floor, while others stood in groups near the loges. Suddenly, one of them left his group and strode between the dancers to the center of the floor. There he stopped and began to sing at the top of his voice:

"Hail, Columbia, happy land
  Hail ye heroes, heaven born band
  Who fought and bled in Freedom's Cause . . ."

Other *Americain* voices took up the song and the orchestra playing the French quadrille faltered and fell silent. The dancers paused uncertainly. Men crowded onto the floor.

An armed Creole thrust his way to the front of the

crowd, turned his back on the *Americains* and shouted at his friends to join him as he sang his own song:

"*Allons, enfants de la patrie*   Arise, ye sons of France to glory

Le jour de gloire est arrive . . ."   Your day of freedom bids you rise

A hurricane of cheering burst from Creole throats. Men rushed their partners from the dance floor and Madelaine saw the fear on the women's faces. She felt none. Her pulses pounded with excitement and outrage. How dare these *Americains* cause trouble here?

"A reel, play us a reel," an *Americain* shouted at the musicians.

"The quadrille, continue the quadrille," Creole voices ordered.

A woman screamed as the Creoles swept toward the *Americains.* Guy, seeking to protect Madelaine, was jostled off balance and she was torn from his grasp. Someone bumped into her from the rear and she stumbled forward, falling. A strong arm caught her, brought her to her feet.

"I beg your pardon," the man said. Though he spoke with an accent, his French was understandable. "I'm very sorry this is happening. May I see you to safety?"

Madelaine looked into bright blue eyes.

"John Kellogg, at your service, *mademoiselle*," the man said.

He was quite handsome, a tall man with red hair and a strong jaw. But an *Americain.* Madelaine pulled away. "Thank you, I can take care of myself."

Where was Guy? She looked about at the shouting, angry men and knew there'd soon be bloodshed. Then challenges, duels . . .

No! Something must be done.

Madelaine tunnelled through the men until she reached a wall, climbed the steps to the highest loge and stood on a bench.

"Listen to me!" she cried, speaking French, for in her

agitation she couldn't find English words. Her voice was drowned by the clamor below.

She put two fingers to her mouth and whistled in the piercing shrill tremolo Guy had taught her when they were children. The noise lessened. Heads turned, looked up. She whistled again.

"Listen to me," she repeated and now her voice could be heard as the crowd quieted and stared up at her.

"*Americain monsieurs*," she said, her words ringing with passion. "Think what you do. Why can't we dance as we choose? We had to be Spaniards for many years but Spain didn't force us to learn the fandango. Now that we've become *Americains*, why should you make us dance the reel?"

A murmur of questions floated up to her in English.

"What does she say?"

"Who is she?"

A shock of red hair thrust above the other heads and Madelaine realized John Kellogg had climbed on a chair. He translated her words into English, then turned to the musicians who were huddled in their box at the far end of the hall and said in French, "Play a quadrille for the lovely and courageous *mademoiselle, s'il vous plait.*"

A few moments later crowd cleared from the dance floor. Men found their partners and formed patterns for a quadrille. Madelaine, still in the loge, climbed down from the bench and looked for Philippe.

There! She waited for him to look up at her, to make some sign to her but he did not, bending over his partner's hand as she smiled at him. He danced with Annette-Louise, who looked charming in a blue muslin dress cut low to show the rounded tops of her generous breasts.

"She'll look like a fat cow by the time she's twenty-five," Madelaine muttered under her breath, then was immediately ashamed of herself. Annette-Louise was her friend, after all, and Philippe was only being careful to mislead everyone.

That's what he was doing, wasn't it?

Why did he have to gaze into Annette-Louise's eyes so intently, laugh so uproariously at her every word? Dancing with her was certainly enough.

"Would you do me the honor, *Mademoiselle* La Branche?" John Kellogg's voice said from behind her.

Madelaine whirled about. "You startled me!"

He bowed. "I'm sorry. I thought you saw me climb the stairs. I'd be honored if you'd dance with me."

About to give him an indignant, "no," she bit back the word as she again glanced at Philippe with Annette-Louise in his arms. She smiled at the red-haired *Americain*. Two could play at Philippe's game.

John Kellogg was a graceful dancer for such a tall man. Not as quick on his feet as Philippe but then no one was like Philippe. *Monsieur* Kellogg held her just right, firmly enough to carry her with him but not tightly enough to embarrass her.

"You discovered my name," she said coolly.

"When you were scolding us, I heard someone say who you were." He smiled down at her, a charming smile. Madelaine began to like this particular *Americain*.

"I've never been so impressed with anyone in my life," he went on. "You're brave as well as being the most beautiful woman in New Orleans."

"You're very kind," she murmured. "Are you on General Wilkinson's staff?"

"No. I'm a doctor with the United States Army."

"Ah, then it's *Docteur* Kellogg and not *Monsieur*. I heard you tell your compatriots what I said to them."

"We're not all barbarians, even though it may seem that way at times. I think every man here felt ashamed when he understood what you told us."

His hair was such an unusual color, not carroty red but closer to auburn. Really, he was most agreeable for an *Americain*.

"You don't seem to be a barbarian, *docteur*," she said, then, catching sight of Annette-Louise's blue dress, lowered her lashes and smiled coquettishly up at the tall *Americain.*

Let Philippe make what he would of that!

Guy was waiting for her when the quadrille ended. When *Docteur* Kellogg introduced himself, he acknowledged the *Americain* stiffly. "You will excuse my sister and myself, *docteur,*" he said. "We must leave."

As soon as Guy joined Madelaine in the carriage, he began scolding her. "Making a spectacle of yourself, whatever possessed you?"

"Someone had to do something," she protested.

"Not that." His tone softened. "Ah, Madelaine, I was proud of you up there in the loge. A true La Branche—fearless and outspoken. It was a dangerous chance to take, but how can I be angry when you were so brave? No, that's not what I speak of at all. This *Docteur* Kellogg—I don't want to see you dancing with *Americains.* They're not like us, will never be like us. Your reputation can't fail to be seriously harmed by any association with one."

"You work for General Wilkinson."

"That's business. Besides, I'm a man."

"I see no harm in *Docteur* Kellogg. His profession is honorable and I'm sure he is as well."

"You didn't see how he looked at you. I won't have my sister's name bandied about in the coffee houses. You will not accept any more invitations from this man or from any other *Americain,* Madelaine. I mean what I say. In any case, I shan't take you to a public ball again until the city settles down. Next thing you know we'll have army patrols at all our dances to keep the peace. Disgraceful."

Madelaine said nothing but her jaw was set. I won't promise, she said to herself. *Mon Dieu!* The *Americain* was far more courteous than some of Guy's friends when they dance with me. No nonsense about letting his hands wander or pressing against me as if by accident.

"Your little friend Annette-Louise is turning into quite a beauty," Guy said.

"I don't care to discuss her," Madelaine said coldly.

"You saw her with Philippe Roulleaux, then. Of course you can't approve. I understand. If they marry you'll lose her friendship, it could be no other way. It's a sad thing to lose a lifelong friend."

Madelaine gritted her teeth. She mustn't say anything, certainly not the furious words that welled up in her. She wasn't angry with Guy now, but with Philippe. Tears gathered in her eyes. Oh, Philippe, she thought, how can you be so cruel?

The next day Guy moved them back to La Belle. "I've been gone far too long," he said. "Fortunately the sugar grinding went well, even though I wasn't here to supervise."

Day after day Madelaine rode to the secret spot where she and Philippe had arranged to meet, but he was never there. She had no way of knowing if she'd missed him by a few minutes or if he'd never come at all.

He can't love Annette-Louise, she assured herself. He loves me. Me!

At the plantation house she was sulky and restless.

"*Mon Dieu*, Madelaine, can you settle to nothing?" Guy asked her. "Where is your embroidery, your fancy work?"

Upstairs, Odalie took her to task. "You be sickening for something, look like, the way you be acting."

"I'm prefectly fine," Madelaine snapped.

"Seem like you ought to smile and be glad your brother be taking a bride soon. She be company."

Madelaine sighed. "Senalda thinks I'm too impetuous. She plans to change that, I'm sure."

"Seem like you be better off do you think about getting your own self married."

Madelaine bit her lip. "I do think about it. The trouble is . . ." Her words trailed off. Philippe's name couldn't be shared with anyone at La Belle, not even Odalie, whom she trusted with everything else.

Odalie nodded wisely. "That no-good."

"He's not a no-good!" Madelaine balled her fists and glared at Odalie, then turned and ran from her room, down the stairs, outside and around the house to the stables.

"Ancin, have Empress saddled," she ordered.

Ancin shot a glance at her morning dress and her uncovered hair but said nothing. Instead of directing one of the stable hands, he fetched the saddle himself as Madelaine watched him impatiently.

Ancin led her mare from the stall and helped her into the saddle, frowning when he saw she wore house slippers instead of riding boots. "You do be careful," he told her.

"I'm sick and tired of being careful," she said over her shoulder as Empress trotted off.

The March day was overcast, promising rain. She rode along an avenue between rows of live oaks whose branches were draped with long moss, turned between two of the huge-trunked trees and made her way along a path leading toward the bayou. As she neared the water, a blue heron flapped up with a squawk of protest, long-legged and ungainly until he was airborne, then a graceful flyer. Something splashed in the bayou water—perhaps the frog the heron had been waiting to spear with his long sharp bill.

Madelaine took a deep breath of the damp air that hinted of decaying vegetation. Today he'd be there, he had to be there. She longed for his touch, to feel his lips on hers, to experience the wild rush of fire in her body when he held her. She closed her eyes as Empress trotted along the bank of the bayou. Philippe, oh, Philippe, I love you so . . .

She rode through the tupelo trees, beginning to green with spring, around the thick growth of willows and on to where a solitary camphor tree spread out its heavy branches. Past the camphor tree and—but there he was! Madelaine let out her breath and spurred her mare.

"Philippe!" she cried.

He turned and took off his hat and she gasped to see red hair glowing in the grey morning. John Kellogg waited for her, not Philippe Roulleaux.

Madelaine reined in Empress so abruptly the mare

reared onto her hind legs. Madelaine controlled her, patting the horse's neck in apology. "What are you doing here?" she demanded of John Kellogg.

"I've been hoping you'd come this way by chance," he said.

"I don't believe you."

He smiled one-sidedly. "You'd be right not to. I confess I've been watching you ride this way. I tried to call on you at your plantation house but your brother told me you didn't care to see me again. I wanted to hear it from you."

She stared at him. "You came to see me?"

He nodded.

"Guy forbids me to encourage an *American*," she said bluntly, not forgiving him for being here instead of Philippe.

"I can hardly help being what I am."

She saw his wry grin and felt a tug of response. She couldn't resist John Kellogg's smile. "I don't always agree with my brother," she told him.

"Good. May I help you down?" He dismounted and advanced toward her.

Madelaine slid from Empress' back before he could reach her.

"This doesn't mean I'll see you again," she warned, walking away from him to a pond where the flat green leaves of water lilies lay like stepping stones to the far side. "There's swamp all through here," she said. "Quicksand. You took a chance when you came this way."

"I felt lucky today."

"Do you have a girl of your own? An *American* girl?"

He turned from her to gaze at the pond. "Not any more," he said.

"But you did once?"

He nodded, still not glancing her way. "She died of yellow fever," he said. "We meant to marry."

"I'm sorry."

He moved toward her suddenly, grasping her shoulders before she could back away. "I can't stop thinking of you," he said. "I don't mean to frighten you but my heart tells me you're the only woman I can ever love."

Madelaine stood still, stunned by the intensity of his words, his bright gaze fixing her in place. His hands were warm through the thin muslin of her gown.

"I—I don't . . ." she began.

"You don't need to say anything. I had to tell you. I wanted to court you properly, to come calling, but your brother made it clear I wasn't welcome."

Madelaine stared into his eyes, her breath quickening. Her blood seemed to race in her veins, infusing her with liquid heat as his face came closer and closer until his lips met hers. For a moment she melted into his arms, her entire being responding to his kiss, then she jerked back, horrified. What was she doing?

She trembled when he released her. "Go away," she cried. "I never want to see you again." Turning on her heel, she ran to Empress, scrambled into the saddle and urged the mare ahead.

"Wait," he called. "Please . . ."

"No," she said. "No, never." She kicked the horse's flank and Empress broke into a lope. But though she fled from John Kellogg, she couldn't escape from the memory of how he'd made her feel. How dare he do this to her?

I hate him, she told herself. It's Philippe I love. Only Philippe.

Chapter 6

A week before Shrove Tuesday, before Mardi Gras, the two-story white columned stuccoed brick mansion at La Belle was filled to overflowing with friends. In the *garconniere,* the guest house to the south of the mansion, men were forced to double up. House slaves rushed about serving the guests and putting the final touches to the wedding decorations. Guy and Senalda had been married before the altar of the St. Louis Cathedral, Father Antoine presiding, and now everyone was at the manor house for the wedding reception.

"La Belle never look so nice, not for long years," Odalie told Madelaine. "*Mademoiselle* Senalda be a beauty, that be for sure." She shook her head. "Got to be saying *Madame* to her now, I be forgetting."

Madelaine said nothing. Senalda Gabaldon La Branche was a beautiful woman. Among the dark Creoles, her blondeness made a sharp contrast, magnifying her attractiveness. Her eyes were every bit as blue as the spring sky and her figure was stunning.

I wish I liked her more, Madelaine thought. Can it be my fault? Am I so difficult? Guy tells me I am, but he's teasing—at least I used to believe he was. Senalda seems to hold me off or else treat me as a child, and she can't be so very much older than I am. She doesn't let me get close enough to her to like her.

"You be a pretty sight in that yellow," Odalie said. "Maybe soon you be smiling instead of looking so cross."

Obediently, Madelaine turned up the corners of her mouth, but she'd never felt less like smiling. I wish it could have been me, she thought. Philippe and I before the altar at St. Louis' receiving the sacrament that made us man and wife, arm in arm at the reception here at La Belle . . .

Yet she didn't begrudge Guy his happiness. Inpulsively, she hurried from her bedroom down the stairs, searching for her brother amid the throng of wedding guests. He stood beside a radiant Senalda, smiling and talking to the Lafrenieres. Madelaine eased in on Guy's other side and put her arm through his. When he looked down at her she rose on her toes and kissed his cheek.

"I'm truly happy for you," she whispered into his ear.

He put his arm about her, hugging her. "She's so lovely," he said, his eyes on Senalda. "How can I help but be the happiest man in the world?"

"Certainly the luckiest," Andre Lafreniere said.

Guy nodded. He *was* lucky to have won Senalda as his wife when every young man in New Orleans had wanted her. And tonight—tonight she'd be completely his, they'd be one. He was scarcely conscious of Madelaine leaving his side, or of talking to the many who came to offer good wishes. Nothing seemed real except Senalda beside him. His wife.

Although Guy tried to limit the toasts he drank, he could feel the wine muzz his head by the time he climbed the stairs behind his bride. The candles on the brass and crystal chandelier cast a soft glow over her fair hair so that she almost seemed to be wearing a halo.

Guy smiled. A saint for a wife wouldn't do, not at all. A memory of Aimee's golden body slipped into his mind and he shook his head, pushing the thought away. Now that Senalda was his, he'd need no *placee*.

In the hall below, the last of the guests sang and tinkled bells in a gentle serenade as Guy and Senalda made their way up the staircase. There'd be others, he knew, waiting beneath the windows of the bedroom, but since it was March they'd be able to keep the windows shut. He grinned, thinking of all the times he'd been among the ones outside.

Senalda preceded him through the door to the bedroom and walked so swiftly toward the dressing room at the far end, traditionally the one La Branche wives used, that he hadn't time to take her in his arms as he'd intended to do, to kiss her and tell her how much he loved her. Guy shrugged off his disappointment. No doubt she was nervous, not quite certain what to expect of the marriage bed.

He strode to the dressing room at this end, always the room of the master of La Belle, unbuttoning his waistcoat as he went. He flung off his clothes and draped a satin-lined silk robe over his shoulders as he padded barefoot toward the high white and gilt bed with its carved posters and elaborate canopy.

Senalda wasn't in the bed. He stood beside it, savoring his anticipation, yet impatient, the wine singing in his veins, fueling his desire.

By the time she emerged from the dressing room, he'd begun to wonder if something was wrong. She walked slowly toward him, her diaphanous white robe drifting behind her.

"You look like an angel," he said huskily.

As she came closer he saw that her face was set, her eyes guarded. She turned her gaze away from his naked body.

"The lamp," she said breathlessly. "Put out the lamp."

"But I want to see you. You're so lovely . . ."

"Put out the lamp," she repeated, her voice rising.

Guy did as she asked. In the darkness she was a dim

white figure, like a ghost. He touched her arm and felt her withdrawal.

"Don't be afraid," he murmured. "I'm your husband, there's nothing to be afraid of."

He drew her toward him, intoxicated by the gardenia scent she wore, took her into his arms and kissed her. She stood rigid for a minute before she answered the pressure of his lips, relaxing against him.

A long bang shattered the silence, a gun shot. Another, then another. Bells clanged, voices shouted.

Senalda flinched and pulled away from him.

"It's but the charivari," he assured her. "They saw the lights go out and so they thought . . ."

"How barbaric! They act like peasants."

"It's merely a custom," he said soothingly. "Come to the balcony with me and wave to them. They'll soon go away if we do."

"Tanguy, I'm in my nightrobe. I won't have them staring at me."

"It's dark, no one can see more than is proper. Come." He put an arm about her waist and urged her toward the double glass-paned doors that led to a small balcony.

Senalda resisted him. "I won't be treated like a servant girl."

Guy sighed. "Sweetheart, everyone respects you."

"You aren't even—you aren't clothed," she protested.

He slid his arm into the sleeves of his robe and tied the sash. "I am now," he said, damping down his growing annoyance. "We'll go to the door." Despite himself, the words came forth as an order.

Senalda said nothing, walking with him to the doors, waiting while he pulled the curtains aside, opened one, then stepped onto the balcony.

A cheer went up.

Senalda slipped from the room to stand by his side and the group below shouted their approval.

"Good night," Guy called down to them.

"Sweet dreams," a man's voice called back. Others laughed.

Guy led Senalda inside and closed the glass door. He guided her back to the bed. He touched the front of her robe, feeling for the buttons. She pushed his hand away.

"*Cherie*," he said, "certainly you don't intend to sleep in your robe."

"I'll take it off myself. You—you get into bed first." Her voice quivered.

He smiled in the darkness. A maiden's fears. He'd be loving and gentle. Guy took off his own robe and slid naked between the sheets.

Long moments later he felt Senalda climb into bed on the far side. He waited a few seconds before he moved close to her and touched her.

"My darling," he whispered, "my love." When he tried to caress her breast he found she still wore a thin night shift. "You won't need this," he told her as he began to pull it up her body.

"Don't," she begged, clutching at his hand. "Do what you must—but don't undress me."

"It's all right," he said. "I'm your husband, Senalda. I want to feel your loveliness next to me with no cloth between. Trust me, *cherie*."

"No, no, I want my gown left on. It's a sin. The other—that's a husband's right but I won't be naked."

Guy sighed. The exhilaration of the wine was gone, leaving him with a slight headache. Have patience, he counseled himself. Gently he slipped his hand under her shift and touched skin that was silkier than the finest fabric from China. He ran his finger along the curve of her hip and along her side until he felt the soft roundness of her breast.

Senalda, rigid, submitted to his caresses.

He leaned over and put his lips to hers. She gave no answering pressure. He let the tip of his tongue trace the outline of her lips, hearing a small sound of—was it protest?

Guy pulled back. "What is it?" he asked. "We've kissed

many times before and always you clung to me, felt pleasure in my embrace, at least I thought you did."

"It was different then," she said.

"But how?"

"I wasn't your wife. A kiss was permitted but nothing more. Now . . ." She fell silent.

"Has my kiss changed so much since yesterday?"

"You want to do more. What a husband does."

"Well yes, Senalda. We're married in the eyes of God and man. It's no sin to love one's wife." Her gardenia scented flesh so close to him made him burn with desire. He lay his palm on her cheek. "I'll show you that love between a man and woman is a heavenly gift, a wonderful feeling."

"I know it's my duty," she said. "I won't refuse you."

Guy rose on one elbow to run a hand over her shoulder down across the wispy cloth, pushing the shift up until he could touch her bared thighs. Her caressed her slowly, finally slipping his hand into the soft warmness between her legs. He heard her draw in her breath. Carefully, he caressed her, clenching his teeth against his own mounting need.

He pushed the shift higher, putting his lips to her breast, his tongue circling her nipple. She hadn't relaxed, he could feel her tenseness. He tried to be patient, to go on touching her, caressing her, but he could no longer control his desire and with a groan he pushed her legs farther apart and thrust himself into her.

She screamed.

He wanted to draw back, knowing he was hurting her, but it was too late. He couldn't stop, but could only hold her to him and thrust within her until his overwhelming need was satisfied.

Afterwards, he tried to comfort her as she lay sobbing next to him, but she turned her back and in a few minutes he fell asleep. He woke in the night and reached for her, but when he felt her flinch from him he moved away from her to sleep again.

In the morning she wasn't in the bed when he woke. He sat up. "Senalda?"

She came out of the dressing room wearing a blue velvet robe, a hairbrush in her hand and smiled at him as though the night had never happened.

I'll make it up to her, he told himself. The next time I'll be more patient. I won't hurt her again.

But as the days and nights passed, Guy found that no matter what he did, no matter how hard he tried to give Senalda pleasure, she could only view the marriage bed as a duty. And a disagreeable one, at that.

In April, after a night of gambling with friends, when he found himself heading up the rue des Ramparts at dawn, he hesitated only a second, shrugged and went on.

Aimee stared at him when he opened her door. Her peach robe had been hastily thrown on and her eyes were still drowsy.

"Guy!" she cried, running to him and flinging herself into his arms, clinging to him, laughing and crying at the same time. She smelled not of gardenias but of woman.

He kissed her, finding her full lips warmly responsive. He picked her up and carried her into the bedroom.

Her body was strange under his hands, yet only when he felt the roundness of her belly did he remember the child. But she wanted him, her eyes, her lips, her body told him. He made love to her and it was like coming home.

Guy visited Aimee often after that. She offered him the physical love that Senalda wouldn't or couldn't give him. Though he adored his beautiful blonde wife, he began to treat her more casually.

Aimee's son, Denis, was born on July Fourth, a day the *Americains* celebrated with fireworks, music and speeches as the birth day of their country. His country. Denis' country. Guy found himself caught in the festive spirit of the day. After all, the child might be his and despite being born a little early and small, he was a healthy, beautiful boy. Besides, it was only polite to help the *Americains* mark this twenty-eighth anniversary.

Still, he didn't really feel the United States was his country. He didn't think of himself or his friends as *Americains*. On July fourteenth, Bastille Day, the Creoles had their own celebration, one that meant more to Guy than the Fourth.

The remainder of the year sped by. Guy assisted General Wilkinson in his dealings with the Spaniard over a contested strip of land on the southwestern border between the Louisiana Territory and Spanish-held Texas.

Guy admired and had confidence in the general until late in the year when a man named Aaron Burr came to New Orleans and spent long hours in conference with General Wilkinson. None of the general's aides, Guy included, were made privy to what was discussed.

The coffee houses buzzed with gossip, rumors that the general was a secret spy for Spain, that he was plotting with Burr to form a western empire of Louisiana and Mexico.

"I don't fancy *Americains*," Andre told Guy. "Still, I believe the governor is honest enough. Why doesn't he arrest General Wilkinson?"

"We might join in Burr's scheme and then take over the empire ourselves," Rafe Devol said. "Louisiana for the Creoles. Nicolas Roulleaux would agree with me, even if you don't, Guy."

In his heart he did agree, Guy thought. In his mind, he knew the Creoles were too few, the *Americains* too many to make any such cloud-castle plan practical. About Burr he wasn't so certain. The man was charming and persuasive. If Burr had Wilkinson in back of him, might not his scheme succeed?

Early in 1806, Senalda told Guy she was expecting his child. He celebrated the news with a party and afterwards, in bed, took his wife into his arms.

"You've made me very happy," he told her.

Senalda lay limply in his embrace. "You mustn't touch

me now," she said. "It's not proper. We mustn't come together as man and wife until after the baby is born."

Guy, who'd been thrilled to the center of his being at the idea of a La Branche heir, couldn't help but think of Aimee, and how she'd welcomed his love-making until the very month of Denis' birth. He turned away, suddenly not wanting to hold Senalda, his desire for her gone. After an hour of trying to fall asleep, he rose, dressed and went to the rue des Ramparts where he spent the rest of the night with Aimee.

The next day he registered Aimee's son in the parish books as Denis La Branche.

Senalda was upset when Guy didn't come back to La Belle for a week.

"Can it be he's been taken ill in the city?" she asked Madelaine.

"We would have heard. He's staying in the townhouse, no doubt."

"No, he's not. I asked Josefina to seek him there. The servants at the townhouse haven't seen him."

Madelaine thought it very unwise of Senalda to trust her maid, Josefina, with such a query. The slave was capable enough as a maid but she was young and talkative. It would be all over the city that *Madame* was a fool for not realizing where her husband was. The slaves, all the people of color knew very well. Certainly Josefina knew, as did most of the Creoles. Even I know, Madelaine told herself.

"Don't fret over Guy, Senalda," Madelaine said. "He'll be home when it suits his fancy."

"Josefina said something about another house in town—a cottage?"

Josefina was a menace. "A—a cottage?" Madelaine repeated, trying to think how to parry Senalda's next question.

"By the fortifications at the edge of the city. Why would Guy have a cottage there?"

Madelaine wasn't fond of her sister-in-law. In truth, Senalda acted as though everyone else was of less consequence than herself. She deplored Madelaine's manners, her demeanor, even criticized the way she wore her hair. It had been months since she'd been able to slip away to meet Philippe because Senalda had once caught her coming into the house in the evening at a time when she shouldn't have been outside. Since then Senalda had taken all too much interest in her comings and goings.

"I—Guy doesn't have such a cottage," Madelaine managed to say.

Senalda's blue eyes narrowed, grew chill. "You're not telling me the truth. I don't trust you, Madelaine. You constantly lie to me."

A spurt of anger thrust words onto Madelaine's tongue. "I'm not lying! If you must know, Guy has a *placee* and she lives in that cottage. It's hers, and that's where he is. With her."

The color drained from Senalda's face. Madelaine put her hand over her mouth, whirled and ran out of the room.

When Guy came back to La Belle that evening, Senalda was waiting, her face pale and set.

"You've been with your filthy quadroon," she burst out as he came under the parlor archway.

Guy stopped and stared at her for a moment, then took a deep breath. "*Madame*," he said between clenched teeth, "it's not a matter for discussion."

Senalda stalked across the room and slapped him, hard. "I'll talk about it if I choose," she cried. "How can you do such a thing to me, to your wife?"

"If you acted more like a wife in bed and less like a stick of wood . . ." he began furiously but she cut him off.

"Animal! Beast! To lie with a black woman when I carry your child!"

Guy's eyes glittered. "Do you think you're the only woman in the world who's ever been pregnant?" he shouted. "I already have a son by Aimee. A boy named Denis."

66

She flew at him, beating at his chest with her fists, screaming and crying. He tried to fend her off but she struggled with him, clawing with her nails, until he finally clamped both her wrists in one hand. "Josefina!" he yelled. "Come here, Josefina!"

The black maid appeared instantly in the archway and hurried to Senalda. "Hush," she said. "Be still, *Madame*."

Senalda was beyond hearing as she alternately sobbed and laughed, twisting her body from side to side, her hair straggling down from its chignon.

Madelaine rushed into the parlor. "Can I help?" she asked, her voice trembling.

"We must put Senalda to bed," Guy told her.

As they led the resisting Senalda from the parlor, Guy saw the other house servants gathered in the foyer.

"Tend to your duties," he ordered harshly and they dispersed.

The three of them managed to get the hysterical woman up the curving staircase and put her to bed. Senalda curled on the far side, her body shaking with sobs.

"Give her something to calm her," Guy ordered and Madelaine hurried to measure a draught of laudanum which Josefina finally coaxed Senalda to swallow.

In the hall outside the bedroom, Madelaine touched her brother's sleeve. "I'm sorry," she said. "I didn't mean to tell her about your *placee* but she kept asking and I . . ."

"It's all right. Someone else would have told her if you hadn't. In fact, I—I supposed she knew. Most wives . . ." He broke off. "This isn't fit conversation for your ears, Madelaine."

She shrugged.

Guy sighed and shook his head. "Senalda will get over this," he said. "She'll be . . ."

"*Mademoiselle* Madelaine!" Josefina's voice was shrill with fear. "Please come. Blood be over the bed. She do be losing her baby."

67

Chapter 7

Guy, devastated with guilt over the loss of the child his wife carried, tried at first to comfort her. Senalda, pale and listless, only turned her face from him and didn't speak. He'd moved to another bedroom during the time of the miscarriage and there he stayed, aware that she wouldn't welcome him back to her bed.

Somehow, soon, they must have a rapprochement, he knew, but he couldn't seem to reach Senalda as she sat wanly in her bedroom, refusing to come downstairs even though Dr. Goodreau had assured her she could return to her normal activities.

Guy wasn't happy, either, about his position with General Wilkinson. At first Guy had thought the stout, red-faced *Americain* rather foolish, but he had learned that the genial manner concealed a ruthless efficiency. Guy tried to ignore the rumors that branded Wilkinson a Spanish spy, conspiring with the *marquis* de Casa-Calvo. After all, Governor Claiborne, under orders from President Jefferson, had sent Casa-Calvo a passport with "best wishes for the health and happiness of the nobleman whose presence has become so unacceptable." Whereupon the angry *marquis* left New Orleans for Spanish-held Florida.

Was it likely the President would tolerate the general remaining as Commander-in-Chief of the United States Army if the gossip about him and the Spaniard had been true?

More rumors drifted down the Mississippi about Aaron Burr recruiting men for a take-over of Mexico and Louisiana. General Wilkinson's name became ever more firmly linked to this conspiracy. Guy couldn't make up his mind if the general was involved in the filibustering scheme or not, and he was torn between resigning his position as aide to the man he suspected of being a traitor and staying on to keep close watch on the general.

The hot months passed, the sugar cane harvesting began, then the grinding. Guy was in the sugarhouse at La Belle with the overseer when a messenger arrived from General Wilkinson requesting that Guy report to him immediately.

Guy hurried to the house to change his clothes. As he came down the stairs dressed for town, he saw Madelaine waiting for him in the foyer.

"I'm worried about Senalda," she said.

"You told me last week. I'm in a hurry now, we'll talk later."

"This can't wait. She's—different. She acts strangely."

Guy sighed. "I know she's not herself."

"Is there anything you might do to—well, to make her take an interest in things again?" Madelaine asked.

Guy gazed at the tip of his boots. He'd let too much time go by without insisting that Senalda accept him in her life, in her bed. The truth was he no longer desired the pale, cold ghost of the haughty beauty he'd married. Yet she was his wife and he knew they must reconcile.

Many months had gone by since the loss of the baby. Perhaps if Senalda became pregnant again she'd improve. As soon as he came back from meeting with the general he'd force the issue.

If he gave his whole heart to wooing her, was there a chance he could make Senalda love him with all of herself? To be his wife completely? If that could happen surely he'd regain his desire for her. Guy struck his fist into his hand. *Dieu,* he'd give it his best try. In a way, he still loved her.

He smiled at Madelaine. "I'll do my best to help Senalda," he said. "Now I must go to the general."

"Burr's threatening New Orleans," General Wilkinson told his aides and officers in a secret meeting. "We'll fortify the city, set up blockades. I intend to ask the governor to declare martial law."

"Burr's coming down the Mississippi?" Major Tomlinson asked.

Wilkinson nodded curtly. "I've informed President Jefferson of the threat against New Orleans, but we can't expect troops to get here before Burr and his men."

"How many does he command?" the major asked.

"Perhaps as many as ten thousand."

The room was silent. New Orleans had the newly formed *guarde de ville,* the city guard, and the Louisiana militia available. Neither were large, nor were they seasoned fighting groups.

"I'll be sending a force of men upriver to watch for Burr's expedition, to strike at him if he slips past the guards at Natchez." The general looked from one to the other. "I'll accept volunteers."

Every man in the room rose, *Americains* and Creoles alike.

"Major Tomlinson, you'll command one expedition. La Branche, Devol, Perrier, arm yourselves and report to the major. I'll see you get a company of soldiers, major. Captain Hock, I plan to send you up to Natchez with a squad. As for you other men, I'll expect you to recruit additional volunteers to patrol the city. Dismissed."

Guy rushed back to La Belle to arm himself for the expedition. He had no uniform except the dress whites he'd worn as aide to de Laussat so he donned hunting clothes and boots. As he came out of his bedroom, Senalda drifted past in the hall. He called her name and she jerked with surprise, turning her head.

"Senalda," he repeated, coming to her and taking her hands.

She gazed at him with oddly blank eyes. He felt a tremor of apprehension.

"*Cherie,* I've neglected you and I'm sorry. I must travel up the river on order of General Wilkinson but when I come back we'll spend time together, just the two of us."

She said nothing.

He touched her cheek gently. "We'll have a child yet, my love, don't despair. Wait for my return." He kissed her forehead and patted her shoulder.

She made no response.

"Senalda!" he said loudly.

She blinked and took a step backwards.

"Won't you wish me good fortune?" he asked.

"Of course," she said, her voice slightly hoarse, as if from disuse.

He smiled, brought her hand to his lips, turned and ran down the stairs, spurs jingling.

Senalda stood staring after her husband. Long after he was gone from the house she remained in the same spot. He'd disarrayed the curtain of grey that hung between her and the world. His voice, his touch had slashed holes through which flowed memories she'd thrown away.

A baby. She placed her hands atop her stomach, one over the other. Her stomach was flat. But there'd been a baby inside her, she remembered. Yes, she remembered.

Where was the baby now? For, although she couldn't find the memory of being brought to bed for the birth, she must have delivered her child. She touched her breasts, found them strangely shrunken. From nursing? These weren't the full breasts of a new mother. The boy was older then, finished with his mother's milk. For hadn't Guy told her the baby was a boy? "My son," he'd said.

71

She even recalled the name. Denis. Of Guy's choosing, obviously.

How thin her arms were. Had she been ill? Of course, that was it, that was why her mind seemed so fuzzy—she'd been ill. Senalda turned toward the room she'd choosen for the nursery.

"Denis?" she called softly as she opened the door. "Denis, where are you? Where is mother's darling boy?"

Guy had been on the Mississippi innumerable times, crossing to plantations on the right bank, visiting others up or down stream, out into the gulf fishing. Travel upriver was always difficult, fighting against the swift current. In their bulky keelboats, poled by ten men to either side of each boat, it took almost a week for Guy's expedition, led by Major Tomlinson, to move the sixty miles up the Mississippi the general had ordered. Christmas passed while they poled upstream.

Boats of all description sailed by them toward New Orleans—*pirogues*, flatboats, keelboats. Most had a few armed men aboard, *Kaintocks* with their squirrel rifles, other men with muskets and pistols, but in none of the boats were the men they sought.

The weather, which had been sunny when they left the city, grew increasingly cloudy. When they landed sixty miles upriver, it was in a chilling rain. They found a stand of pines and the men immediately split into two groups, the Creoles setting up camp together, some twenty of them, separate from the thirty-odd *Americain* soldiers and keelboatmen.

"A damn bunch of gaudy peacocks in them fancy clothes," one of the *Americain* keelboaters muttered to a companion. "Do they think we're gonna toss a ball?" He minced about, imitating the steps of a quadrille.

Guy pretended not to understand. He spoke English far better than his fellow Creoles but it was likely the *Kaintock* didn't realize this and so the remark wasn't intended for his ears. There was no sense in taking offense. A fine group of guards they'd be if they began to fight among themselves. Yet anger smoldered deep inside him.

He was glad the *Americains* didn't know French, for Jean Perrier constantly pointed out their faults. "Hogs are clean and dainty by comparison," Jean complained. "*Mon Dieu,* what filthy pigs."

Two days after they landed, January first, 1807, dawned cold and misty. As the sun rose, Guy saw the shrubs about the campsite glittered with frost. He shivered in his greatcoat and held his hands out to the morning fire, wishing he was back in New Orleans, making New Year's visits with his friends from house to house, enjoying life.

Was Aaron Burr really coming? There'd been so many rumors. Spanish soldiers marching to Baton Rouge to join Burr, a flotilla of armed *Americain* volunteers, added to at every stop along the Ohio and Mississippi Rivers as Burr floated down toward New Orleans.

Guy didn't trust General Wilkinson. He knew the man's disarming manner hid a shrewd brain, a devious mind that might very well have conspired with Burr in the beginning and now, feeling Burr's was a losing cause, conspired against him. He, personally, had caught the general in more than one lie.

Yet who could risk the chance of Burr arriving in New Orleans with enough armed men to take over the city? That's why Guy had come to this cold and uncomfortable spot to begin with, there was little point in grousing about what he'd felt had to be done.

"I say they're a bunch of God-damned sissies, each and every one of the froggies," a hoarse voice said loudly, slurring the words so Guy could scarcely understand them.

Without turning his head, he glanced toward the *Americain* tents. A buckskin-clad *Kaintock* keelboater stood with his hands on his hips, staring toward the Creoles. One of the soldiers tried to pull him down by their fire.

"What's he saying?" Jean Perrier demanded. "What insult does that *cachon*, that pig, shout at us?"

73

"I couldn't understand him." Guy lied. "He's drunk."

"I know that word he uses. Frog. He dares to call a Perrier a frog?" Jean's voice rose and the *Kaintock* took a step toward the Creole tents.

"You talking to me?" the *Americain* demanded?

"*Oui, cachon,*" Jean called, glaring at the man.

"I don't know frog talk but I know when I'm being called something nasty," the *Kaintock* said.

"What's he saying?" Jean asked Guy.

All the Creoles were gathered around Jean and Guy. More of the *Americain* soldiers as well as other keel-boaters joined the *Kaintock*. Guy's muscles tensed.

"Attention!" Major Tomlinson's command was as icy as the morning wind. He walked between the two groups of men. "I'll have no brawling in camp," he warned. "Any man who breaks the rule will find himself under arrest. Is that clear?" His eyes drifted over the men, lingering on the keelboaters, before he allowed the soldiers to return to their breakfasts.

For three days there were no further incidents as the men took shifts watching the river, two men at a time. That night, as Guy was coming off from his turn at sentry duty, he spotted Jean slipping out of his tent. The smoldering fire cast enough light so Guy could see Jean wore his sword buckled about his waist.

"Ah, Guy." Jean patted the sheath significantly. "I plan to seek out the *Kaintock* and challenge him. "I've been watching and listening. He's called Whiskey Joe Banks and I know where he sleeps."

"Have you forgotten the major's order?"

Jean held up his hand. "The duel won't be in the camp, no, we'll fight upstream at a spot I've found."

"The *Americain* will have his choice of weapons," Guy reminded him. "Have you ever fired a squirrel rifle?"

Jean shrugged. "If I can shoot one rifle I can shoot another."

"And can you also use a knife with the skill of a keelboatman? Don't be a fool, Jean. A challenge is wasted on such a lout as Whiskey Joe. Besides, we're here on a mission, not to quarrel with one another."

"Do you dare to call Jean Perrier a fool?"

Guy sighed. "Calm down. I'm just trying to make you see this isn't the time or place for a duel. Whiskey Joe didn't actually insult you in any case. He was drunk, that's all."

"I don't believe you. He called me names and you refused to tell me what the words meant. Do you take sides with the *Americains* over your own people?"

Nothing Guy said could sway Jean and, finally, Guy stood among the ten men gathered on a rise along a row of moss-hung oaks to watch the duel between Whiskey Joe and Jean. As Guy had feared, the boatman chose knives, wicked instruments with long curved blades.

Three lanterns hung from branches of the trees, casting a sinister glow over the scene. Guy knew that Jean had never fought with a knife. Creoles regarded knives as implements for skinning game or cutting cane. Certainly not for a duel between gentlemen. *Le bon Dieu* only knew how many men Whiskey Joe might have knifed up and down the river. The only thing in Jean's favor was that the boatman was half-drunk.

"I'm a roaring rip-snorter and I can lick an alligator one-handed," Whiskey Joe shouted, waving his knife above his head.

"En garde," Rafe Devol cried, acting as Jean's second.

"Go to it!" exclaimed the boatman standing by Whiskey Joe.

The duellists circled one another warily. Jean dodged aside from a feint by the *Americain*, who immediately lunged again, narrowly missing the Creole. They circled again.

Guy held his breath, watching. "Use the bedamned knife," he urged Jean inaudibly, for it wasn't proper to shout advice to duellists. "Strike at him when he rushes you."

An explosion split the air, the crack of a rifle. Guy spun

around, searching the darkness. Another shot. Six soldiers double-stepped into the open from the pines, lantern light glinting on leveled gun barrels. For a moment, Guy thought he was looking at Aaron Burr's men.

Major Tomlinson stepped into the light. "Perrier, Banks, you're both under arrest," he snapped. "Drop the knives and submit quietly. I'm in no mood for argument after being roused from my sleep by your foolishness. Do you think I issue orders to hear myself talk?"

Under the unwavering rifles on the soldiers, both men threw their weapons to the ground.

"You'll be confined in a tent with guards set," the major said as Jean and Whiskey Joe were marched off. He smiled for the first time. "Confined in the same tent. I trust you'll enjoy each other's company." He turned to the onlookers. "As for the rest of you, keep this in mind before you decide to flout camp rules."

The next day the Creoles avoided Guy and, as he approached his friend Rafe, even Rafe hesitated before he returned Guy's greeting.

"What's the matter with everyone?" Guy asked.

"They think you told the major."

Guy's eyes widened.

"*I* don't believe you'd turn against us," Rafe said, but there was a hint of a question in his words.

The next two weeks dragged on, Guy a pariah among his fellow Creoles. When the news came on January eighteenth that Aaron Burr had been arrested near Natchez the day before, and that his force had amounted to only sixty men, Guy felt it was an ironic anticlimax.

Chapter 8

IN the foyer of the plantation house, Madelaine tried to smile at her sister-in-law. Behind Senalda, the front door stood open and a cold January wind rattled the tear-drop crystals of the chandelier. The setting sun slanted dull redness onto the polished tiles.

"Please stay inside," Madelaine said. "You haven't your pelisse on or even a shawl. You mustn't catch a chill."

Senalda held out her hands imploringly. "Why won't you help me?" she asked. "I know my son is out there, lost in this terrible swamp country. I've searched and searched but . . ."

Madelaine took her hands. "Senalda, come upstairs. Josefina has a hot bath ready for you, the tub is in your room." Her heart contracted with pity for the gaunt, bedraggled figure who stood in front of her.

Senalda looked twice as old as she was, her beauty faded. Madelaine had tried time and again to convince her that she had no baby, but Senalda wouldn't listen to her. Day after day Senalda searched the house and grounds for an imaginary son. Denis, she called him, amd Madelaine felt a *frisson* of unease every time Senalda said the name. She knew that Guy's *placee* had a boy named Denis.

77

Guy, please hurry home, Madelaine prayed under her breath. *Hurry.*

When she'd coaxed her sister-in-law up the stairs and into Josefina's care, Madelaine withdrew to her own room, where Odalie sat mending one of her mistress' gowns.

"Odalie, I'm at my wit's end," she said. "I don't like to think about locking her in her bedroom but what am I to do? If that field hand hadn't seen her go into the swamp yesterday and followed her, she'd have died. The quicksand would have swallowed her and no one would have known. We can't watch her every minute."

"*Monsieur* Guy be home soon. Maybe he help *Madame*."

"I hope so. Oh, how I hope so."

Later that night, when she was ready for bed, Madelaine walked quietly to Senalda's door and eased it open. Seeing Senalda on the bed, she beckoned to Josefina to come to the door.

"You must watch her carefully tonight," Madelaine whispered. "We can't have her outside in the dark."

"She never go out, be it dark," Josefina said.

"She's getting more and more restless. We must take no chances. Sleep in front of the door."

Josefina nodded, glancing slyly at Madelaine. "She do be talking about that Aimee when she take her bath," she said.

Madelaine frowned at her. It seemed every slave in the house had overheard the quarrel last year that had culminated in Senalda's miscarriage. Still, they'd probably known well before that about Guy's *placee* and the son she had. House servants seemed to know everything.

"I watch *Madame* good," Josefina said, eyes downcast.

"See that you do." Madelaine turned away from the door and returned to her own room, troubled and uncertain. Should she have punished Josefina for daring to speak Aimee's name in her presence? *Dieu* only knew Senalda said the name often enough, demanding to know who

Aimee was, where she lived. She seemed to have forgotten entirely about the *placee* business which was just as well.

Every day Senalda seemed to sink deeper into a morass of confusion and agitation. When Madelaine had stopped her from going out this afternoon, the wild look in Senalda's eyes had been more chilling than the winter wind.

Senalda kept her eyes closed when Josefina bent over her. Everyone in this house was against her, she knew that. No matter how they smiled and pretended concern, no one would help her find Denis.

She'd asked and asked about Aimee. Tanguy had said the name, she recalled that clearly. Who was this person? Yesterday she'd asked one of the field hands, threatening to have him whipped if he didn't tell her. She'd frightened him into revealing where Aimee lived. Now she clutched the knowledge to herself.

Rue des Ramparts.

She lay very still, eyes shut, hearing Josefina fuss about the room, straightening, putting things away. Finally the glow of light on her eyelids faded and she knew Josefina, believing her asleep, was planning to prepare for sleep herself.

To sleep in this bedroom in front of the door. Madelaine had told her to. They thought she couldn't hear as they whispered and plotted against her. Where was Tanguy, why had he left her alone?

Senalda waited, listening for Josefina's snoring to begin. When she heard it, she opened her eyes. The lamp was turned very low. Josefina lay on a straw pallet next to the bedroom door so that the door couldn't be opened. Senalda's eyes turned to the windows that were really glass doors leading onto the balcony. Outside, next to the balcony, thick vines of wisteria clung to the stuccoed brick walls. Once, a long time ago, hadn't she stood on that balcony with Tanguy while voices shouted below?

Carefully, Senalda rose from the bed. She saw Josefina's old black shawl folded on the floor next to the pallet and, tiptoeing, picked up the shawl and flung it over her shoulders so it covered much of his white nightgown. She crept to the glass doors and very slowly eased one open, freezing in place when it creaked. Josefina grunted and turned over.

Senalda waited, then inched the door farther open until she could slip past it onto the balcony. She pulled up her gown and bunched it around her thighs, tucking in the ends to hold it in place, climbed onto the balcony railing and clutched at the vines of wisteria.

On the way to the ground, strands of the vine ripped loose under Senalda's feet and she almsot fell, but she hung on grimly with her fingers until her bare toes found new holds. She realized when her feet touched the cold ground that she'd forgotten her slippers. It didn't matter, the important thing was that she'd escaped. She was free now to find Aimee.

As she headed toward the city she prayed to the Virgin. "I must find my child, Mary. You, who lost your beloved son, aid me in my search. Mother Mary, guide my steps."

Senalda sighed, remembering Sister Ana in the Convent of the Blessed Miracle near Madrid. Sister Ana had been like a mother to her, more beloved than her own mother, whom she rarely saw. Sister Ana had urged Senalda to pray that God might lead her to a religious vocation. Senalda had been of two minds. She knew men admired her and the knowledge was like wine but she still felt at home, protected, behind the convent walls where she'd spent so much of her life.

Her mother wouldn't hear of such a notion. "You'll marry well, Senalda," she said. "You'll marry money."

Tanguy was wealthy, but she'd married him because he didn't frighten her as much as some of her other suitors. With his arm in a sling he'd been a romantic figure, she'd felt he needed her to take care of him.

After the marriage . . . Senalda put her hand to her heart. No, she wouldn't remember. She couldn't. All she knew was that Tanguy wasn't with her. Where was he? Why wasn't he helping her to find their son?

A bobcat screamed in the darkness to her right, startling her. So many wild animals in this country, the swamps filled with them, with snakes and birds and plants that fought each other for room. Too much life and growth, a choking green profusion. Not like Spain's hills and fields which had never threatened her.

Everything and everyone was against her here. The cold damp ground hurt her feet, the chill night breeze froze her—and they'd taken her son. Wings brushed her face and she bit her lip to keep from crying out. A bat? An owl? Senalda hurried on.

She reached the river road along the levee. She knew the way, she'd follow the road into town. When she'd walked for some time, she heard horses' hooves and the rattle of wheels. She shrank into the roadside shadows. A loaded dray passed her. Fortune smiled. The driver hadn't seen her. She clutched the shawl closer and went on.

Senalda slipped through the streets of New Orleans uncertainly, keeping away from the light, avoiding everyone. She had only a vague idea of where the rue des Ramparts was, although she knew from the name that the street must be near the fortifications at the edge of the city.

When she finally came onto the rue des Ramparts, Senalda walked along the row of white cottages.

"It be the last," the slave had told her, standing in the stubble of cut cane. His eyes had showed white all around the brown, like the eyes of a frightened horse.

He hadn't wanted to tell her, but he was afraid. Of her, maybe, and not the whipping she'd threatened, for when she'd seen herself in the mirror it was like looking at a stranger. How had she grown so thin and starey-eyed?

The last cottage. What would she say to Aimee when she found her? Senalda's steps lagged. Could Aimee help her? Would she? No one talked of Aimee at La Belle, no one said who she was. Except Tanguy. He'd mentioned her name. If only her memory was better.

She'd ask Aimee to help her find Denis. Yes, that was it. Aimee knew where Denis was. Hadn't Tanguy said so?

Senalda's bare feet made no noise on the wooden porch. Her hand went to the door. Locked. She tapped at it, waited, knocked again, louder.

"Who is it?" a voice asked through the wood.

"I come from Tanguy," Senalda said, smiling at her cleverness, for Aimee might not know her name. "Let me in."

The locked clicked, the door opened. Senalda stared at the pretty woman in the doorway holding a lamp. A very pretty woman. "Aimee?" she said.

"Yes. Who are you? What does Guy want?"

Senalda started forward and Aimee fell back to let her come in. Senalda closed the door. "Where is Denis?" she asked.

"He's sleeping, of course." Aimee's glance took in Senalda's bare, bleeding feet, the shawl covering a night dress. "What do you want?" she asked, a tinge of alarm in her voice.

Senalda looked hard at her. A quadroon? Was Aimee Denis' nursemaid? But why did she keep him here in New Orleans, so far from La Belle, so far from his mother?

"I've come to take Denis home," she said.

"What? What are you talking about?"

"If Tanguy hadn't gone away, this wouldn't have happened," Senalda said. "What right do you have to hide my son from me?"

Aimee edged away, her yellow eyes wide. "I don't have any child of yours," she said. "Denis is my own son."

"You lie! Denis is mine and you've stolen him. Give him back to me immediately!"

"You're mad," Aimee gasped. "I know who you are now, they told me your mind was gone and they were right." She backed farther away. "Get out, get out of my house."

Senalda ran at her and Aimee ducked to the side, clutching at the lamp to keep it from overturning. Senalda hurried past her and into the tiny hallway. She peered into the gloom of a bedroom, heard a child cry out.

"Maman, maman!"

Senalda plunged into the room toward the sound of the child's voice. She stumbled against a cot, bent and felt warm flesh under her hands.

"Denis," she cried, "oh, thank God I've found you."

She snatched him up and turned to see Aimee in the doorway, still holding the light.

"Put him down," Aimee shouted.

Senalda looked quickly about, seized a poker from beside the tiny fireplace. "Let me by," she said.

The child in her arms began to struggle and cry.

"Give me my boy," Aimee sobbed, slamming the lamp onto a table and lunging at Senalda. "Give him to me!"

Senalda slashed with the poker but Aimee's rush knocked her over backwards and the three of them crashed to the floor in a tangle. Senalda lost her grip on the boy.

"Maman!" Denis screamed. Aimee reached for him.

Senalda felt the poker still in her hand. She lifted it and swung at Aimee's head, once, twice. Aimee fell back and Senalda raised the poker and hit her again and again until her arm grew tired and the poker fell from her grasp.

She looked down at Aimee's bloody head. "It was your own fault," she said. "You shouldn't have taken my son." She turned to Denis who was shaking with convulsive sobs, kneeled down and picked him up.

"Come, darling, *maman* will take you home," she crooned.

Chapter 9

MAJOR Tomlinson and his men disembarked in New Orleans in a driving rain. Guy, though eager to get home to La Belle, accepted Rafe Devol's invitation to stop in a coffee house, not wanting to refuse Rafe's peace offering, but when they stepped inside Turpin's, he looked around and regretted his decision. Nicolas sat at a front table with his younger brother and Marc de la Harpe. Guy would have to pass their table to sit down.

Nicolas raised his eyebrows at the sight of Rafe and Guy in their bedraggled clothes. He leaned over and said something that caused Marc to laugh and Philippe to scowl.

Guy gritted his teeth and went past to another table. No use to borrow trouble. Since he hadn't heard what Nicolas said, it was folly to decide the words were about him, mocking him in some way.

Mon Dieu, it was good to be back in the city, to return to civilization. The *Americains* could have the wilderness for all he cared. They and the Indians. He glanced about at the other patrons, hoping to spot Gabriel, and noticed to his surprise that everyone was watching him with eyes that slid away when his gaze met theirs. The place seemed unusually quiet.

He leaned to Rafe. "Do you imagine they think us heroes? Or possibly fools?" He gestured with his head toward the watchers.

Rafe looked about, frowned. "I think it's you they're interested in."

Guy shrugged. Perhaps word was already out about the aborted duel at the camp. He'd ignore them, have his coffee and go home. He was wet and tired and regretted his impulsive decision to volunteer for the Burr expedition. It had accomplished nothing. Worse, now he was mistrusted by Creoles who once liked him.

As he and Rafe left the coffee house, Guy heard a buzz of conversation begin before the door closed behind them. He caught a word of two.

". . . mad . . ."

". . . blood all over . . ."

"Do you suppose we've missed a noteworthy duel?" he asked Rafe.

"Who knows?" Rafe's voice was cool and Guy cursed himself for reminding Rafe of what had happened.

"I'm off for La Belle," he said, clapping Rafe on the shoulder. "Give my regards to your parents."

"And mine to your lovely wife," Rafe said as they parted in the rain.

Old Louis, who'd been his grandfather's body servant and was now Guy's butler, opened the front door of the manor house as Guy climbed the steps onto the porch in the gathering dusk.

"We be happy to see you, *Monsieur* Guy. Most happy." But old Louis wasn't smiling.

Guy shed his wet hat and coat. "I'm just as happy to be back," he said. "I'll want a bath and . . ." He broke off as Madelaine came running into the foyer, calling his name.

"Guy, oh Guy, I'm so glad you're here. It's been terrible." She flung herself at him, heedless of his damp clothes, and began to sob against his chest.

An ominous chill went through him. Madelaine had never missed him this much before. He grasped her shoulders and held her at arms-length from him.

"What's wrong?" he demanded. Where's Senalda? Is she all right?"

Tears streamed down Madelaine's face. "No," she sobbed, "oh no."

He shook her a little. "*Nom de Dieu*, tell me!"

"Senalda—she—I had to—oh, Guy, I had to lock her in the storeroom."

"You what?" He stared at his sister, thunderstruck. "You did what?"

Madelaine pulled away from him and wiped at her eyes with a handkerchief. "Senalda's gone mad, Guy. It wasn't safe to—to . . ."

"How dare you do such a thing to my wife?" he demanded. "Take me to her immediately."

She bit her lip, new tears welling. "There's worse to tell . . ." she began but he grabbed her shoulders again.

"Take me to Senalda, I said!"

From upstairs he heard a child begin to cry and he stared in the direction of the sound, then back at his sister.

She sighed, saying only, "Come with me."

Madelaine hurried toward the back of the house with Guy following close behind. As they passed the house slaves he noticed with a fragment of his mind that not one wore a welcoming smile, but scuttled out of the way, avoiding his eyes.

On a nail beside a room he remembered as small and windowless, hung a key. Madelaine lifted it down and inserted the key into the lock, turned it, and hesitantly pushed open the door. She stood back to let him enter.

A ceiling lamp turned low cast a dim light. Empty wooden shelves told of the room's former use. A bed and commode took up most of the floor space. Atop the covers, her gown rucked up to expose her nakedness, lay— *mon Dieu!* This emaciated stick of a woman couldn't be his beautiful Senalda!

Madelaine eased past him to pull down the gown and put the bedclothes in order.

"I tried to tell you," she said in a low tone as he walked to the bedside.

The gaunt woman on the bed opened her eyes and they were the same blue he remembered. This was his wife. He sent Madelaine an anguished look. "Why did you put her here? How could you?"

"You don't understand . . ."

"I understand you've locked a very sick woman in a windowless cell. How could you be so cruel?"

"She—she escapes, Guy. She climbs out windows and she . . ." Madelaine broke off, started again. "She bites and scratches the servants, too. They won't take care of her, they're too frightened. I—she doesn't hurt me. But I can't watch her all the time. This is the only way I can—protect her."

"I want her taken upstairs to her own bedroom immediately. The servants bedamned—I'm master here, they'll do as I say."

He looked down at Senalda and tears blurred his vision. He dropped to his knees beside the bed and gently took one of her hands. "*Cherie*," he whispered.

Senalda looked into his face with no sign of recognition. "Denis," she said in a thin, sad voice. "I hear him crying. Bring him to me, bring me my son."

Hair rose on Guy's neck. He dropped her hand and rose, turned to face Madelaine. She spread her hands.

"I keep trying to tell you," she said. "While you were gone . . ."

A dull thud came from the front of the house. The front door slamming. Guy stepped into the corridor. He heard Louis' voice raised in protest. Someone, a black woman from the sound, demanding, her voice drowning out Louis'.

"The *monsieur* is home, you don't lie to me, old man, lest you wish to suffer."

Guy strode toward the foyer, stopped short when he

saw Louis cringing away from a tall mulatto woman. She wore all white, even her *tignon* was white, and he was reminded of someone—of Aimee's sister, Estelle. This woman was older, but she looked like Estelle.

"What do you want?" he asked her. "What are you doing in my house?"

"You know who I am," she said, crossing her arms and looking directly at him. "You know."

She had to be Vedette Rusert, Aimee and Estelle's mother. The voodoo queen. No wonder old Louis was frightened.

"I know who you are. Why are you here?" he demanded.

"I came for my grandson. He don't belong in this house."

Guy blinked, a terrible conviction forming. The child he'd heard crying, Senalda asking for Denis . . . But how was such a thing possible?

He took a step toward Vedette. "Where's Aimee?" he asked. "Is she all right?"

Her eyes blazed. "Aimee lies in stone, if you call that 'all right.' You give me back Denis, she brought him here, where he don't belong."

"Aimee brought him here? I don't understand."

Vedette raised her arms straight up, flinging back her head. "He don't know, the man don't know," she said, eyes fixed on the foyer ceiling. "*Bon Dieu*, he don't know."

Vedette brought her gaze down to fix Guy's once more. She glided toward him until she was inches away. "That woman you marry brought Denis here. She killed my Aimee and took my grandson. He is mine. I want him. Where is he?"

Upstairs the child cried out as though in answer and Vedette whirled and dashed up the stairs, reappearing moments later with Denis in her arms. The boy stared wide-eyed at Guy who, stunned, hadn't moved.

From the direction of the storeroom a wild cry rose. "Denis, Denis!"

Vedette, on her way to the front door, paused, her dark gaze sliding toward the sound of Senalda's voice. She shifted the child to one arm, reached into a pocket of her gown and, before Guy realized what she meant to do, she hurried past him toward the storeroom.

He ran after her. Madelaine stood in the corridor, key in her hand. The storeroom door was closed. Vedette fumbled with the knob a moment, turned away and slipped down the hall toward the rear door.

"Wait," Guy called, but she paid him no mind and when he followed her outside, she and the child she carried had disappeared in the misty drizzle of the night.

He walked slowly back along the corridor. Louis stood beside Madelaine in front of the storeroom, staring in horror at the door.

"*Gris-gris*," Louis muttered.

Guy saw that a bundle of black fur and white feathers hung from the doorknob. He snatched it off and thrust it at Louis.

"Burn this abomination," he ordered.

The old man backed away, his eyes white-ringed with terror. "Don't be making me touch no voodoo *gris-gris*," he pleaded.

Guy, about to shout at Louis, clenched his fists. Voodoo. No use to blame Louis, the slaves believed in voodoo. He took a deep breath, let it out slowly. "I'll take care of it," he managed to say.

Louis bobbed his head in thankfulness and backed away, then turned and fled down the corridor.

Madelaine clenched the key in a whitened fist. "What—what is that thing?" she asked.

"Some kind of voodoo charm, it's meaningless." He spoke firmly to reassure his sister, although he'd been shaken to his soul by Vedette. The *gris-gris* in his hand seemed inexplicably foul to him and he strode to the back door and flung it into the night.

When he came back to the storeroom door, Madelaine handed him the key. He looked at her. "Is it true what she said?" he asked, knowing the question was useless, for Vedette hadn't lied.

Madelaine nodded, her face pinched and white.

He said nothing for a moment, then unlocked the storeroom door. "We must bring Senalda upstairs," he said. "I'll watch over her."

Senalda was so light in his arms he felt as if it was a child he carried. He bore her into the bedroom they'd once shared and laid her gently on the bed.

"I'll take care of you, *cherie*," he murmured.

She didn't open her eyes or answer.

Guy stayed with Senalda constantly for the next two weeks, watching her fade each day. She wouldn't eat, took almost no water, and seemed to be in a trance. He couldn't bring himself to lay next to her, so he slept in a chair drawn up beside the big bed.

At night he left a candle burning and one morning, early, before dawn, when the night's candle had almost guttered out, he woke suddenly, believing he'd heard his name. He leaned over to look at Senalda. Her eyes were open, staring at him, and he thought she knew who he was for the first time since he'd come home from upriver. He touched her cheek very gently and her lips quivered as though she was trying to smile. Her eyelids fluttered closed and she stopped breathing.

When he went to rouse Madelaine, he found Louis at the top of the staircase by the grandfather clock. Incredulous, he watched as Louis stopped the pendulum so the clock no longer ticked. Louis looked up the stairs, saw him and nodded solemnly.

"I be knowing," he said. "I always knows when somebody in the family die."

By dawn, all the clocks in the house had been stopped. Black crepe hung on the outside of the front door.

In a daze of grief, Guy had the coffin made and ordered the black hearse with its matched pairs of black horses. He sat through the service at St. Louis Cathedral, hearing not a word, and watched silently as the lavender coffin was carried into the cold stone of the La Branche vault.

When Madelaine touched his arm, to have him come away with her, he shook his head. She persisted and he looked into her eyes, red-rimmed from crying and patted her shoulder.

"I'm all right. I want to be alone for a time."

Reluctantly, she left him, everyone left, and he was alone by the vault.

He saw Senalda before him, smiling and haughty in her blonde beauty as she'd been when she descended from her uncle's carriage the first time he'd set eyes on her. That was his Senalda, not the pitiful remains in the lavender coffin.

But where had his Senalda gone? How had she become someone else? He realized he'd never really understood her and now it was too late, forever too late.

He bowed his head and prayed for the Virgin Mary to intercede for her soul. Sometime later he looked around, saw that the sun's rays slanted, the day waned. Guy left the cemetery and made his way toward the river, to another, smaller graveyard. Once there, he opened the gate and went inside. Two mulatto women glanced at him as they moved away, leaving. No one else was in sight.

He walked between the vaults, searching, and came to one that the setting sun touched to rose-red.

LaMotte. Aimee LaMotte.

Her name was carved below an angel holding a wreath.

Now, at last, tears came to Guy's eyes. "Forgive me," he murmured brokenly. "Forgive me, Aimee, for you weren't to blame for what lay between my wife and me. May you find your place in heaven."

He dropped to his knees, covered his face with his hands and wept for both his loves.

When he rose at last, he was startled to see a white figure standing next to him in the dimness of early evening.

"Vedette!" he exclaimed.

"No, I'm Estelle," the woman said.

He let out his breath. "How is Denis?" he asked.

"I've brought him to Aimee's cottage," Estelle said. "My mother says he shouldn't be raised in her house."

"She seemed determined to have him," Guy said grimly. "But I'd much rather have him with you. Stay in the cottage as long as you like."

"My mother only wished to have Denis in his rightful place," Estelle told him. "That wasn't La Belle. She says the cottage is his home."

"Yes." Guy knew he'd never use the cottage again. "I'll see there's a settlement made for you to take care of Denis," he added.

Estelle nodded as though it was no more than she expected. "Aimee was so gentle, she never would have harmed anyone," she said. "And she truly loved you."

He bit his lip. "I know that."

Estelle stared at him. Was that hate he saw glowing deep within her eyes? Something stirred inside him as he met her gaze, a desire as dark and unfathomable as her eyes. He was appalled. He thought she recognized what was happening to him for her brows drew together and she turned, slipping into the evening shadows without a word of farewell.

Guy was left alone with the dead.

Chapter 10

"So now they tell us no more Negroes from Africa? Ah, these *Americains*, always seeking to inconvenience us." Andre Lafreniere removed his cigar from the tray on the coffee house table and took a puff. He blew out the smoke and smiled wisely. "What they don't know won't hurt them, eh?"

Guy nodded. African Negroes were untrained and wild, sullen at being captives. Guy felt he could understand—he'd be as bad if someone tried to force him into slavery. He, like all the Creole planters, preferred Caribbean-born blacks from the West Indies. It was against the law to import them, so men living on the islands at the mouth of the Mississippi, the Baratarians, made a good living smuggling Caribbean slaves into New Orleans.

The Baratarians charged more for their product but, *Dieu*, an amenable, trained black was well worth the extra money.

"I have perhaps ten Africans left in my fields," Andre said. "Trouble-makers, most of them. The whip cures them only for a time." He shook his head.

Guy didn't hold him with whippings and mutilations. What he wouldn't do to an animal he certainly wouldn't do to a human. If, now and then, a slave had to be shot, that was a fact of life. You destroyed those who would destroy you, animal or human, black or white. All Creoles lived with an uneasiness, for they were outnumbered by the blacks—if the slaves and free persons of color were counted together. There was always the nagging fear that the free Negroes might join the slaves in a bloody revolt against the Creoles.

"Isn't President Jefferson a planter himself?" Andre went on. "Perhaps he breeds his replacements, then, for a man wouldn't cut his own throat."

"Jefferson's president, not king," Guy said. "Congress passed the law prohibiting the African slave trade. We're governed by a republic these days."

"But not, I think, one such as *la belle* France."

"We'll have our own state congress when Louisiana joins the union of states," Guy said. "A house of representatives and a senate."

"So?"

"So you should think about being elected to this state legislature, Andre. How else can Creoles run Louisiana?"

Andre laughed until he choked on the smoke from his cigar. "Me, writing laws? Come, Tanguy, how would the planting get done, the cane-grinding? Who would run the plantation?"

"The same ones who run it now, while you and I sit in this coffee house. Our overseers." Guy grinned at the older man. "We'd be right here in New Orleans, able to be home every night."

"Ah, I see. You plan to be in this legislature and you wish me to come along for company."

Guy sobered. "I don't always agree with you, Andre, but you want what's best for Louisiana, for the Creoles, and so do I. We can work together. Unlike—others."

Andre shot him a sharp glance. "Nicolas Roulleaux intends to be in this congress of ours, too?"

"So I've heard."

"I'll consider what you say." Andre held out his cigar

and regarded the glowing tip thoughtfully. "Certainly we Creoles must make our own laws. Having an *Americain* for a governor is bad enough." He sighed. "Ah, why didn't the great Lafayette accept the governorship when it was offered to him?"

"I'd rather see the *marquis* de Lafayette in charge of Creole affairs, too, but we could have worse than Claiborne. He tries to be honest."

Andre ground out his cigar and leaned across the table. "Never mind the politics, Tanguy. How do things go with you?"

Guy didn't answer for a moment. Less than a month had gone by since his return from upriver and he still couldn't speak easily of the tragedy. He took a deep breath and forced a smile.

"Improving," he said.

"And Madelaine, how is she?"

"She's well enough." Guy frowned as he spoke. Madelaine was too quiet, seemed to brood in her room much of the time. When Gabriel had called on her, she wouldn't see him. He must do something to further their match. And soon.

In the parlor at La Belle, Madelaine put her hands on her hips and glared at Odalie. "I don't know why you won't talk about Vedette. I saw her in this very house. I saw her hang that *gris-gris* on the door, it isn't as though I don't know she's a voodoo queen."

"Be none of your business about charms and such." The black woman's face was closed and stubborn. "You do leave voodoo alone. Unlucky to be talking about Vedette."

Madelaine flounced from the parlor and climbed the stairs. It was no use to try to make Odalie tell her what she needed to know. Vedette was certain to have love powders for sale, if she could only find where to contact Vedette.

Voodoo love powders were a silly idea, maybe, yet everyone whispered of how well they worked, of men who never looked at another woman after a love potion was dropped into their food or drink.

Philippe had made no effort to contact her in over four months. She'd been afraid to leave La Belle because of Senalda . . . Madelaine closed her eyes and gripped the banister rail for a moment.

Poor Senalda. It was over now, may her soul be with the saints.

But what was Philippe doing?

Madelaine entered her bedroom and sat on the bench before her vanity mirror. Was she as pretty as Annette-Louise? How many times had Philippe danced with Annette-Louise in these four months? Did he call on her? Had he ever kissed her? Her hands clenched into fists.

"He loves *me*," she whispered.

Her glance caught the reflection of the silver filagreed pin in the shape of a butterfly that she wore on the bodice of her black gown. She frowned. Annette-Louise had given her that pin. Quickly she unfastened the butterfly, rose to thrust it from her sight among her other ornaments, then paused as an idea struck her.

Odalie would tell her nothing about Vedette but Josefina was something else entirely—younger, flighty. If she promised Josefina this silver pin, the slave would tell her whatever she wished to know.

That evening, Madelaine listened to Guy's plans for the late spring, plans for her. Small gatherings, since they were in mourning, outings on Lake Pontchartrain in the old summer house there, an *intime* dinner party—just a few close friends like Gabriel Davion . . .

Madelaine took a deep breath. "I look on Gabriel as a friend, just as you do," she said. "I'm fond of him, but nothing more. Why don't you see that Gabriel and I are not in love as a man and woman should be to marry? He'd marry me, I believe, just to please you, his best friend. I wish to please you, too, but I can't marry Gabriel."

"Women change their minds. It'll do no harm to be with him. Is there someone else you'd care to invite?"

An imp of mischief put words in her head. "There's that handsome *Americain* doctor. Is he still in New Orleans?"

Guy scowled at her and she laughed. "You look so stern. Quite like that painting of *grandpere* in the drawing room."

Guy smiled uncertainly. "You're joking then about the *Americain*."

"And you don't consider it a joking matter." She shook her head. "It used to be you who'd play tricks on me. You've become so serious since you started working for the *Americains*."

"Not *for* them. *With* them. There's a difference."

She made a face. "That's what I mean. You're so serious. All you need now is to grow a set of whiskers and you'll be a second *grandpere*."

After dinner they played a game of backgammon, their first in many months. She beat him so easily she knew he wasn't concentrating. Had he really loved Senalda as much as she loved Philippe? Could he love both Senalda and the *placee*, Aimee?

She thrust away a stray thought of John Kellogg. She didn't love him, she hardly knew him. His kiss had taken her by surprise, that's all. Her response was accidental, it meant nothing.

But if Guy could love two women at the same time . . . ?

No, she loved only Philippe, would always love only him.

And Philippe loved her. Did he also love Annette-Louise?

How she wished she could talk to her brother about Philippe, and the way she felt about him. She hated to go behind Guy's back, but he left her no choice.

Madelaine heard the faint boom of the nine o'clock cannon from the Place d'Armes. The slave curfew. "I think I'll go to bed," she said. Impulsively, she kissed

Guy's cheek. "I wouldn't trade you for any other brother in the world," she said. "I know you want me to be happy."

And he did, she knew that. He couldn't help his feelings any more than she could hers. It made her feel all the more guilty as she waited behind her closed bedroom door for him to retire. He'd go upstairs when he'd drunk enough brandy to make him drowsy and, once he was in bed, the only problem would be avoiding Odalie's sharp eyes and ears—and to gain the cooperation of Josefina.

Though she felt guilty about deceiving Guy, she wasn't going to change her mind.

Just as Madelaine had suspected, Josefina was willing to do anything for that silver butterfly.

"I be knowing Vedette. She dance voodoo maybe tonight," Josefina said. "Got to listen for the drums."

"You must take me, Josefina. To where Vedette is. Tonight."

Josefina's eyes widened with fear, but narrowed when Madelaine dangled the silver pin in front of her. "I do that," she whispered.

"Don't you dare tell anyone."

Later, as she waited in her room, Madelaine wondered how far she could trust Josefina, who was a born intriguer. She turned the silver butterfly in her fingers and the pin pricked her flesh, drawing blood.

When the house quieted, Madelaine crept down the stairs and let herself out the back door. A half-moon slid from behind the clouds. Did she hear the throb of drums or was that the beat of blood in her ears? She was excited and frightened and when a dark figure stepped out of the shadow of an oak, she put her hand to her mouth to stifle her gasp.

"Drums," Josefina whispered.

African drums. Madelaine had seen one once in the slave quarters at La Belle, a long hollow log open at one end with a goatskin stretched over the other. The next time she'd looked, the drum was gone and she never saw it again.

"The dogs might follow us," she whispered to Josefina.

"Dogs be tied in the stable," Josefina assured her.

She followed the black woman, flitting between the oaks like a wraith, to the bank of Bayou le Chat. She could hear the drum beat more clearly along the water—a low throbbing. Neither of them should be out in the night. For Josefina it was after curfew. For herself, unheard of.

Josefina halted beside an old *pirogue*, half-hidden in the reeds along the bank. "Do you give me the butterfly?" she asked.

Madelaine held out the silver pin. Josefina affixed it to her dress, stood dreamily feeling the pin with her fingers.

"Must we cross the bayou?" Madelaine asked.

"Here we cross, yes."

Josefina poled them quickly across the dark water. Madelaine helped her draw the old boat onto the opposite bank. Josefina took the lead along a narrow path running through the undergrowth.

The sound of lighter drumming joined the boom, boom of the big drum and soon Madelaine saw a glow ahead, a fire, and, silhouetted against the light, a man's form. She grasped Josefina's arm, slowing her.

"Just be Tomas," the black woman said. "He be waiting for me."

Tomas? Madelaine didn't know a Tomas, but, whoever he was, it was obvious that Josefina hadn't kept quiet about tonight's escapade.

"Who else knows we're coming here?" she demanded.

Josefina's eyes glittered. "I tell Scipion when he go to town, say to tell Tomas we be here."

Madelaine groaned inwardly. Scipion was a stable hand—had he passed the word to Ancin? If he had, Guy would be after her, for Ancin told him everything. And whoever this Tomas was, he may have told others.

Josefina slipped from her and hurried ahead, joining Tomas. Madelaine followed them slowly. Should she go back? She'd come to find the voodoo queen and buy a love potion. Was she being foolish? Now that Josefina was with her current lover she'd likely forget everything else and leave Madelaine to shift for herself.

The rattle of pebbles shaken in a gourd and a rhythmic clacking Madelaine couldn't identify accompanied the drums. She was very close. Give up now? She shook her head, and increased her pace until she saw a clearing ahead of her where dark bodies gathered beside a fire. Josefina and Tomas lost themselves among the other blacks.

Uncertain of what to do, Madelaine ducked behind a tangle of vines and edged nearer to the crowd of squatting Negroes who'd formed a semi-circle near the fire. Suddenly a woman leaped into the half-circle, almost directly in front of Madelaine. Although the vines concealed her, Madelaine shrank back, for the woman was Vedette.

But, *mon Dieu*, how changed! Vedette weaved to the beat of the drums, arms undulating. She wore knotted red handkerchiefs bound about her loins and breasts, her *tignon* was fiery red, the knots standing up in front like horns. A necklace of small bones hung around her neck.

The drummers were to the left of the voodoo queen. A man sat astride the big drum that lay lengthwise on the ground, slapping the skin head. Another Negro beat the smaller drum. Two shook gourds and a tan-skinned Negro ran a long bone up and down the toothed jawbone of a horse. The hair rose on the nape of Madelaine's neck as the rhythm quickened. The sounds, the sights were like nothing she'd ever experienced.

Her fear of Vedette mingled with excited anticipation as the *voodooienne* turned to the right to face a large painted box on a raised altar, inscribed with strange symbols and drawings. Madelaine saw an iron mesh was set into the front of the box. Tiny bells on Vedette's ankles tinkled as she gyrated toward the box, chanting.

L'Appe vini, Le Grand Zombi

L'Appe vini pou fe gris-gris.

Over and over she intoned the words, her voice rising to a frenzy as she writhed and swayed before the box.

"Aie, aie!" the crowd shouted. *"Voodoo Magnan!"*

With a suddenness that made Madelaine blink, a man leaped in front of Vedette. Naked, except for a few red handkerchiefs knotted about his loins, he sprang into the air, the bells on his ankles jangling. Madelaine watched open-mouthed, pushing the vines apart to get a better view, her eyes never leaving the two dancers.

He was a giant Negro, his skin glistening like black onyx in the flames. On each cheek three long lines of tattooing rayed out. An African, for Creole blacks had no tattooing—it was forbidden.

"Eh! Eh! Bomba hen, hen!" the man chanted.

He picked up Vedette and stood her atop the box. Her jerking became more violent. She flung her arms toward the night sky and her head rolled on her shoulders as though her neck was broken.

"Aie, aie!" the crowd screamed, all of them swaying in rhythm.

Vedette leaped off the box, writhing and shaking, seized the mesh and yanked it away. She reached inside and brought out a mass of coils, a huge snake that she caressed as it twined about her body. The man whirled around her, chanting, sweat gleaming on his naked skin. He was so very black. Madelaine touched her tongue to her dry lips. The drums invaded her body until she felt their beat in her bones. Her hand went to her bodice, unbuttoning the high neck for she felt she couldn't breath.

Suddenly the man jumped into the air to land inches from the vines that concealed her. Without pausing in his dance, he stared directly into Madelaine's eyes. She couldn't tear her gaze from his. Slowly he extended his hand toward her. His glinting black eyes held her as though she were a bird and he the snake.

Without willing it, Madelaine's hand came from the vines to meet his. With a shout he pulled her free of the tendrils and into the firelight. Her body began to sway as he danced in front of her.

"Eh, eh! Bomba hen, hen!" the crowd shouted, rising as one to their feet. Black bodies clustered about her, dancing, men with women, Vedette with the snake.

Madeláine's hair loosened and tumbled down her back as she stamped her feet to the drum's rhythms and twisted her body to match the primitive gyrations of the tattooed black.

"Houm! Dance Calinda!" a voice cried.

"Voodoo Magnan. Aie, aie!" others shouted.

How the snake coiled about the voodoo queen! As though it felt the drums, moved to their beat. Madelaine tore at the buttons of her gown, stifled inside her clothes. Part of her seemed to stand aside and look on in amazement as she stepped out of her dress and threw it aside but she couldn't break the spell of the drumming and the dance.

"Bomba, bomba, bomba," her partner chanted.

"Aie!" she answered, in unison with the crowd. *"Aie, aie!"*

Closer and closer he danced, leaping into the air, bells tinkling. As she undulated next to him she could feel the heat of his naked flesh. Her lips parted, she gasped for breath. All around her women threw off their clothes, bodies glistening with sweat, twisting, writhing snakelike as the men leaped and pranced.

She must—she must . . . Her hands were feeling for the fastening of her petticoat when she was grasped by the waist and whirled away from the tattooed black giant.

Madelaine fought against her captor, turning her head to stare into the face of Philippe Roulleaux.

Philippe half-carried Madelaine through the throng of naked, dancing blacks. No one interfered, the Negroes seemed scarcely aware of them. Still dazed by the dancing, by his sudden appearance, she clung to him as he strode beyond the firelight and down the path.

"Philippe," she murmured.

He set her onto her feet, his hands on her shoulders. "Madelaine, what were you thinking of to come here?" He shook her as he spoke, his voice throbbing with anger. "*Mon Dieu*, what might have happened to you if Tomas hadn't told me!"

She blinked at him, saw his pale face in the light of the half-moon. "Tomas?"

"Yes. Tomas, our coachman. He said a La Belle slave was bringing you to the voodoo. Tomas knows about us because of the carriage. I could hardly believe you'd do such a foolish thing but I came here anyway. Luckily."

Madelaine's lower lip quivered. He sounded almost like Guy scolding her. She flung her arms around him, tears in her eyes. "Philippe," she cried, "don't be angry. I love you so."

He groaned and his hands slid from her shoulders to crush her against him. His lips came down on hers demandingly. Her body throbbed with the drums, a fiery pulsation. His lips moved down her throat to the top of her breasts.

"Madelaine, *cherie*," he murmured.

He lifted her and, carrying her in his arms, pushed through the bushes along the path to a tiny clearing. As he put her down, her loosened petticoats slipped off and left her clad only in her chemise. She pressed against him, molding her body to his. He held her tightly, staring into her eyes, his face only inches away.

"This is madness," he said. "I'm mad for you, to have you, *mon cherie*, but . . ."

Her kiss stopped his words.

Philippe's hands caressed the curve of her hips, cupped her buttocks to hold her firmly to him. A tingling desire grew within her, a need crying to be satisfied. When he put his lips to her breasts through the thin batiste of her chemise, she pulled away and, with a quick sinuous motion, pulled the chemise over her head. She stood naked in the moonlight.

He caught his breath. Keeping his eyes on her, he hurried to remove his clothes. She stared in fascination at his revealed maleness, put out her hand and touched it, marvelling at how different he was from herself.

How wonderfully different.

When he caught her to him, she moaned at the feel of his flesh on hers, his throbbing hardness pressing against her. The drums pounded, pounded, both without and within her, urging her, driving her.

Somehow they were on the ground, his hands on her breasts, then his lips.

"Philippe," she breathed, "please . . ." She didn't know what she wanted him to do, only that he must, he must, or she would die with desire.

"My beautiful, my love," he whispered.

His hands stroked her thighs, then moved between her legs, gently pushing them apart. His body slid over hers, his hardness probing, entering, thrusting against something that yielded with one knifelike stab of pain, gone so quickly she had no time to cry out before she was overcome with pleasure.

Madelaine arched to him, wanting more and more of the wonderful, terrible sensation. Her fingers dug into his back as, unable to speak, she murmured incoherently.

She was in a glittering night of pulsating darkness where fiery serpents writhed inside her in a dance of ecstasy. Flames skyrocketed into the blackness, a fireworks of release, and she felt herself fragment into delicious wonder.

Philippe cried out, moaned, they held one another tightly, their hold gradually relaxing. He moved, turned onto his side, next to her. "I love you very much," he said. "We shouldn't have . . ."

"Hush. I won't listen. It's a part of our love so it must be right. So wonderful, Philippe. I never dreamed anything could be like this."

"You're mine forever, sweet Madelaine. No other man shall have you, I swear, no matter what may happen."

"Yes," she said, "I'm yours, always."

He sat up. "*Mon Dieu*, how am I to get you home? You in your petticoat. Ah, my love, you're a wanton."

"For you," she said fiercely, shoving away the memory of the moment she'd danced with the giant slave, when she felt the heat of his body . . .

"A wanton only for you, Philippe."

Chapter 11

WHEN they came onto the path, Madelaine saw, with disbelief, her black gown hanging from a branch of a shrub.
Philippe swore and stared back toward the voodoo fire.

"Josefina," Madelaine said, putting on her dress. "She
remembered me and brought the gown." But she felt a
chill, for whoever had hung the gown on the bush might
well have seen her with Philippe, seen them making love.

Not Josefina. The slave was with her own lover, Tomas,
and would have forgotten Madelaine.

The tattooed African? No, he wouldn't care about her
clothes.

Vedette? Madelaine shivered, suddenly certain the
voodoo queen had been the one, but she said nothing to
Philippe.

"Why haven't you come to our meeting place?" she
asked him. "It's been four months."

"I came many times. You didn't. I thought you no longer cared."

"I couldn't get away much. Senalda . . ." Her words
trailed off. It was better not to speak of poor Senalda. "I'll
meet you there again. Philippe. Tomorrow?"

106

He put his arm about her, guiding her along the path. "No, not tomorrow. The next day, in the afternoon."

She stiffened. "Why not tomorrow? Is it because you must see Annette-Louise?"

He laughed. "Annette-Louise was your idea, not mine. She's a pretty little girl, but I'm hopelessly in love with a far more lovely woman. I've given my heart away to her and have nothing left for poor Annette-Louise." He paused and kissed her, his lips warm on hers.

"I came tonight because I thought you didn't love me," she said when they were walking once again. "I hoped the voodoo queen would help me." She couldn't bring herself to say Vedette's name.

Again he laughed. *"Dieu,* I've little need for you to give me love potions. I think of you constantly as it is." His voice changed, grew serious. "You must promise me you won't go out at night again on foolish errands. It's not safe."

"I'm not afraid of the night animals, the wildcats and such. And the slaves wouldn't harm me."

"I'm not thinking about the animals. The slaves—well, who can really trust them? But there are also the *Americains*—those *Kaintocks* off the boats—wild and more dangerous than any animal."

"Not all the *Americains* are like them." Why was she baiting Philippe this way? Some mischievous devil guided her tongue for she agreed entirely that it was foolish to be abroad at night without an escort.

He stopped abruptly, grasping her shoulders and glaring into her face. "Have you been seeing that red-haired soldier? That *Americain*? Answer me!"

"No," she said. "Oh, no, Philippe."

But she had, though it was months ago. Philippe's question made the memory spring vividly to her mind. Not only had she seen John Kellogg, but she had enjoyed his kiss—try as she might to forget the feeling.

She clung to Philippe's arm. He was the one she loved. After what happened tonight she'd never love another.

*   *   *

Seagulls swooped over the blue water, their cries shrill and plaintive. Madelaine, drowsy from the heat and the wine she'd drunk, watched the birds glide on the wind. Although it was cooler along Lake Pontchartrain than at La Belle, the July day was sultry.

"You dream, perhaps, of another," Gabriel Davion said from his place beside her on the gallery of the old summer house.

The gallery was netted against the mosquitoes, but a few had gotten past, as usual. One hummed in her ear and she picked up her ivory fan to wave it away. "It's so warm," she murmured, ignoring his comment.

Guy had left them alone purposely, she knew. He'd arranged the picnic in the summer house on La Branche land near the lake and invited the guests, all the while hoping she would say "yes" to Gabriel. So far she'd managed to forestall a marriage proposal.

Gabriel leaned toward her. "You've changed these past months, Madelaine," he said. "I see you're no longer a child." Although his glance didn't miss the curve of her body under the light blue muslin gown, she realized he meant more than that.

"I've had to grow up," she said.

"Yes. Such misfortune must have been difficult for you. But the change seems deeper. You ever look at me differently."

Madelaine blushed. She hadn't known he was aware of the long, considering gaze she'd turned on him earlier. She'd been wondering what it would be like to marry Gabriel, to be bedded by him.

Not that she wanted such a thing! Each meeting with Philippe, each time they lay together, made her love him all the more passionately. She eyed Gabriel, fluttering the fan between them. Since she'd experienced what a man and a woman could share, she no longer regarded Gabriel as a brother—even if she had no desire to marry him.

"I could never marry you," she said abruptly.

His eyes widened.

"I know you haven't asked me, but surely you realize that Guy has been pushing us together with marriage in mind. He wants it, I don't."

"Madelaine, I . . ."

"Let me finish, for I may not gather the courage to speak so bluntly again. I've always been fond of you, Gabriel, but I don't love you. Please don't tell me that I could learn to. It may or may not be true, but I don't wish to try to love you. We aren't meant for each other, Gabriel, and I want you to be free to find a wife who can love you as you deserve, because I can't. Annette-Louise Courchaine, perhaps. She's sighed over you from the time we were children."

Gabriel took a deep breath and let it out slowly. "I can't deny I was about to propose to you. I have long admired you, and I've watched as you've grown into a beautiful woman—a woman of character and charm."

"Be honest, Gabriel. You aren't hearbroken by what I've said, are you?"

He smiled a bit sadly. "I'd be honored to have you for my wife. But, no, though my heart pains a trifle, it's intact."

Impulsively, she leaned over and kissed him on the cheek. "I've always liked you, Gabriel. Can we not remain friends?"

He nodded. "Do you love another, Madelaine?"

She lowered her eyes. It wouldn't be wise to reveal too much to Gabriel, for he was Guy's best friend. "You embarrass me," she murmured.

When she looked at him through her lashes she saw his skeptical glance. Gabriel knew very well she wasn't easily abashed. But he didn't press her. She brushed away a mosquito from her arm. The shadows were lengthening, encouraging the pests to swarm, and more were getting past the netting. Her head had begun to ache from the glare of the sun on the water. The picnic was over, and it was time to go home.

In August, Annette-Louise visited Madelaine at La Belle. Flushed and excited, she clutched at Madelaine's hands.

"Just think," she said, "Gabriel has spoken to papa and we're to be married in three weeks. I never dreamed he noticed me. All the time I thought . . ." She stopped, eyeing Madelaine.

"I'm happy for you," Madelaine said honestly. "Gabriel is a wonderful man, and I know he'll make you very happy. I suspected you still nourished a *tendresse* for him, even though you have flirted constantly with Philippe." What pleasure it gave her to say her lover's name.

"Oh, Philippe." Annette-Louise waved her hand as if to dismiss the possibility that she could ever *seriously* consider him as a suitor. "He's amusing, but I could never marry him. I could never feel for him as I do about Gabriel." She sank into a chair, and removed her fan from the pocket of her dress. *"Mon Dieu* but it's hot." Peering at Madelaine from behind the waving fan, she added, "You really are glad to hear the news. And to think that I once thought Gabriel was in love with you!"

"He has always loved me as a sister. He helped Guy raise me. We could never take one another seriously because of that. I'm *very* fond of Gabriel, as I am of you, and I know you'll have a good marriage—a loving marriage. It makes me very happy."

Ah, Philippe, she thought, if only you could approach Guy so we could be married. If only this foolish feud didn't stand between us.

Annette-Louise brushed a mosquito from her hand. "I sweat these pesky bugs grow worse every summer," she said. She lowered her voice, leaning forward. "Have you heard about the sickness in the city?" she asked.

"Summer fevers."

"No, no, it's worse. *Maman* whispers and doesn't think I hear." Her voice dropped so low Madelaine could barely hear her. "Bronze John. Yellow fever. Many are ill. Some have died."

Yellow fever. Governor Claiborne had lost his wife and little daughter to the disease two summers ago. Annette-Louise herself had been sick with yellow fever five years ago.

"You're safe from Bronze John," Madelaine reminded her. "He doesn't visit twice."

"But Gabriel—what about him?" Annette-Louise cried.

"You truly do love him," Madelaine said. "Don't worry, he's as healthy as Guy. Bronze John will pass him by this summer, too, as he has every other year."

She wasn't speaking merely to soothe Annette-Louise's fears. It did seem that newcomers to New Orleans, like the governor's wife, were the ones most likely to come down with yellow fever. It struck *Americains* and visitors from Europe far more often than those born and raised in Louisiana. And it killed them more often, too. Annette-Louise hadn't been so very sick—she'd been out of bed a week later. Her skin had barely turned yellow at all.

Bronze John seemed to avoid the slaves almost entirely.

"Marie Thibodeaux has died," Annette-Louise went on in her hushed, frightened voice. "*Maman* was told she vomited black for days before she went. Remember how fair she was, such pale skin? It turned the color of cantalope flesh—a hideous orange-yellow."

"Don't dwell on such things. Think of your trousseau, your wedding gown. Surely your parents will give you the grandest marriage ever seen inside St. Louis since it was built. I can't wait to be there."

Annette-Louise smiled tentatively. "*Maman* says I'm to have pearls sewn into the lace of my gown," she said. "And the neckline—" she touched her finger between her breasts—"down to here, just think! It's the very latest from Paris."

"You'll look enchanting."

The first week in September, Madelaine recalled her words as she sat in a pew watching her friend standing with Gabriel before the altar of St. Louis. Annette-Louise was enchanting, a vision in white lace and silk, the luster of the pearls on her gown no fairer than the glow of her skin.

Ah, I'm so envious, Madelaine thought. Why couldn't it be me standing before Father Antoine, with Philippe beside me? All because of some ancient disagreement that no one even remembers correctly anymore.

The church wasn't crowded because of the epidemic in the city. People hesitated to gather in groups lest Bronze John join them as an invisible guest. Still, a scattering of friends and relatives braved the scourge. Later, they drank to the newly-weds' health in the Courchaine townhouse.

Whether from the champagne or the enervating heat that hung over the city, heavy with the stench of the rotting garbage by the levee, Madelaine began to feel queasy. She asked Guy to take her back to La Belle before the reception was over.

"Are you ill?" Guy asked, peering at her closely as he helped her into the manor house.

"No, it's merely a headache."

"Your eyes look strange," he said. "Glassy."

Madelaine tried to laugh but only mustered a faint smile. "Even a headache is suspect these days," she said.

"The city's using the dead carts again," Guy said. "So many have been dying each day that St. Louis Cemetery can't keep up with the burials. The *Americains* have their army doctors working night and day with our own doctors." He hesitated, then went on, "I understand that Dr. Kellogg is foremost among them. Governor Claiborne praises him highly."

Madelaine hadn't thought of John Kellogg in weeks. As she let Odalie help her to bed, she saw in her mind's eye the strong planes of his face, his auburn hair. It was strange for her to think of him as a doctor, tending to the ill and dying, for he was so vibrantly alive.

112

She was sick. It was more than a headache, her neck and back hurt and her legs cramped until tears came to her eyes. She began to shake, shivering so that her teeth chattered. Odalie piled more quilts onto the bed, then ran down to the kitchen fire to warm bricks, for there were no others fires lit in this hot month.

But Madelaine was cold, chilled to the bone. She ached all over. By the time Odalie had placed the heated bricks around her, she had to fly across the room for a basin because Madelaine began to retch, vomiting until nothing came but bile, green and bitter.

Time ceased to have meaning. Shapes hovered over her in a fog, Odalie, Guy. Once she thought she recognized Dr. Goodreau but when she looked again, he wasn't there. Visions flitted through her mind. The tattooed black man with snakes writhing about him, his eyes glinting hard as onyx. Vedette, slipping through the house, up the stairs with a *gris-gris* in her hand.

"No, don't let her," Madelaine tried to say, for she'd die as Senalda had died if the *gris-gris* were hung on her door, but she was too weak to say the words.

Philippe held out his arms, but she couldn't move to embrace him. He faded into nothingness.

She retched and vomited everything Odalie gave her, hearing the dread word muttered as Odalie emptied the basin. "Noir." Black. She was vomiting black as did those who died from Bronze John's visit.

The tattooed slave loomed above her, gigantic. Black. Darkness was all around. His arms were snakes as black as he, reaching for her, to coil about her and crush out her life.

Frantically she tried to call out but no words came. A light, she must have light to save herself. The glow of a candle, the red of a fire. Red . . .

John Kellogg brushed a strand of hair from his forehead as he stood looking down at his patient. He'd never gotten used to this moment, the instant the spirit fled from the body, leaving nothing behind but a cast-off shell.

He bent over and gently closed the staring eyes.

"No!" The cry came from behind him and he was thrust aside as Annette-Louise cast herself onto her husband's dead body.

"Gabriel, oh, Gabriel," she moaned, hugging him, kissing his face.

The priest had come and gone, as desperately busy as the doctors in this season of sickness and death. John knew the widow must grieve, but it would do her no good to give way to hysteria.

"*Madame*," he said, touching her arm, "come with me."

She paid no attention, tears streaming down her cheeks as she clutched at her husband's unresponsive hands. When John motioned with his head, the black woman in the doorway stepped into the room. He grasped Annette-Louise's arms firmly and pulled her to her feet.

"Oh, no, no," she sobbed.

"You must come away," he told her. "You must rest. Pray for his soul, for he's with God now—didn't Father Antoine tell you so?" He guided Annette-Louise to her maid, a sensible looking black woman, who put her arms around her mistress to comfort her.

John walked with them to the door. "You must rest," he told Annette-Louise. He looked at the slave. "Give your mistress the medicine, a spoonful from the blue bottle, so she'll sleep."

The maid nodded, tears in her eyes. "Come along, *cherie*," she said.

After letting himself out, John walked wearily down the steps into the courtyard and across the paving-bricks to the street gate. He'd never been so tired, even when the army had been campaigning in Indian country. He must rest, he'd prescribe sleep for himself as he had for *Madame* Davion.

The acrid stench from burning tar stung his eyes and clogged his nostrils as he reached the *banquette*. He

114

doubted the smoke did much to prevent the spread of yellow fever—yellowjack, they called it in the army—but at least the smoke masked the festering stink of the decaying refuse along the *batture*, the ground between the river and the top of the levee.

He'd spoken to Governor Claiborne about the way the Creoles dumped nightsoil and garbage into the Mississippi River from the levee. It was all very well in the winter and spring when the water ran high and the waste was carried into the gulf, but in hot weather, when the river fell, the noisome stench of the refuse surely must contribute to disease. The governor agreed, but said the practice was impossible to stop.

He liked New Orleans, despite the sanitary problems, and he liked the Creoles. He got along better with their doctors, many of whom were trained in Paris, than he did with most of the American ones. Mercury in the form of calomel and blood-letting were in favor among his American colleagues, but he couldn't bring himself to follow either course in treating his patients. The logic behind treating an already ailing patient with a potent poison such as mercury was beyond his grasp.

As for bleeding, it seemed as barbaric as anything the Indian medicine men practiced. He didn't even own one of the small bronze cubes that a doctor pressed to the back of his patient's neck to bleed him. A touch of a spring released a flock of tiny knives that cut into flesh like cats' claws. Then, to keep the blood flowing, a cloth saturated with turpentine was stuffed into a glass, lit, and when the flames had almost died out, the mouth of the glass was clapped over the wounds, creating a vacuum to suck out the blood.

John shook his head. He'd never seen a diseased patient improved by this practice. The Creole doctors tended to try supportive measures: giving the patient fluids, keeping him clean and warm—methods that did no harm.

Sometimes it seemed to John Kellogg that a physician helped his patient the most when he did the least.

He reached his quarters, opened the gate and was immediately met by a slave carrying a letter. No matter who it's from or what it says, he told himself, I'm going inside to bed. He unfolded the paper and read the note.

Dr. Kellogg: My sister, Madelaine La Branche lies ill with yellow fever. In her delirium she calls your name. I fear for her life. Will you please come?

Tanguy La Branche

Chapter 12

John Kellogg sat beside Madelaine's bed, her black maid, Odalie, asleep in a rocking chair behind him. Madelaine's skin was fire-hot with fever, but her pulse, instead of racing to match the increased heat of her body, was ominously slow. A bad sign. He raised her head and trickled another spoonful of sweetened lemon water between her parched lips, watching closely to make sure she didn't choke.

Her skin was dark yellow from the disease. Her eyes, when he lifted the lids to check them, were glazed and unseeing, the sclerae as yellow as her skin. He remembered her as she'd been at the ball where they'd met—beautiful, magnificent in her righteous anger at the quarrels of men.

"I won't let you die," he muttered aloud. "Madelaine, you mustn't die."

Her eyelids fluttered and opened. He saw her eyes try to focus on his face as he bent over her. She blinked, and he thought he caught a gleam of recognition in her eyes before they closed again. A spoonful at a time, he trickled more lemon water into her mouth.

"Swallow," he urged her. "Swallow, Madelaine, the water will help you."

"I go fetch more for you to give her." Odalie spoke from behind him and he nodded. The Negro woman was as devoted to Madelaine as if she'd been her own daughter. It spoke well for the treatment of slaves at La Belle.

He wasn't used to the idea of one human being owning another, for there'd been no slaves on or near the Connecticut farm where he grew up. His father hired help when it was needed. When he went away to school he learned about slavery and its justifications, but the idea of human bondage was abhorrent to him.

"How is she?" Guy spoke from the doorway.

John turned to look at Guy's red-rimmed eyes, his haggard face. Without answering, he looked back at Madelaine, reached to feel the pulse at her temple. Faster, yes, definitely more rapid.

"I think the tide has turned and she's on her way back to us," John said. "The "us" had slipped out, and he saw Guy frown at the word.

"You're certain she's better?" Guy asked, looking dubiously down at Madelaine's yellow face.

As if in response, Madelaine's eyelids quivered. "Water," she whispered. "Water."

Madelaine's recovery was quite rapid, though her strength returned slowly. John Kellogg called daily.

In early October, Madelaine sat before her vanity mirror watching Odalie arrange her hair. The slave had cut it during the illness, for everyone knew that long hair sapped one's strength. How strange it was to see herself with short curls all over her head.

"I look perfectly awful," she complained. "My skin is still yellow, and my hair looks like a child's."

"You be alive," Odalie said. "And you looks just fine. That doctor, he see you when you look ready to die, he be the only one coming today."

Madelaine sighed. Odalie was right, John had seen her when she looked really terrible—her first look at herself in a mirror in the beginning of her convalescence had made her shudder. Still, she couldn't help longing to see her old familiar self in the mirror instead of this short-haired stranger. She wanted John to think of her as attractive.

His face was one of the few things she remembered about the worst of her illness, the lurking darkness lightened by the red flare of his hair, showing her the way back to life, his voice saying her name, keeping her with him so she didn't slip into the black void.

Yet she must discourage him from coming to see her now that she'd recovered. She couldn't deny the bond between them, couldn't even deny that she felt more than a patient's confidence in her doctor when he took her hand to feel her pulse, but her love belonged to Philippe now and forever, and it was wrong to enjoy the company of another man so much. Besides, Guy had begun to glower at John's continued visits. How long would it be before her brother would feel compelled to forbid them?

Madelaine sighed again. She'd seen no one but John and her brother since her illness. She wasn't well enough to call on Annette-Louise, who, still grief-sticken over Gabriel's death, was in seclusion at her parents' home. What a terrible tragedy for Annette-Louise, to find love only to have it snatched away so quickly.

When would she be strong enough to rendezvous with her Philippe again? she wondered. She closed her eyes, dreamily recalling the feel of his lips, his hands, his body.

"There," Odalie said, "you is new-made."

Madelaine stared at her reflection. Curls tumbled over her forehead and ears in a style that reminded her of drawings she'd seen of Napoleon's Josephine. She actually looked quite elegant. She smiled at Odalie, catching her hand and pressing it affectionately.

Odalie helped her to walk to the chaise lounge and drew a silk coverlet over her.

"A charming picture," John said as he came into her boudoir. "You look radiant, Madelaine."

She held out her hand and he took it, feeling automatically for the pulse at her wrist. She laughed and pulled her hand away. "No need for that—I'm better, much better. In fact, I'm certain coming here forces you to take time from more pressing duties."

"But none I enjoy more."

He smiled at her, looking into her eyes in the intent way he had, a way that made a forbidden prickle of excitement stir inside her. She'd never forgotten the day that John had kissed her on the bank of the bayou.

She lowered her eyes. He's not for you, she reminded herself. You don't want him and even if you did, Guy would never allow it. Her brother, in mentioning how grateful he was for Dr. Kellogg's care, had obliquely pointed out that John wasn't only an *Americain*, but a poor one at that, born into an insignificant family.

Never mind that Philippe was also forbidden. She was committed to Philippe, body and soul. To dally with John would be unfair to Philippe as well as to the *Americain*.

Madelaine looked at him earnestly. "You must stop your visits to La Belle," she said. "Guy is beginning to misunderstand your reasons, and I don't want any unpleasantness between you."

"He doesn't misunderstand my reasons."

She twisted her hands together. "I can't continue to see you."

"Because of the way your brother feels?"

"No. Because I—I love another man."

All trace of a smile left his face. He leaned forward as though to take her hand again but she kept her fingers firmly clasped together. His lips touched hers, gently but firmly.

"Have you forgotten?" he asked softly when she drew back—a second or two later than she should have.

"It makes no difference what I remember. I love another and won't see you again. It's not right."

He straightened. "Madelaine, I'd hoped—I meant to ask you . . ."

"There's no hope. Don't ask me. The man I love is a

Creole, and he's everything I want. You and I are too different, and besides—I don't love you. There's no possibility I'll change my mind." She blinked rapidly, hoping he wouldn't see the tears in her eyes. He might misinterpret them and believe there was a chance.

She loved Philippe, of course she did, and yet sending John away made her feel like her heart was breaking.

"I'm leaving New Orleans, my unit's been transferred. I was going to ask you to come with me—as my wife."

She shook her head. Traveling with John—where would they go? To the *Americain* cities in the east? To the capital, Washington? Or to the western wilderness? Something in her responded to the lure of other places, of strange sights. And how would she feel when John came to her at night, when he . . .

No! What could be the matter with her that she thought of such things?

"Please, John—go now," she said. "I can't talk about this any longer. Please go." Her voice broke on the last word.

"I won't forget you, Madelaine," he said.

She thought he meant to kiss her again and lowered her face into her hands, afraid of what might happen if he did. She heard the door close softly. When she glanced up he was gone.

John Kellogg didn't return to La Belle.

In the scant warmth of a November afternoon, Guy trotted toward the rue des Ramparts on his bay gelding, Marquis. Since Estelle had taken Denis to live in Aimee's cottage, he had found himself visiting there often. To see the boy, of course. Denis was going on three, and was bright and talkative.

Certainly Estelle didn't offer herself. Even when he made it clear he was interested in her she'd avoided a response. He was both attracted and repulsed by her. She was dark for a quadroon—darker than he cared for—not plump enough, and definitely not accommodating. Yet when her dark eyes looked at him, something equally dark stirred inside him, something he'd never felt for another woman.

As he approached the cottage, Denis hurtled off the porch.

"Papa, papa," he shouted, holding up his arms. "Ride me, ride me."

Guy lifted Denis onto the horse, kicked Marquis into an easy canter and rode the length of the street and back. He dismounted and, perching Denis on his shoulders, went into the cottage.

"*Tante, tante,*" Denis called, "papa is here."

Estelle came from the kitchen. "I have shrimp jambalaya, if you're hungry," she said by way of greeting.

"I didn't come to eat," he said. "I came to see the boy."

"Denis was to attend a birthday party," she said. "Of course I won't take him now."

"He'll go," Guy said. "I wouldn't want him to miss the party. A boy can never be too young to learn to enjoy parties. Where is it?"

"But two doors away. For Henri de la Harpe. He's four years old."

"I'll have coffee while you take Denis," Guy said.

Estelle fixed the coffee, poured him a cup, dressed Denis in his best clothes and left the cottage. Guy emptied his cup, poured another and waited for her to return, feeling anticipation rise with each passing minute. He'd never been alone with her in the cottage.

When Estelle came through the front door he was standing just inside. She stopped, looking at him, her dark eyes unreadable.

"Go into the bedroom," he ordered.

She raised her chin, still meeting his gaze, saying nothing. He grasped her arm.

"Didn't you hear?"

She nodded but stood her ground. He tightened his hold and pushed her ahead of him toward the bedroom.

"It's customary for a woman to agree to an arrangement," Estelle said, resisting. "I haven't heard you ask."

"Asking bedamned! You *know* I want you."

"I don't agree to have you." She twisted in his hands to stare at him. "I don't agree."

Her eyes glittered with some emotion he couldn't identify. Hate? Certaintly not fear. He was determined to have her, though he'd never taken a woman against her will.

He yanked her close to him and held her, kissing her savagely, his hands tight against her buttocks. Her mouth was hot and he tasted blood where he'd forced her lips against her teeth. The taste drove him wild. He lifted her lithe, slim body, and carried her to the bed. Tearing her clothes away, he caressed her bared breasts, putting his tongue to her nipples, nipping them with his teeth, his hands stroking the smooth skin of her thighs.

At first she tried to writhe away from him, but suddenly her breath came faster, and her mouth answered his hungrily. When he touched her between her legs he found her ready for him, and he stared in triumph into her eyes, seeing the glitter for what it was—passion.

"You want me as much as I want you," he said hoarsely, hurriedly taking off his clothes.

She fought him as he eased his body over hers, twisting from underneath him. He held her writhing body close, feeling his desire mount as she squirmed against him, her breath hot on his throat.

He gripped her legs and forced them apart, thrust inside her ferociously. She moaned, her arms around his back, holding him to her in a fierce embrace as she plunged wildly beneath him in untamed and open passion, uttering animal cries, head back, mouth open.

Her nails raked his back, her teeth sank into his shoulder as she lost herself in her feral rush of desire. She was a wildcat. Her insatiable need multiplied his own passion until he lost all sense of time and place, driving into her again and again in a fury, unaware of anything except the panting woman beneath him.

She shrieked in release, a high-pitched sound he'd never heard from a woman. As she continued to move her hips hard against him, he spent himself convulsively within her.

When he finally rose to wash and dress, Estelle lay as he'd left her, on her back, legs apart, arms flung to either side, eyes closed.

He studied her as he dressed, the rise and fall of the high peaked breasts, the slim waist and flat belly, the thrust of her pelvic bones under the brown velvet of her flesh. His shoulder throbbed where she'd bitten him, his back smarted from the scratches. His eyes lingered on the secret part of her that had throbbed so violently against him.

Tonight—yes, he'd come back tonight when Denis was asleep and take Estelle again and again until she admitted her desire for him, told him how much she wanted him, and begged for his touch.

Guy visited his sister's room when he returned to La Belle. The red-haired Kellogg had somehow saved her from death, had willed her back to life in a manner Guy didn't understand, for Dr. Kellogg had done nothing Dr. Goodreau hadn't also tried to do. He could never repay the man, and yet he was grateful that Kellogg's army unit had been transferred to the Mississippi Territory. He'd never permit Madelaine to marry an *Americain*, and she'd seemed far too interested in this one.

"See, I'm much better," Madelaine said to him. With her short curls she looked like the little girl he remembered from the years of his childhood.

"Soon I'll ride Empress again," she went on, "and you can take me to a dance, dear brother."

"You still need to rest."

She pouted. "I won't be coddled. Tonight I'll be down to dinner. By next week I'll be ready to mount Empress. You'll see how well I am. I may even challenge you to a game of backgammon."

"Not tonight," he said hastily.

She laughed. "All right. I'll let you rest up for it. Tomorrow night."

When dinner was over and Madelaine had retired once more to her room, Guy drank a glass of brandy in the library before hastening to the stables. Ancin had Marquis saddled and ready.

As he loped toward town, Guy pictured himself opening the cottage door, imagined Estelle staring at him, her dark eyes guarded for now she knew how he could make her feel, knew she couldn't resist his love-making.

She might try to offer him food. He'd wave it away, insist she share the wine he was bringing with him. The red of the burgundy would match the color of her lips—those sensuous lips that had enticed him from the first. He spurred his horse.

She'd drink the wine, feel it warm her blood as he kissed her lingeringly. He wouldn't carry her to the bedroom. No, he'd caress her as they sat on the divan together. He'd run his hands over that soft skin until she was wild with desire, unable to control her need and then . . .

Guy smiled.

Would he say her own words back? "I don't agree to have you"? Make her caress him until he did what she wanted?

Marquis stumbled, almost pitching Guy over his head. The horse regained his footing but began to limp. Guy cursed, dismounted and, in the dark, ran his hands down each of the gelding's legs, finding he'd thrown a shoe. Damn.

Guy led the horse the rest of the way into town, stopping at a livery stable with a blacksmith shop attached. He left Marquis there, and hired a rig to take him the rest of the way.

It amused him to ride to Estelle's in a buggy, as though he intended to take her to a Quadroon Ball. He might even do that someday, he thought. As he reached the house, he noticed that the only light shone from the bedroom window.

Ah, he'd really surprise her. He still had his key—he'd slip in quietly, and perhaps catch her disrobing.

Guy tiptoed up the steps, making certain his boots didn't click on the porch, slid the key carefully into the lock, and eased the door open. He crossed the living room silently, and was almost to the bedroom door when a wild shriek rent the air. He froze momentarily. He'd heard that same sound this afternoon.

Rage rose inside him. Who was with her? He strode to the door and looked inside. The two brown bodies writhing on the bed in the lamplight cast dancing shadows on the wall. He started inside the bedroom, feeling for his pistol, then held. He shook his head. He ran from the house and wrenched the buggy whip from its socket, then raced back inside.

He'd made no attempt to be quiet and the man had risen from the bed and put on his breeches.

"You!" Guy exclaimed, staring into Francois' angry eyes.

The sight of Francois lashed him into a murderous fury. How dare Francois touch what belonged to him, to Tanguy La Branche?

Guy stepped back and raised the whip.

Francois sprang backwards, reaching, Guy saw, for his sword cane. Guy flicked the whip so it caught Francois across the back. Francois jerked, missing his grasp at the cane, which clattered to the floor and rolled under the bed.

Guy brought the lash down, again, again. Francois bellowed in pain as the leather slashed across his face, his shoulders. He'd never whipped a man before, but the desire to wound Francois, to punish him, humiliate him, inflamed Guy.

"No, no!" Estelle screamed, flinging herself from the bed. Guy, unable to arrest his next stroke, saw the whip lash across her breasts.

"The window, the window!" she cried. "Francois, the window!"

126

Francois hesitated.

"Papa, Papa," Denis sobbed from behind Guy. Small hands hugged him around one leg. "Scared, Papa."

Francois dived across the bed and smashed through the window. Guy, trying to free himself from Denis' grip, heard the clatter of hooves as Francois commandeered the buggy.

"I told you!" Estelle screamed at Guy, standing beside him naked, blood oozing from a thin line across her breasts. "I said I didn't choose to have you. Selfish, selfish, you don't listen."

Denis buried his face against Guy's thigh and wept noisily.

Guy picked up the boy and thrust him at Estelle. She reached out her arms automatically, taking Denis.

"I intend to kill Francois," Guy said, his voice taut with anger. "Kill him like the dog he is."

Chapter 13

"Ah, Guy, *mon ami*, the quadroon belles from Cuba surpass anything you've ever seen," Rafe Devol said, leaning across the coffee house table, eyes sparkling. "There's one you must see for yourself, because words can't do her justice. We all want her, but she hasn't chosen a man yet.

"Her name is Roxanne St. Luz. Skin like moonlight, breasts like melons, a waist so tiny a man itches to span it with his hands."

Guy nodded absently, his mind on the vanished Francois. No one had admitted to seeing him since that night on the rue des Ramparts. Guy thought that some of his friends looked askance at him, as though, knowing why he searched for Francois, they couldn't understand why he hadn't killed the man on the spot.

Guy took a certain perverse pleasure in having humiliated Francois with the whip, just the same. And, although it appalled him to recognize such a darkness within him, he secretly relished the knowledge he'd cut Estelle across the breasts with the same whip, accident or not.

"So why not come with me this night to the Quadroon Ball?" Rafe went on. "Roxanne will certainly be there."

The Cuban free Negroes were actually transplanted

128

Santo Domingo blacks, and everyone knew that the quadroons from Santo Domingo were the most beautiful of all black women. Such a woman might take his mind off Estelle and her perfidy, and rescue him from her spell. Guy smiled at Rafe.

"Yes, perhaps I'll join you. I haven't been to a Quadroon Ball in several years. A man shouldn't deprive himself like that, *n'est-ce pas?*"

The ball was to be held, as usual, at the Conde Street ballroom where Guy had met Aimee four years earlier. It seemed like a century ago. Once, the Quadroon Balls had been for the free men and women of color, and white men attended as they pleased. Now the free men of color weren't permitted to attend, except as musicians. Slaves, of course, had never been eligible.

The Negroes sang one of their *gombo* songs about the change, poking biting fun at the situation, calling the black slave *cocodrie*, a crocodile, the free man of color *trou lou lou*, fiddler crab.

Milatraisse courri dans bal	Yellow girl goes to the ball
Cocodrie pote fanal	Nigger lights her to the hall
Trou lou lou	Fiddler man
C'est pas zaffaire a tou?	What is that to you?
Trou lou lou	Fiddler man
C'est pas zaffaire a tou?	What is that to you?

Guy told his man at the townhouse, Leroy, to lay out his new claw-hammer tailcoat with the black velvet collar, his fawn trousers and green waistcoat. Since he'd made up his mind to go, he'd go in style.

By the time he and Rafe arrived at the Conde a full moon had risen. Many of the quadroons were already in the hall with their chaperones and Rafe kept nudging Guy, pointing out one girl after another whose dark eyes promised secret delights.

"There's Ancelin Otray, the tiny girl with skin the shade of topaz—exquisite, is she not?"

"But where is this Roxanne?" Guy asked.

As he spoke, a murmur of voices made him turn his

head. Entering the room was a young woman dressed in pearl-white silk, her skin almost the shade of the gown. The bodice dipped so low that all of her upper breasts except the nipples showed, and the gown's high waist, emphasized by the rose silk ribbon, pushed her breasts to even greater prominence. Guy stared, as did every man in the room.

He knew this must be Roxanne St. Luz. She was every bit as magnificent as Rafe had described her. Desire rose in him. She was what he wanted, what he'd have. Let Estelle take her *cochon*, her pig lover. What was she to him? Guy started across the room toward Roxanne.

Nicolas Roulleaux reached her first. Guy stopped, watching Nicolas bow to her. *Sacre bleu*, were they fated to choose the same women forever?

"Ah, *Monsieur* Roulleaux." Roxanne's voice was clear and soft. Obviously she knew and liked Nicolas, for her smile was brilliant. They moved off to dance together.

Guy walked up to the older woman who'd been standing next to Roxanne—her chaperone. Remnants of beauty in the woman's face made him certain she was Roxanne's mother.

"You are Roxanne's *maman*?" he asked.

"Oui."

He bowed. "I'm Tanguy La Branche. I haven't had the pleasure of meeting your daughter, but I am most interested in doing so." He knew that this woman, like all mothers and chaperones of the quadroons, looked out for her daughter's best interests, and that she'd not only recognize his name but would know that La Belle was a richer plantation than En Dela, the Roulleaux holdings.

"If you'll be patient, *Monsieur* La Branche, I'll bring Roxanne to meet you in a few minutes." She smiled at him, an attractive woman, despite grey hair and a thickened waist. He noticed that her eyes didn't smile, but observed him guardedly—though with obvious interest.

Guy returned to Rafe, who stood talking to Bernard de Marigny.

". . . asked me to warn the left bank planters," Bernard was saying as Guy came up.

Rafe turned to him. "Bernard says Joubert Le Moyne from upriver thinks we're in for trouble. There's been a mulatto going from plantation to plantation talking to the slaves. Joubert thinks this man preaches revolt."

"Joubert's no fool," Bernard put in. "His slaves have been restless ever since the mulatto was seen at D'Argent, his plantation. He's warned all the right bank planters."

A slave uprising! The fear of a revolt was always in the back of every planter's mind—every Creole's mind, for that matter, for the whites were outnumbered by the blacks—free colored and slaves. There was no certainty who the free Negroes would ally themselves with if the slaves revolted. Now it appeared that a free man of color was agitating for a revolt.

"Did Le Moyne have any idea of who the mulatto is?" Guy asked.

Bernard shook his head. "He's not certain of anything. Just that we should be on our guard, for the mulatto had no business being on his plantation and ran off when he was challenged by the overseer. Joubert's slaves haven't settled down since, and he doesn't like the looks of it."

Guy tried to think if the slaves at La Belle had acted any different of late. Not the house servants, certainly.

"*Monsieur* La Branche." Guy turned to see Roxanne's *maman* behind him.

"If you'd care to wait in the *'tite salon*, I'll bring my daughter to meet you."

Guy nodded to Bernard and Rafe and followed her to the rear of the hall, where four small rooms had been partitioned off from the dance floor. She indicated the second on the right with a tilt of her head, and left him.

Guy chose to stand rather than to sit on the small divan. He frowned in concentration. Could he completely trust any of his slaves if an uprising began? Odalie, perhaps. She'd see to Madelaine's safety if he was unable to.

131

As for the rest, no, he couldn't be sure of them. Even old Louis might well follow this mulatto leader.

He was still brooding over Bernard's story when Roxanne's *maman* appeared in the doorway and ushered her daughter inside.

"*Monsieur* La Branche, my daughter, Roxanne St. Luz."

Roxanne smiled as brilliantly at Guy as she had at Nicolas. No doubt her *maman* had whispered to her, telling her who he was.

"I am most pleased to meet you," Roxanne said.

Her breasts were so perfect and round they hardly seemed real. Her face was round, too, with a small nose and sensual lips that cried out to be kissed. She was adorable and she knew it.

"I'm charmed to meet you," he said. "May I have this dance?"

"I would love to dance with you," she told him, each word dropping from her coral lips like a pearl. She was too good to be true.

A quadrille was forming as he led her through the door. He put his arm around her, feeling the tininess of her waist for himself, the enticing curve of her hip. Before he could take a place with her in the dance, Nicolas appeared, glowering. Roxanne made a sound of distress and slipped from his grasp to run to her *maman*.

"I've spoken for her," Nicolas said.

Guy lifted his eyebrows. "And has she chosen? I think not."

Nicolas narrowed his eyes and Guy felt a tingling anticipation run through him. A challenge was coming and this time he'd kill the *batard*, the bastard.

He was dimly aware of men shouting and someone running toward them, but he didn't deflect his attention from Nicolas. He smiled thinly, insolently, waiting.

"Nicolas!" Philippe clasped his brother's arm. Nicolas shook him off without looking at him.

"Leave me. This is none of your concern."

"It's everyone's concern," Philippe cried. "The slaves have revolted! They've killed at least one man upriver and are heading for New Orleans."

Both Nicolas and Guy stared at him.

"We're arranging to meet in the Place d'Armes, mounted and armed, to go after them," Philippe said. "Hurry!"

Because of his experience in the trek upriver after Aaron Burr, it was agreed that Guy would lead a group of eight men, Philippe Roulleaux among them. The entire unit of forty-odd men was led by an older planter, Rene LaCasse, who'd survived a slave uprising in Santo Domingo in 1791.

"Every last slave who defies us must die," LaCasse warned them. "This is not time for leniency. Kill—don't attempt to take prisoners."

By midnight they'd crossed the river and had their horses trotting along the levee road, heading upstream. Flames from a fired grinding mill, shouts, and sporadic shooting guided them to the fighting. As they neared they heard a woman screaming from the manor house of the plantation, keening, wailing, the high-pitched sound setting the teeth on edge.

A man raced toward them on a lathered horse. A dozen pistols were pointed at him before they realized he was white, an overseer.

"Black bastards killed her husband," the man said. "Cut off his head. Can't get her to leave him. Must be a hundred niggers on the rampage. They're stealing horses now. They got cane knives, clubs . . ."

"We'll flush 'em out," Guy said, spurring his horse toward the stables.

"They got guns," the man called after him.

Guy rode on, pistol in his hand, his eight men galloping behind him. As they neared the stables, a shot rang out and Guy's horse staggered. He urged Marquis on and the gelding stumbled ahead for a few yards, then dropped to his forelegs. Guy pitched forward, over the horse's head to the ground. He pushed himself to his feet.

"Look out!" a Creole shouted.

A dark wave rolled from the stable, some blacks mounted, others afoot. Shouting and cursing, they dashed onward, the firelight glinting on knives and the brass of gun mountings.

One of Guy's men fired his pistol, though the blacks weren't in range.

"Hold your fire!" Guy ordered. He unsheathed his sword, pointed it toward the Negroes. "Attack!" he yelled to the mounted men milling about him.

The horses raced past him. Guns blazed. A Negro came at him on foot, cane knife swishing through the air with a deadly hiss. Guy sidestepped and drove his sword into the man's neck. Blood spurted onto him as the slave dropped. Guy yanked his sword free, ducking quickly as another black swung a club at his head. Guy twisted, turned, and came up with his sword to face his attacker.

He'd lost his pistol when the horse fell, but his sword kept the club-wielding slave at bay. When the man rushed him, Guy waited until the moment was right, then lunged forward. His sword reached its mark, and the black fell, screaming, to the ground, his hands pressed against the mortal wound to his chest.

Guy heard a horse pounding toward him and looked up, expecting to see a Creole riding to his aid. Instead he saw a Negro astride a gigantic white stallion, the man as massive as the horse.

"Die," the black chanted, "die, die, die!" He brandished a curved saber, the steel gleaming red.

Guy ran, knowing he was easy game on foot with no gun. If he could get behind the oaks . . .

The white horse thundered toward him, and Guy knew he had no time to reach the stand of trees. Hooves pounded, pounded. Guy turned to face his doom like a man. The white horse was nearly on him. He raised his sword defiantly, seeing the giant black's tattooed, hate-contorted face, the tattoos flaring out on the cheeks like rays of a dark sun.

Another horse brushed past Guy, almost bowling him over, and slammed into the white horse. Both horses staggered and angled to the left. A pistol cracked, the white horse reared, another shot, horses galloped toward Guy, the giant on the white horse wheeled back toward the line of fighting blacks.

"I winged him," Philippe Roulleaux said, reaching a hand to Guy. "*Dieu*, but he was a big one. I think I've seen him before somewhere."

Guy sprang up behind Philippe and they raced after the other Creoles, swerving off to intercept a riderless chestnut horse. Guy dismounted and vaulted onto the back of the chestnut and, sword in hand, rode toward the fighting.

"Wilkinson's sent an army unit," LaCasse shouted to the Creoles. "His messenger just arrived. We're to contain the slaves until the army gets here to finish them off."

Guy searched the red-lit night for the big black on the white horse, determined to meet him on equal terms and vanquish him. He caught a flash of white heading away from the plantation, angling toward the swamps behind the cane fields. He took off in pursuit. Another rider cut in front of him and fury swept through Guy. How dare anyone challenge his right to kill the tattooed giant?

"Get back, he's mine!" Guy yelled, spurring the chestnut forward.

The white horse sprang ahead—the black had heard him—but the second horse stopped. Guy instinctively slowed. He'd assumed a Creole was after the fleeing slave, as he was, but with the flames behind him and only the light of a full moon, who could be certain?

"Who waits for me?" he called.

"Welcome, brother," the man called back. "It is I, Francois, waiting to settle the score between us."

Francois! Was he the mulatto who'd been agitating the slaves? Had Francois planned the uprising?

"Does fear of me make you tarry?" Francois taunted.

"*Cachon!*" Guy shouted, urging his chestnut forward. As he drew close, he saw that Francois held a pistol. He checked his horse.

Francois laughed mockingly. "No, I won't shoot you, little brother. I see you have your sword. So do I have mine. We'll dismount and discover how much the pupil has learned from his teacher. You first."

Francois kept the pistol trained on him as Guy slid from the chestnut, then Francois dismounted, flung away the gun and faced him, sword in hand.

"*En garde!*" he cried. "To the death!"

Dieu, how he hated Francois! It came to Guy that he'd always hated his half-brother, this sardonic dark man who bore the La Branche name, and who looked so much like him.

He forced himself to loosen his tight grip on the handle of his sword. One of the first lessons—hold the rapier firmly but not tightly. Guy took his position a few feet from Francois.

Francois bore in at him with a stroke like lightning, and Guy felt the blade slash his coat sleeve as he arched away from the thrust. He turned, turned again, feinted to the right, thrust to the left, only to find Francois' sword parrying his every attempt.

"I taught you everything, brother, do you think you can fool me?" Francois mocked.

Guy ducked away from a swift jab, circled. *Be unpredictable*, Francois had always told him. *Fool your opponent.* He had demonstrated to Guy many of the ways one might be unpredictable. It would be no use to try any move he'd learned from this master swordsman—Francois would anticipate his every thrust and feint.

The white light of the full moon showed him Francois' smile. A confident smile. There'd be no use to bore in heavily, for Francois would disarm and kill him quickly. He had to outwit him. How could he?

Francois attacked again, feinting, slashing. Guy felt the point of the sword prick his side, felt the blood run from a shallow cut along his ribs. A near thing. Stop thinking, he warned himself. Start fighting.

Guy darted right, then left, and got past Francois' guard enough to tear a strip from his shirt sleeve. The man wasn't invulnerable, he must stop believing he was.

Thrust, parry, duck, circle away, parry, thrust.

Blood trickled from Guy's cheek now as well as from the wound in his side. He'd made another cut in Francois' shirt but hadn't drawn blood. Every time he feinted, Francois knew exactly where he'd attack and met his thrust halfway.

Stop feinting. Have every thrust be just that—an attack. Would it work? He'd have to be careful, skillful, not go charging in. That way lay certain death.

Guy circled, circled again, heard Francois' taunting chuckle. Don't let him anger you, he warned himself. He means to rattle you—you're a dead man if you let him.

"Running away, brother?"

Guy suddenly realized that Francois had always hated him. He, Tanguy, white, the La Branche heir.

Guy circled yet again. In the moonlight, Francois' face was a tan mask. Suddenly Guy twisted and struck, tearing into the cloth of Francois' shirt front. Guy thrust again, leaped back to avoid a *riposte*, pretended to feint but carried through on the thrust, felt the blade sink deep into Francois' chest. Francois staggered back and the blade sprang free, dark with blood.

Now Francois gave ground, moving back, back, Guy following cautiously, uncertain how badly he was hurt, aware that Francois was a master of deception. Francois sank to one knee, coughing. Guy came in, sword ready, then paused. He couldn't run him through. Not a man down, injured. He couldn't do it.

Francois scrabbled about on the ground, Guy stepped back, sickened and repelled. A pistol cracked. A bullet grazed his ear.

The pistol! That cursed Francois had been faking, had deliberately gone after the discarded pistol in order to shoot him. He sprang forward, seeing Francois stagger to his feet, determined not to give him time to reload. As Guy positioned his sword for a final thrust, Francois spoke.

"You've already killed me, brother," he whispered, and fell forward at Guy's feet.

Chapter 14

MADELAINE let Empress have her head, knowing the mare would take her to the small rise near the bayou where she and Philippe met secretly. There was no hurry, for he wouldn't be coming today—the men were still rounding up straggling rebels from the slave uprising of two nights ago.

Guy would be furious if he knew she was out alone. Odalie had insisted she take one of the dogs along and Madelaine had obediently untied Guinevere, Guy's new hunting dog, promising Odalie she wouldn't go far.

It wasn't so very far, after all. Besides, those rebellious slaves were undoubtedly hiding in the swamps across the river, not anywhere near La Belle. Only one field hand was missing from La Belle and that slave had already been counted among the dead.

Philippe had rescued her brother! Excitement rose in Madelaine's breast every time she thought about it. Surely there was a chance that Guy would listen to Philippe now, and consider his request for her hand. While it was glorious to be with Philippe in secret, she longed for them to be married, to be openly and honestly together.

Like Annette-Louise and Gabriel had been. True, their happiness had been cut short, but his baby now comforted

Annette-Louise. Little Gabe had been born almost nine months after his father's death. Ah, to hold Philippe's son!

The winter had been mild so far, but today the sun hid behind a grey overcast and the sweep of the wind along the bayou made Madelaine huddle in her riding jacket. No need to worry about her staying out long in this weather. A red-winged blackbird flew in front of her, the splash of scarlet on its wings bright against the grey-green dimness of the moss and the cypress.

The bull alligator who occasionally roared a challenge from somewhere down the bayou was quiet, and it was too cold for the frogs, so she moved in a stillness unbroken except by the creak of her saddle and Empress' occasional whuffling. Guinevere darted here and there but flushed no game.

Perhaps she should turn and go back.

No, she wasn't a child to be frightened by grey silence. She'd ride as planned to the trysting place and then return home. Dr. Goodreau had recommended a daily ride and she'd done her best to carry out his prescription through the months. She felt and looked her old self.

Did John Kellogg carry a picture of her in his mind as he'd last seen her, wasted and yellow? Where was he now? Did he sometimes think of New Orleans, think of her? She shrugged. He was an army man as well as a doctor and no doubt had forgotten her already. Didn't they say soldiers had hearts like artichokes—a leaf for every woman?

She'd remember John as long as she lived. He'd saved her life as Philippe had saved Guy's. She owed John much—though not her love. Yet she often dreamed of him, dreams where it was he, not Philippe, who embraced her, and she'd wake with flushed cheeks and pounding pulse.

The spot where she met Philippe, where they lay together, was a tiny knoll of higher ground, surrounded by water oak and tupelo gum and hidden by a tangle of vines. The gums were barren of leaves now, but the rise was still concealed by the underbrush. Today she didn't dismount to open the secret passageway and lead Empress inside. Instead she sat for a moment, thinking of Philippe.

Guinevere ran to the bushes ahead, smelling the ground nearby. She growled, and the mare stomped and snorted.

From behind the vines came an answering nicker. Madelaine's eyes brightened. He'd come after all!

She slid off the mare and pulled back the vines, leading Empress through the tunnel of green and yellow growth into a tiny clearing. Guinevere dashed in ahead of them and began barking excitedly.

Madelaine stopped short. A huge white horse confronted her, his neck smeared with rusty stains. Guinevere circled warily about something on the ground beside the horse, whining.

"Oh!" The exclamation was jolted from Madelaine, her hands flying to her mouth too late to hold it back.

A black man lay unmoving in the yellow grass. Blood soaked his blue shirt and trousers and pooled on the ground beside him. Near his feet—Madelaine bit her lip to prevent herself from screaming—was a severed arm laying palm outstretched, a long-bladed knife next to it. Unmistakeably he'd cut off his own arm just below the elbow.

When Guinevere nudged the arm with her nose, bile rose to Madelaine's throat. Hurriedly she called the dog to her. She knew the man had to be a rebel slave. She must gallop back to La Belle and . . .

He raised his head and looked at her, his eyes glazed and dull from pain and loss of blood. She saw that he was a giant of a man, and noticed with dismay the tattoo marks on his cheeks. She recognized him.

The black she'd danced with at the voodoo.

He was too weak to stop her, she could easily mount Empress and rush from the clearing, but Madelaine didn't move. There was something in his eyes—not a plea for help, not a threat, but something she'd seen in the glare of captured hawks. A fierce pride.

Had he been a *candio*, a chief, in Africa?

They'd hang him. Already captured black rebels

dangled from trees across the river as a warning to the other slaves. Madelaine swallowed. Slowly she approached him, averting her eyes from the severed arm. His head dropped back, his eyes closed. She was frightened, but something drove her on.

Madelaine could see that he'd tried to bandage the stump of his right arm, but had apparently been too weak to complete the grisly task. The rag was soggy with blood. Madelaine took a deep breath, fighting to control nausea. She retreated behind Empress and lifted up her riding skirt to tear at her petticoat. The cotton was too strong for her to rip. Gagging, she retrieved the black's cane knife with its discolored blade and slashed at her petticoat, tearing a wide strip from the bottom.

She wrapped the white cotton around the stump, seeing with horror that the bloody tissue looked charred. She pulled the bandage tight, remembering how Odalie always applied pressure to a wound to stop the bleeding. The black groaned once, but showed no other sign of consciousness. She used the knife again to cut the ends of the cotton into small strips, tying them around the bandage to hold it on.

Blood oozed from the stump, staining the white cotton. As she put the knife on the ground, she noticed that its blade was blackened rather than blood-stained. She saw the remains of a small fire. Understanding flooded through her. He'd deliberately seared the stump with the heated blade of his knife in an effort to stop the bleeding.

The severed arm caught her eye, and before she could wrench her gaze away, she saw why he'd cut it off. There was a terrible wound above the wrist where the ends of shattered bones protruded.

She stood up, staring down at the black. He couldn't stay here, for surely Philippe would come—if not tomorrow, the next day. Besides, Guinevere knew he was here and Guy often took the dog out with him. The dog would likely lead her brother here, Madelaine decided.

She knelt beside the man again and whispered into his ear.

"*Candio*," she said. "*Candio*, listen to me. You must listen. I'll bring food, a blanket. But then you must take your horse and find another hiding place. They will find you here."

She couldn't tell if he heard, or if he understood. His eyelids quivered, but he made no other move, no sound.

Madelaine had little trouble collecting food and a blanket, and no trouble at all bringing the supplies to the secret place. But when she came back to La Belle again, she realized she must try to conceal the remains of her petticoat from Odalie's sharp eyes.

She changed into a different gown, and brought the wadded-up petticoat downstairs in her embroidery bag. An oak fire burned in the parlor. Madelaine, alone in the room, thrust the petticoat in among the glowing logs. The cloth smoldered a moment, then burst into flames. The acrid smell of burning cotton crept into the room.

By the time Odalie came into the parlor, the petticoat was ashes. Odalie sniffed the air, remarking, "Somebody be burning what don't belong in no fireplace."

Madelaine said nothing, her fingers busy with needlework.

That night Odalie had more to say. "You be missing a new petticoat. I be looking and it gone."

Madelaine shrugged.

Odalie eyed her sternly. "You do be taking up with that no-good again, that be what. Fine, indeed, when you be losing a petticoat. Don't look good to me, and that be the truth."

"I wasn't with him."

Odalie's glance was dubious. *"Mari napas trouve dan vitivere,"* she said. "You don't find no husband in a haycock."

"Odalie! What a thing to say to me."

The black woman snorted. "You know what I say be true. Trouble come."

143

The next day it rained, and Madelaine stayed home. The following day she approached the trysting place with trepidation. Would the one-armed black lie dead on the grass? Was he still there, waiting to be discovered by Philippe?

She pushed aside the concealing vines and led Empress inside, her heart beating fast with fear. The clearing was empty and the rain had washed the blood away, as well as the ashes of the fire. There was no sign the black had ever been there.

A bell tinkled, a tiny sound that made her freeze with shock, recalling the ankle bells the black had worn at the voodoo dancing. She whirled around. No one was behind her. No one was in the clearing. At last she saw what made the sound. A little bell tied to a vine near the entrance. She stared at it, realizing he'd left the bell for her.

Quickly she worked it loose and thrust it into a pocket. Philippe mustn't see the bell lest he suspect a rebel slave had been here. Philippe must never know she'd helped the black, any more than Guy must know. They wouldn't understand—she scarcely understood herself, only knew she'd done what seemed right.

Philippe came soon after she arrived. As he embraced her, she lifted an eager face for his kiss, but pulled back after a few moments.

"I haven't seen Guy yet today," she said. "Were you able to speak to him?"

Philippe sighed. "Not about you, not about us. When I rode up and greeted him yesterday he only nodded. It was a miserable day to search the swamps with the rain pouring down. Yet your brother was determined to flush out the slave on the white horse who'd tried to kill him, and so he kept searching, though the others gave up one by one and returned home."

Philippe didn't notice her start of surprise. *Mon Dieu*, she asked herself, had she helped the very man Guy was hunting?

"I stayed with your brother," Philippe went on, "for I

knew I'd shot the slave and expected we'd come on him, wounded and helpless."

Madelaine shuddered.

"I'm sorry I must speak of such matters to you," he said. "They can't be pleasant to hear."

"Go on," she urged.

"Soon only we two were left, Guy and myself. I talked of the enmity between our families, intending to ask him to end the feud by allowing us to wed." Philippe shook his head. "I never had the chance. He turned on me with no forgiveness in his face.

" 'I owe you a debt, for you saved my life,' your brother said, haughty and cold. 'This has nothing to do with what stands between our families and has for these six generations. I'll go to my grave hating the Roulleaux name and those who carry it. Never expect friendship between us, debt or not.'

"Madelaine, I hated him at that moment, even though I tried to go on with what I wanted to say. He cut me off.

" 'I prefer not to speak to you again,' he said. 'Please leave.'

"What was I to do? I left. To stay was to risk a challenge and, while I'm not a coward, it would be death for me to face the man who killed the fencing master, Francois."

Madelaine was silent a moment, then grasped Philippe's arm. "We'll run away," she said eagerly. "Oh, Philippe, that's what we'll do. We can marry in some place far from our families and be happy together forever."

He put an arm about her. "We can't run away," he said.

She pulled away. "Why not?"

He looked at her helplessly. "So many reasons. Money. I'd have to have money to buy land to grow cane, for I know nothing else. Nicolas manages the money. If I eloped with you, I'd have to take money without his knowledge. I couldn't do that."

Tears came to her eyes. "You don't love me."

145

"I do love you. I love my brother, too. Nicolas raised me, and took me everywhere with him so I wouldn't be alone. He's my father, my friend, as well as my brother. How could I run off without telling him? It would be a betrayal."

"How does he feel—would he feel—about us?"

"Like your brother, I'm afraid. Nicolas has already told me he wishes I'd managed to find someone else to rescue rather than Tanguy La Branche."

"If you really loved me you'd find a way to marry me," she said stubbornly.

"Perhaps Father Antoine . . ." His words trailed off. They both knew the priest would have nothing to do with a marriage not fully approved by both families.

"Ah, Madelaine, I do love you—more than life itself," he said, putting his arms about her and drawing her close. "I think of you all the time, and dream of holding you. If you'd died of the fever I'd have died myself, I think."

She melted against him, her body aflame with the need for him, only to draw back a moment later.

"This place—I can't, Philippe. Not here."

"What's the matter? This is ours, has always been ours." He tried to take her in his arms again.

She pressed her hands against his chest. "No, no, we must go somewhere else. I want you to make love to me, but not here. Never here again." She shuddered.

Later, farther up the bayou, beneath the concealing branches of a massive oak, they joined in the ever new delight of their passion.

At the end of July, Estelle sent word to Guy that he was to come to the cottage. He'd avoided her since the November night he'd discovered Francois in her bed, sending Leroy from the townhouse to bring Denis to him there, choosing times when Madelaine was at La Belle. The boy pleased him, and he decided to send Denis to

France to be educated soon. It wouldn't do to leave him with Estelle.

At first Guy planned to ignore her summons, but curiosity plagued him into riding to the rue des Ramparts.

Tiens, but the city grew. The *faubourg,* suburb, of the *Americains* would soon be as large as where the Creoles lived. Houses sprang up almost daily, it seemed. The more people, the quicker Louisiana could be admitted into the union of states. If one must be *Americain,* it was better to be a full-fledged state than a territory, of this he had no doubt.

On the other hand, he didn't care to see New Orleans fill with *Americains.* Already Protestant churches flourished in the town. What heresy would be next?

Since 1724 the *Code Noir,* the Black Code, had ruled that not only must the Roman Catholic religion be the only one allowed in Louisiana, but that it must be taught to slaves by their masters. The *Americains* changed much of the Code, though, leaving mostly the sections pertaining to the Negroes: No marriages permitted between Negroes and whites; manumission of slaves by masters over twenty-five or by such master's will; no concubinage.

The last provision wasn't enforced, of course . . .

Estelle opened the door to him. Guy looked about for Denis as he entered.

"Denis is playing with Henri down the street," she said, divining his glance.

"You asked me to come."

"Yes." She led him toward the bedroom and, after a brief hesitation, he followed.

Just inside the bedroom door, Estelle stopped and gestured toward the foot of the bed. He stepped past her and saw that Denis' old cradle had been taken from storage. For a moment he didn't realize there was a baby in the cradle. He stared at the child.

Estelle reached in and picked up the infant, a very tiny child, he noticed, far smaller than Denis had ever been. She thrust the baby at Guy. He backed away.

"Take him," she said, her dark eyes glittering.

Guy made no effort to hold out his arms, and after a time she laid the infant on the bed and undressed him. The boy woke and began to scream, waving his arms and kicking vigorously. He was small, but certainly sounded healthy enough.

"What do you think?" Estelle asked.

"He's small."

"He came early, two days ago. He wasn't to be born until August. No wonder he's tiny, he wasn't finished growing." Her voice was angry.

Yes, of course it was Estelle's baby, whose had he thought it might be? He'd let it be known he didn't care to hear Estelle's name mentioned, so no one had told him of her pregnancy.

"His name is Anton. Does that suit you?" she asked.

"What has his name to do with me?"

"I said he wasn't meant to be born so soon—you can see for yourself it's true. He was made in November of last year. Whether the father was you or Francois, the boy is certainly a La Branche and must be acknowledged."

Chapter 15

By January of 1810, Guy entered Anton La Branche in the parish register as his son. He came to see both boys often, though his relationship with Estelle remained cool and distant.

Anton was indeed a La Branche—he looked very like Madelaine had as a child, though he was much darker. He was darker than Denis, too, who, as far as Guy could tell, didn't resemble anyone except Aimee. Sometimes he felt neither child was his blood son, but he'd grown fond of Denis and even baby Anton, whose merry smile was enchanting. He'd continue to see them, and make certain they were educated.

The year went by, and Guy had not taken a *placee* since that bastard Nicolas had stolen Roxanne for his own. As 1811 came and went, Guy began to worry more about Madelaine remaining a spinster than he did about his own needs.

In November, he sat in on the constitutional convention at Tremoulet's Coffee House, afterwards again urging Andre Lafreniere to run for the legislature.

"Me draw up laws? I'm no lawyer," Andre protested.

"You don't need to be. Any Creole of sense can decide

what's best for Louisiana. You can't deny you're a man of sense."

Andre grinned. "Well, it's true I wouldn't let them change our name. Imagine wanting to call *la belle Louisiane* after the President. Can you imagine if we had to become the state of Jefferson? Never! I'd blow the lot of them sky-high before I'd allow such an abomination!"

After the parties and celebrations ushered in the new year of 1812, Guy decided he could wait no longer to speak frankly to his sister.

"Madelaine," he told her at breakfast during the second week of January, "you must think of marriage."

"I have."

"And?"

She gazed across the table, her face somber. "What if I were to say I was in love and wanted to marry an *Americain*? Or a—a Roulleaux? Would that make you happy?"

"Be serious."

"Perhaps I am serious."

"You know Dr. Kellogg is no longer in the city. He's been gone for almost five years. Surely you don't still think of him. As for a Roulleaux, I find your mention of them in bad taste. Certainly not in the least amusing. I'd see both Nicolas and Philippe dead before I'd let you marry either of them."

"It seems I'll have to remain a spinster then, since you've eliminated all possible suitors."

Guy sighed. "I don't understand why you won't be logical. There are many eligible young men who'd be pleased and happy if you'd encourage them. Yet you flutter among them like a butterfly, never landing anywhere. Soon they'll all take wives and you'll be too old for the young blades."

She shrugged. "No one suits me. Please don't concern yourself on my account. Senalda has been dead for five years and you're still single. You carry the name, not I."

He stared at her, knowing she must be thinking, as he was, of the old Roulleaux curse about the La Branche name dying before the seventh generation. Nonsense.

150

"I realize you have two free black sons," Madelaine went on, "but since neither of them can be a La Branche heir, shouldn't you be the one to consider marrying?"

"I intend to marry," he snapped. "Someday." Madelaine never seemed to understand that it wasn't proper for her to mention the boys.

"Someday I, too, plan to marry," she told him. "Why don't we drop the subject before you become angry? There are many other matters you might speak of—the marvelous steamboat of the *Americains* at the dock, for one. I'm told she can travel upriver as easily as down."

He said nothing for a moment, then grinned reluctantly at her. "I'll miss you when you do leave to marry," he told her. "And, yes, the *New Orleans* sails readily up the Mississippi. A strange-looking craft with both sails and her steam-powered paddle wheels. The unfortunate thing is that two *Americains* have exclusive rights to steam navigation on the river in exchange for building and operating the steamboats. Always they seek to shut out the Creoles."

"Can't someone challenge this so-called right?"

"In the courts. The matter would drag on for years while the *Americains* continued to enjoy their monopoly."

"Still . . ."

He nodded. "As you say, it should be done."

On the last day of April, Louisiana became the eighteenth state to join the union, just in time to be included in the United States when Congress, at President Madison's request, declared war on Great Britian.

By August, two British warships bottled up the mouth of the Mississippi and goods began to pile high on the New Orleans docks—a hundred thousand bales of cotton, thousands of pounds of sugar and tobacco in hogsheads.

The coffee houses buzzed with indignation. After all, were not those English pigs traditional enemies of Frenchmen?

In August of 1814 the British burned the Capitol in Washington, infuriating *Americains,* though the Creoles felt little, not yet used to being a part of the United States.

151

But when the British joined the Spanish in Florida, New Orleans took notice—Florida was much closer than Washington. The Creoles might grumble about *Americains,* but the British were enemies.

In November, General Andrew Jackson defeated the British at Mobile Bay. He then took over Pensacola, ousting the British who were "guests" of the Spanish governor there, after which he marched toward New Orleans to command its defense as the British fleet, with upwards of fifty sail, set forth from Jamaica, heading for the mouth of the Mississippi.

Andrew Jackson rode into New Orleans on December first, the cannon of Fort St. Charles thundering their greeting. Guy stood in the drizzle among the spectators, Madelaine by his side, staring at the tall thin general whose iron-grey hair bristled from his head like porcupine quills.

"Is it true he married his wife before she was divorced from her first husband?" Madelaine asked.

"I hear he still carries a bullet in his shoulder from one of the many duels he's fought over that rumor," Guy told her.

Jackson's fierce blue gaze raked the crowd, meeting Guy's for an electric second before sweeping on.

"*Faucon,*" Guy said. "The man has the eyes of a hawk."

"See how thin he is. He doesn't look well to me. Perhaps he needs good Creole food to fatten him up."

Madelaine caught her brother's arm. "Is it really true there'll be a battle here?"

"I've been telling you so for over a year."

"But there's been no fighting near us. I thought it was only worry on your part." She stared up at Jackson who was being greeted by Governor Claiborne and Mayor Girod. "Now, seeing him, I begin to believe you. He's altogether like a bird of prey. He'll attack."

"I'll be with him when he does," Guy vowed grimly.

A motley group of men formed Jackson's army. General Coffee brought twelve hundred Tennesseans, eight hundred of them mounted. Major General Carroll came behind him with three thousand Tennessee militiamen. Major Hind rode in with his Mississippi dragoons. Major General Thomas sent a message saying he was heading to New Orleans with twenty-three hundred Kentucky militia.

In the city itself, Creoles and free men of color flocked to join volunteer and militia groups. Guy, with thirty other young Creoles, joined John Beale's Volunteer Rifles. Since all were excellent marksmen, they became sharpshooters, wearing a uniform of blue hunting shirts and wide-brimmed ebony-black hats.

At first Jackson rejected offers of help from Jean and Pierre Lafitte and their crew of Baratarian privateers, calling them "hellish banditti." But the Louisiana legislature saw things differently, and agreed to grant the Baratarians amnesty for past crimes if they would serve with the United States Army. Jackson soon relented. The general needed men who knew the bayous and coulees below the city, since the British fleet lay offshore in the gulf and he had no way of knowing which of the thousands of waterways they might choose for their landing barges.

With Jean Lafitte's help, Jackson narrowed the possibilities down to five. An attack by way of the Mississippi River was the least likely, the general felt, since he'd reinforced the two forts at the entrance from the gulf. There was the possibility of an attack from the north via Lake Pontchartrain, from the east through Lake Borgne, from the west via the River La Fourche, or from the south through Lake Barataria. The last was unlikely with Lafitte on the American side.

In December, when British vessels drove Jackson's fleet of gunboats from Lake Borgne, east of the city, sinking or capturing them all, part of the question was answered. The attack would come from the east. But now there were miles of bayous and coulees between the lake and the city to worry about, and no way to keep an eye on every one. The two most obvious routes from the lake were via Villere's Canal or via Bayou Terra Aux Boeufs. Reinforcements were dispatched to both.

As La Belle was all too near Villere's Canal, Guy hurried to the plantation to insist Madelaine leave.

"But why?" she asked.

"The plantation's directly in the path of any British troops that might slip past the sentries," he said. "You can't stay in the house another day. Why are you so stubborn? All the other women have left the left bank plantations below the city—why won't you listen to reason? How can I go off and fight knowing you're not safe?"

"If they burned Washington, won't the British do the same to La Belle if no one is here to stop them?"

He threw his hands in the air. "President Madison couldn't stop them. What chance have you?"

Madelaine bit her lip, looking about the familiar rooms of the manor house. Generations of La Branches had furnished the house, bringing heirlooms from France. She knew and loved everything in the place.

"If you say I must go, I will," she said, "but I intend to see that more of our belongings are sent ahead to the townhouse. I'll supervise the servants in the loading of the wagons, and then I will leave."

"You must be in New Orleans before nightfall."

"Yes, I'll leave as soon as I see the wagons go off."

"You must promise. Beale allowed me only enough time to come and warn you, and I must go now. The Rifles are on the alert for an attack."

"I promise, Guy. I'll leave La Belle and follow the wagons into town. It's hours until sunset—stop worrying and return to your unit."

"I'll have the wagons brought up before I leave." He started out, then turned to look at her. "British officers may be gentlemen, Madelaine, but their soldiers, like ours, are not. There's serious danger for you here."

"I promised you I would leave, and I will. Please go ahead, Guy. Don't keep on at me. The sooner I get the servants started with the loading, the sooner I'll be in New Orleans."

When Guy had ridden off toward the city along the levee road, Madelaine began showing the house slaves what to pack into the wagons. All but Odalie would be staying at La Belle.

"What they be like, the British soldiers?" Josefina asked. "Maybe they will kill us all?"

"You'll be safe enough," Madelaine said. "If they do come here, which I hope they don't, just serve them as you would any Creole. They'll not hurt you."

Guy had said that the British had incited the Chitimacha Indians to rise up against the Creoles, and would probably urge the slaves to do the same, but Madelaine had no intention of saying such a thing to them.

"Be careful with that ormolu clock," she warned Josefina, who seemed ready to drop it. "Put it in the second wagon with the tapestries."

Josefina was back in a few moments, the clock still in her hands. "Ancin say the wheel be broke off, he need to fix it before you go. We be taking everything out of the wagon."

"Well, put the clock in the first wagon, then."

"Can't."

"Why not?"

"Ancin say that no-good Bris be halfway to New Orleans by now, he whip up the horse with the first wagon half-loaded, say he ain't coming back to La Belle."

"Why didn't Ancin tell me? Just wait until I see that Bris!" Madelaine debated sending someone after Bris, decided it would be a waste of time. None of the slaves except Ancin would be able to make Bris return to La Belle, and she needed Ancin here. There'd been only the two wagons left since Guy had taken the others for army use.

"Ancin trying to keep the wheel on, he don't be running to tell you. He yell at Bris, but Bris don't stop."

Madelaine sighed and went out with Josefina to look at the damaged wagon.

"Axle be broke. I be making a new one," Ancin said.

"How long?"

"Take some time." He squinted at the sky. "By sundown, maybe."

Madelaine bit her lip. She could follow the runaway wagon into town, leaving more than half of what she meant to take from La Belle behind, or she could wait for Ancin to make the new axle.

"By sunset," she repeated.

"Somewheres like that, *Mademoiselle*."

Guy would be furious if she waited. Still, he'd be with Beale's Rifles, not at the townhouse, so he'd never know. And she'd be keeping her promise, she'd be following the wagon into town. A bit later than she meant to, that's all.

"You fix the wagon," she told Ancin. "Let me know the minute it's ready."

At dusk, Ancin was still struggling with the wagon by lantern light. He gave a dozen reasons why it took so long, one being that Bris usually "handled the wood."

As it grew darker, Madelaine was forced to consider two options: she could ride into New Orleans now, without the wagon, or she could wait and hope the wagon would be ready to use by morning.

She decided to wait.

Before sunup, when the sky had barely begun to lighten, Odalie shook Madelaine's shoulder, rousing her.

"Hurry, we got to be going. He say right now, got to go right now."

Madelaine sat up. The usually unperturable Odalie was trembling, the brown of her eyes ringed with white.

"What's the matter? Who told you this?" Madelaine demanded.

"Bras Coupe. He say they coming. Them British."

Bras Coupe. Cut-off Arm. Madelaine had heard his name whispered by the slaves before. And cursed by the Creoles.

"He say give you this." Odalie held out a tiny bell that tinkled as Madelaine took it from her.

Madelaine had guessed that the legendary Bras Coupe, the renegade slave who lived in the swamps and eluded all pursuers, was the giant black she'd once helped. Now she was certain.

"Rouse the others," she told Odalie. "I want that wagon loaded if it's ready." She went to the wardrobe, and pulled out some clothes.

"The wagon be fixed. Bras Coupe, he say hurry, that don't be looking like we got time to load that wagon."

"I'm not going to leave my belongings for the British!"

"Stubborn, never did see such a stubborn," Odalie muttered as she hurried from the room.

Madelaine dressed rapidly and ran downstairs, where bleary-eyed servants were stumbling in from their quarters.

"The wagon," she cried. "Load the wagon. Start with the pile of things in the foyer."

Soon after the sun rose, the repaired and loaded wagon was ready to go.

"Ancin, you stay here and keep order among the men," Madelaine ordered. "Odalie and I will drive the wagon ourselves, with Empress tied behind. Keep the dogs in the stables, I don't want them following us."

He gazed past her with slack jaw, not answering, seemingly stupified. Madelaine turned to see what he stared at and confronted a soldier in a red tunic and plumed helmet.

"Miss, I fear you are my prisoner," he said in English.

A British soldier!

Madelaine didn't answer. I won't let them know I understand English, she decided quickly. She drew herself up haughtily. *"Je ne comprends pas,"* she said.

"Prisoner, prisoner," the soldier repeated, louder. She thought he must be an officer for he wore more gold braid than the redcoats she saw behind him.

"Prisonnier?" she cried. *"Allez-vous-en! Laissez-moi tranquille."*

The British officer shook his head, not understanding that she'd told him to go away and stop bothering her. He motioned toward the house, then toward her, an unmistakeable invitation for her to go inside. Head high, she sailed past him into the house. He followed her, leaving the front door open.

"Does anyone here speak English?" he asked. He gestured to the soldiers by the wagon and three hurried to join him in the foyer.

"Anglais?" she repeated. She pointed her finger at him. *"Anglais."* Indicating herself, she added proudly, "Creole. *Francais.*"

The officer shook his head. "We should have brought along a few interpreters," he said. "Any of you men know frog talk?"

All shook their heads.

Frogs? Madelaine thought indignantly. English pigs!

"Captain, have your soldiers search the house for any other Creoles, then post pickets and move the men forward," the officer ordered. "I think I'll handle this pretty little one on my own."

As the redcoats filed in through the front door, Madelaine burst into tears. Odalie ran to her side, taking her in her arms, scolding the British for upsetting Madelaine. They didn't understand her words but could hardly miss their intent.

"I'm sorry, miss," the officer said to Madelaine.

She sobbed louder.

He made no effort to stop Odalie when she led Madelaine from the foyer.

"Take me toward the back," Madelaine whispered to the black woman.

Odalie stiffened momentarily but went on, crooning to Madelaine as she directed their steps to the rear of the house.

The pickets would guard the back door as well as the front, Madelaine reasoned, but they wouldn't expect her to escape through a window. The best choice would be the small one near the storage room, which was covered from the outside by a hibiscus bush.

"You can't come with me," she whispered to Odalie. "Pretend you're still talking to me. When they find I'm gone, you pretend I tricked you. But I must get away, I must warn General Jackson."

"You do be careful," Odalie said.

She helped Madelaine force her way out the tiny window. Twigs caught at Madelaine's clothes and pulled her hair as she dropped to the ground between the bush and the house. She peered through the branches in alarm—surely the crackling had alerted the pickets. She saw none.

The levee road was undoubtedly swarming with British, she'd never get through. She'd have to hide in the swamp and make her way past the soldiers. She'd been in the swamps, yes, but could she keep from getting lost or mired in quicksand?

She'd have to try.

Madelaine tucked up her skirts, eased from behind the bush and ran for the high fence separating the yard of the manor house from the fields.

"Stop her!" a voice yelled.

She scrambled over the fence, racing across the stubbled cane fields toward the moss-hung cypresses, voices shouting behind her. She flung herself between the cypresses, her feet sinking into the swamp muck. Whirling to look behind her, she saw soldiers halfway across the field in pursuit.

She ploughed on, up to her knees in the mud, unable to hurry. They'd be on her in moments.

She was trapped.

Chapter 16

MADELAINE stared back toward the cane field, now hidden by the cypresses, as she tried desperately to extricate herself from the muck of the swamp. She heard a redcoat shout—close, so very close.

A hand gripped her around the waist, lifted her free of the grasping mud. She whirled, ready to strike out with her fists, determined not to be easily captured. Then she saw the black face of the man who held her.

Bras Coupe.

Without a word, he hoisted her over his shoulder, then plunged deeper into the swamp, leaping from log to tussock to escape being mired. From behind them, Madelaine heard men call to one another, heard a dog bark. Bras Coupe glanced over his shoulder.

"You go in this tree," he said, easing her onto the ground beside a cypress. "Stay. I be coming back."

He boosted her to the first branch and she climbed into the concealing grey moss that hung in long thick strands. She crouched on a limb, unable to see through the moss surrounding her.

She heard English voices.

"Something moving over there—is it her?"

"Must be. Come on."

"Bloody swamp!"

Squelching sounds, fading, then a whining bark from directly beneath her. Clutching the branch with one arm, Madelaine leaned to part the moss.

To her horror, she saw Guy's favorite hound, Guinevere, standing with her front paws on the trunk, looking up. The British must have untied her, hoping she'd lead them to Madelaine.

As she had.

"Go away," Madelaine said softly. "Go home."

Guinevere paid no heed, barking as if to invite Madelaine down to join her. The dog would give her away, beyond a doubt, when the soldiers came back, as they soon would, to investigate the barking.

Madelaine hesitated, then dropped to the ground. Guinevere fawned at her feet as she bent to seize a fallen limb to use as a club. She looked at the dog's trusting brown eyes.

I can't do it, she thought. No, I can't.

The soldiers would be back any minute. There might be others after her. She'd be captured. The British would march into New Orleans unimpeded, take the city, for who knew they were so close? It would be her fault.

Biting her lip, Madelaine raised the heavy branch and, with all her strength, struck Guinevere between the eyes.

The dog fell without a sound. Tears running down her face, Madelaine hauled the dog's body into the mud and, as it settled, threw the dead limb on top of it, snatched up two more and tossed them onto the body, jumped for the first tree limb, caught it, and swung herself into the cypress again, climbing into the concealing moss. She stifled her sobs with her clenched fist thrust between her teeth as she huddled next to the trunk.

A terrible end for the faithful Guinevere. She'd had no choice, none at all, but Madelaine felt she'd never be able to forgive herself. She heard voices again, the noise of men blundering through the tangle of vines and squelching in the muck.

"I tell you the barking came from over here."

"I don't hear it now. Don't see no bloody dog, neither."

Madelaine held her breath. Would they discover the dog's body?

"I hope to hell the frog bitch sunk ten feet deep in that bloody quicksand."

"The devil's own country."

"The major'll have our asses if we come back without her."

"She must've gone into the quicksand. What else could've happened to her?"

"Right. That's got to be what happened."

The voices diminished. A frog was she? Well, frogs were at home in a swamp. She'd show those British!

Madelaine heard the splashing fade. She stayed where she was, waiting.

"Come down. They be gone." Bras Coupe's deep voice sounded from beneath her.

Madelaine, skirts still tucked up, dropped from the tree. "You saved me. How can I thank you enough?" she said. "Now I must ask you to help me find a way to get into the city without the British catching us."

He stared down at her. She'd never seen such a big man. She remembered his eyes glittering in the voodoo firelight, remembered him lying helpless in her trysting place. His eyes were dark and unreadable. She sensed his tremendous strength as an almost tangible force, causing her breath to quicken in—was it apprehension?

"I must get to General Jackson before the British destroy New Orleans," she said.

He grunted.

She realized suddenly he didn't care whether the Creoles or the British controlled the city, for he was apart from all white men. Why should he help one or the other?

"I take you," he said. "Me, Ashanda. Your feet go after mine."

He turned from her and twisted between vines, heading deeper into the swamp. Madelaine followed, watching his feet, trying to step exactly where he did. On and on he led her, across coulees and through tangled vegetation, and as time went by she began to wonder if he was taking her toward New Orleans at all.

She was completely lost. Was he, instead, bringing her to a hiding place amidst the swamp tangle that only he knew of? Her heart thudded in her chest from exertion and from a shadowy tension.

At last he stopped and waited for her, then pushed aside the underbrush to show her the cane fields. She recognized the manor house at de la Ronde—they'd bypassed Villere and La Coste. He pointed toward the river.

"Safe here. No soldiers."

She understood he feared to come into the open lest he be taken prisoner by white men.

"You're known as Bras Coupe, aren't you?" she said. "I won't tell anyone you helped me. You'll be safe in the swamps."

"They be calling me Bras Coupe. Me, I be Ashanda."

"Ashanda."

He nodded, smiling for the first time.

"Is there anything I can do for you? Leave food somewhere? Clothes?"

He shook his head. "I help you, not New Orleans," he said. "You. Once you help me. My spirit and your spirit touch at voodoo. I know you. You know me. No master, no slave. The same, you, me."

Equal, she thought. He means we see one another as equals. She looked into his proud face, a face that denied he'd serve others except at his own choice.

"Yes," she said. "The same." She took his hand, holding it a moment between both of hers.

"Goodbye, Ashanda," she told him.

Madelaine turned and left the shelter of the swamp and ran across the field toward the river. When she glanced back there was no sign of him.

163

She reached New Orleans on a borrowed horse just before noon and galloped straight to Jackson's house on Royal Street. A flustered aide led her to the general.

"The girl claims she has knowledge of the British, sir."

"They're at La Belle," Madelaine cried, struggling to find the correct English words to tell her story. "The British surprised me early this morning. I escaped through the swamps." She located La Belle for him on the map he had spread out on a table.

"Seven miles away," he muttered. "Only seven. Was every picket asleep? We're caught unprepared, damn it!" His voice grew hoarse with anger and she realized he'd forgotten she was there.

"By the eternal they shan't sleep on our soil. I'll smash 'em, so help me God!"

Just before two o'clock in the afternoon, the signal gun at Fort Charles roared three times and the bells of St. Louis Cathedral began to toll. All around the city soldiers sprang to arms.

Guy, with the rest of Beale's sharpshooter unit, saddled his mount and fell into formation.

"It'll be a night attack," Beale told his men. "General Jackson's sending the Navy schooner *Carolina* downstream to bombard the British. The ship'll start firing at exactly seven o'clock. A half hour later the *Carolina* will send up red, white and blue rockets—our signal to begin the land attack."

At dusk, Guy's unit followed their commander in the vanguard of the men led by Jackson. Guy's heart beat fast in anticipation of the fight to come. Mist rose from the river to shroud them, eighteen hundred soldiers against at least as many British. Behind him marched Choctaw braves with painted faces, next to the Indians came Daquin's Battalion of Free Colored. A diverse and motley group of men, all united to fight the British.

As Jackson halted them at de la Ronde's plantation,

Guy realized with a pang that not only did the British occupy La Belle, but the battle might well be fought on his own land. What would happen to the plantation?

Thank the saints Madelaine was safe in the townhouse.

Jackson formed the troops into a line from the swamp to the river, setting up two artillery pieces on the river road. They waited in the deepening darkness, undiscovered by the British, for the *Carolina* to begin shelling. To Guy, keyed for a fight, the waiting seemed interminable.

A thunderous, flame-spitting roar came from downriver. Another, then another as the ship's guns cut loose. On and on the barrage went until Guy wondered if there'd be any British left alive for him to fight. How could any man live through that terrible hail of ball and grapeshot? The thought that some of the shells must be dropping on La Belle made him clench his teeth, but he quickly thrust the notion into the back of his mind. This was no time to worry about his holdings. If the British weren't defeated, of what use would be any Creole's plantation?

Acrid smoke drifted upriver. The pounding guns fired almost without pause, the noise numbing. He strained his eyes, watching for the rockets.

There!

Red, white and blue arched in the sky, scattering and falling. The *Carolina*'s guns fell silent. Beale called out sharply and Guy followed him with the rest of the unit to the left of Jackson's line, to protect general Coffee's flank. Through the dark and mist and smoke it was difficult to distinguish friend from foe. Soon Beale admitted they were lost and headed his troops back toward the river. In a few minutes they encountered marching soldiers. Guy expelled pent-up breath when he saw the men didn't wear red coats.

"Where's the first division?" one of Beale's horsemen called in English to the foot soldiers.

"*Richt* here!" a man shouted back.

Guy froze at the sound of the words. Not even the most ignorant *Kaintock* spoke English like that. Before he could

165

move, the strange soldiers rushed toward him. He swung up his gun and fired. A man went down. As Guy's horse leaped over him, Guy heard a voice call in the same strange dialect, ordering them to surrender.

Highlanders, he thought, remembering how the Scots fought with British troops.

"Men," Beale's voice said, "ride like hell out of here."

Hooves pounded as the unit fled, but a few moments later, with the Highlanders well behind them, Beale called a halt. Ahead were more soldiers. Friend or foe? Guy gripped his gun.

"Are you the Ninety-third?" a man called in English from the darkness.

"That's right," Guy shouted, knowing Jackson had no Ninety-third.

English soldiers hurried toward them, asking how things were going. Beale's men easily disarmed them and brought thirty British prisoners with them when they rejoined their own line, a prize that helped ease the humiliation of discovering they'd lost half their own unit to the Highlanders.

From the darkness far to the left came the firefly flashing and the stuttering pop of dozens of muskets. General Coffee's Tennesseans were attacking. The crack and flare of British guns answered. The rattle of musket fire spread along the line until the curses and shouts of the men were drowned out. Only the eerie ululation of the Choctaws' war cries rose over the din.

Jackson's line advanced, then fell back when reinforcements strengthened the British. Slowly but steadily Jackson's men withdrew, fighting all the way. The *Carolina*'s guns took up again, firing on the rear of the British lines.

Load, fire, load, fire. Bullets came so close to Guy that he heard their whirr. Gradually the firing lessened, became sporadic. The shelling from the ship stopped.

"Retreat." The official order came down the lines. "Retreat and regroup."

Jackson stopped the withdrawal behind the embankment

of the Rodriquez Canal, an abandoned and almost dry mill run, now knee-deep in rain water, where they huddled through the rest of the chilly night.

The morning dawned cold, the cane stubble sparkling with frost, the fields soon hidden, though, by a heavy mist rolling in from the river.

Guy knew the old sugarmill run extended from the river for over a thousand yards before ending in the swamp. He could see it was five feet deep and about twenty feet wide, with an embankment of dirt piled between them and the British. Did Jackson plan to fight from this entrenched position?

After a tense hour of waiting for an attack that never came, Jackson ordered the men out to dig a *fosse*, a ditch, along the downstream side of the banked wall of the old mill run to make it harder for the enemy to reach them when the British did attack. All the wet soil was added to the existing embankment, building it up several more feet.

The general sent runners into New Orleans to bring slaves and shovels, and Governor Claiborne was ordered to send all available fighting men. Jackson rode along the line, directing the digging, while Jean Lafitte helped the *Americain* engineers set up their cannon. As the day dragged on, the mist turned to rain.

To think it's Christmas Eve! Guy told himself, hearing the distant bell of the cathedral. Madelaine, in the townhouse, would be drinking *cafe brulot*, spiced coffee with brandy, before going to mass. Guy hadn't missed spending a Christmas Eve with Madelaine since the time on the keelboats when he'd volunteered to go after Burr.

Guy took his turn the next day digging the *fosse* in the rain, throwing the mud onto the raised embankment on the side facing the British. Who could ever have believed Tanguy La Branche would celebrate Christmas Day laboring in a ditch? He closed his eyes and prayed for the success of General Jackson.

That night, around the sputtering camp fires, the

Creoles of Beale's unit sang *Ave Maria*. When they finished, they heard *Americain* voices raised in song.

> *While shepherds watched their flocks by night*
> *All seated on the ground*
> *The Angel of the Lord came down*
> *And glory shone around . . .*

Guy listened, tears in his eyes.

The morning sun rose, warm and welcome. The engineers had placed cotton bales in the bottom of the run and laid planks across them so the men no longer had to stand in icy water as they waited for the British attack. But Jackson's men weren't in the ditch now, having camped on the New Orleans side of it, wondering when they'd begin to fight.

Although British cannon destroyed the *Carolina* on the twenty-sixth, leaving only the older, slower, *Louisiana* on the river, there was no land attack. The twenty-seventh passed.

On the morning of the twenty-eighth, Guy watched a tiny brown rail skittering along the edge of the ditch, searching for breakfast. A flock of geese flew overhead. Patches of mist hung over the cane fields.

Suddenly a tremendous hissing brought him to his feet. With a shattering roar a rocket burst directly overhead. Then another, and another, all with the same hair-raising shriek. To his left, one of Lafitte's men, Dominique You, shouted an order and a cannon roared. British cannon replied. In the midst of the roaring cannon, Guy heard a band playing.

He jumped into the ditch and climbed on the firing step to peer over the embankment. He caught his breath.

Columns of red-jacketed, white-trousered troops marched between the buildings of Chalmette Plantation toward the cane fields, toward him. Battle flags waved, bayonets gleamed in the fitful sunlight. He swallowed. *Mon Dieu,* there were so many!

Guy glanced toward the *Americain* flag, the Stars and Stripes, flying above him. He heard the guns of the *Louisiana* thunder. Flames burst from the plantation buildings, almost all of them at the same time, as red-hot shot fired the combustibles planted there by *Americain* engineers two days before. British soldiers fell, but the ranks closed up and came on. Cannon roared from all along the embankment. More soldiers dropped, and before the British line was close enough for Guy to fire, they wheeled about, still in formation, and marched from the field.

The next three days passed with only occasional skirmishing near the swamp. The *Americains* celebrated New Year's Eve with fiddle music and square dancing, the Creoles enjoying with them their "good ole Nongela," the Monongahela rye whiskey, and laughing at the sight of gaunt woodsmen, arm in arm, swinging each other in the vigorous dance.

General Jackson ordered a review of the troops on New Year's Day, with civilians from New Orleans invited to journey downriver to watch. Creoles and *Americains* began arriving at eight o'clock in the morning. The bands tuned up and the troops assembled, ready to march as soon as General Jackson appeared at the rude plank reviewing stand.

Suddenly the fearsome hiss of a Congreve rocket threaded through the strains of *Le Chant du Depart,* bursting overhead with a crash that silenced the band. The rockets were harmless enough, though their sound frightened the horses. When the British cannon began to roar, though, the civilians fled back toward the city. Guy ran to his post, seeing Dominique You atop the embankment, blood running down his arm, fist raised at the unseen enemy artillerymen.

"Shoot at me, will you? Miserables!" Dominique cried. "You will pay. *Nom de Dieu,* how you'll pay!"

On and on the cannonade roared, until a heavy cloud of acrid smoke hung over the field. When the British artillery fell silent, Guy peered anxiously toward the enemy lines but could see nothing through the smoke. The line waited tensely, but still no attack came.

As the days passed, the *Americains* amused themselves with wrestling matches, the Creoles with cockfights. A week went by. Before daybreak on the eighth, British rockets roused Jackson's men.

Guy stumbled through the early morning fog to his position in the lines, rubbing his hands together to warm them. This had been the coldest night yet. He looked over the embankment. Undoubtedly another false alarm. Across the fields, the mist was thinning as an icy breeze blew off the river.

"Dieu!" he exclaimed involuntarily when the mist lifted abruptly, revealing two long columns of redcoats advancing not six hundred yards away. Each column looked to be at least sixty men wide and only *le bon Dieu* knew how many men deep. The British soldiers wore white crossbelts secured on their chests with square brass buckles, a fine target.

Guy checked his gun, checked it again, fidgeting as he waited for the order to fire. There came the Highlanders, wearing red and green kilts instead of trousers. The bayonets glinted in the rising sun.

No bands played today, though the skirl of the bagpipes sounded eerily in the dawn. Along Jackson's line the men watched silently. Would the order to shoot never come? The enemy was four hundred yards away. Three hundred.

"Feu a volonte." The command came to the artillery. "Fire at will." The gunners blew on slow matches and thrust them onto the cannon's touch holes. Shot flew at the redcoats.

British cannon took up the challenge, shooting over the heads of their advancing infantry. Smoke rolled over the troops. An officer behind Guy yelled, "Get ready to fire, boys."

All along the line musket hammers clicked to full cock. Redcoats appeared through the smoke and Guy aimed at a mounted officer prancing beside his men.

"Fire!"

As smoke roiled, hiding the British, Guy saw the officer topple from his horse. He smiled grimly. Guy stepped back off the firing step, letting the man behind him go forward to fire while he reloaded, for the line was three men deep so no time was lost.

When he stood again on the firestep he nodded with satisfaction at the great gaps in the British line. Good shooting. But still they came on.

"Up, up the bayonets!" a redcoat officer shouted, a tall officer on a bay charger. His scarlet coat shone with gold lace.

"I'm gonna get that pretty fellow!" a Tennessean cried.

Rifles cracked and the horse fell heavily, the rider tumbling to the ground where he lay, unmoving.

"General Gibbs is hit!" a British officer shouted.

The decimated columns of redcoats wavered, turned and fled for their own lines. Only the Highlanders remained in formation, still facing the withering fire.

There was a lull and then Guy, stepping up to fire again, saw that a mounted British officer was rallying the men behind the Highlanders. More redcoats appeared, some carrying *fascines,* scaling ladders, to span the *fosse* and climb the embankment. They ran toward his lines and he aimed, fired, and saw a Highlander go down as he let the next man take his place.

An *Americain* to his left in the ditch moaned, clutching a shattered arm while blood spurted everywhere. Guy sprang to the man's side, yanking off his own neckerchief to tie tightly above the wound. Guy uncapped the soldier's canteen and handed it to him.

The man took a deep draught. The pungent reek of whiskey rose to Guy's nostrils—it wasn't water the canteen held.

"That helps, it does," the man said weakly. "I thank ye. Timothy O'Donnell never forgets a kindness and I'll do the same for ye someday."

Guy grabbed up his musket and, as he rammed shot

into the barrel, he saw a plumed British helmet rise above the embankment. Muskets cracked, red blossomed on the soldier's forehead and he fell back, disappearing.

On the firing step once more, Guy waited a moment before aiming. The redcoats were again retreating, the mounted officer who'd rallied them earlier, dashing among the stragglers, shouting. As he watched, a shot flung the officer from his horse.

A cry went up from the British line.

"General Packenham!"

For a moment more of the redcoats came on, then suddenly all their troops were in rout, running away from the fighting, stumbling and falling as musket shots continued to pick them off. An untold number of British soldiers lay on the field, dead or too badly hurt to move.

Guy woke the next morning to hear bells pealing from the towers of St. Louis Cathedral. Other church bells joined in.

Victory bells. The Battle of New Orleans had been won!

Chapter 17

"You hardly spoke to Annette-Louise," Madelaine protested to Guy when she came back into the townhouse after seeing her friend to her carriage.

They were living in the city until a new manor house could be built. Not downriver, on the left bank, where La Belle lay in ruins, but on La Branche land near Lake Pontchartrain where Guy had his slaves clearing fields to plant cane.

"Didn't I greet Annette-Louise? Ask after her health?"

"You know what I mean. You swept into the room and swept out with little Gabe. She had to collect him from you when she was ready to leave."

"The boy needs the company of men. He's too much with women."

"You're very fond of Gabe."

Guy nodded. "He reminds me of his father." He cocked his head, eyeing Madelaine. "I begin to detect a sinister plan in Annette-Louise's frequent visits, dear sister."

"She comes on my invitation!"

"That's the point I make. It finally dawns on me you're trying to pair us up, marry me off to Annette-Louise."

Madelaine smiled. "You must admit it would be a perfect match. Gabe needs a father and who would make a better one than his own father's best friend?"

"And what about me? What about poor Annette-Louise? You'd throw us together, willy-nilly, just so Gabe would have a father?"

Madelaine made a face. "You used to say she was the prettiest of all my friends."

"She's very pretty, but I hadn't thought of marrying her. Or anyone, for that matter. And I don't know that she'd have me. All Annette-Louise ever says to me is, 'be careful of Gabe.' "

"What chance do you give her for any other conversation? And, dear brother, I happen to know Annette-Louise has always admired you."

"I'll promise be a gracious host on her next visit—no more." Guy grinned at his sister and left her in the parlor, striding from the house to the stable where Ancin waited with General, Guy's newly purchased black stallion.

He intended to ride down the river road to what was left of La Belle, perhaps for the last time. An *Americain* merchant had made him an offer for the land and he needed the money to develop the new sugarcane plantation on Lake Pontchartrain.

All the hogsheads of sugar stored in the La Belle warehouse had been destroyed in the fighting. The house had been burned, and two slaves killed. Luckily, he'd moved most of his livestock before the British took possession, but nothing could make up for the loss of the processed sugar. He had nothing to show for the entire year's yield.

They weren't penniless, but the new plantation would show no profit for several years, so he could certainly put the *Americain's* dollars to good usage. Besides, he didn't want La Belle any longer. It was dead and gone. Like Senalda. Like Aimee. And Gabriel.

Guy rode out of the courtyard into the street. Since the battle with the British he'd been mired in *melancolie*. Everything seemed an anticlimax.

Certainly what had happened after General Jackson's

triumphal entry into New Orleans on January twenty-third had left a bad taste in everyone's mouth.

Guy thought back to that exciting day, when every balcony and rooftop on the general's route had teemed with cheering people. In the Place d'Armes an arch of triumph curved imposingly atop Corinthian columns. Two lovely young ladies, one Creole, one *Americain,* stood on pedestals to either side. The girls, dressed in Grecian draperies, represented Justice and Liberty. Other beautiful maidens graced pedestals between the arch and St. Louis Cathedral, each holding a banner with the name of a state or territory.

Andrew Jackson, unsmiling, his face gaunt and sallow, yet immaculate in full-dress uniform, marched down the carpeted path to cannon salvos and the shouts of the people. Cheers went up as he stepped beneath the arch, stopped, and was crowned by Justice and Liberty with the laurel wreaths of a victorious hero.

Abbe Dubourg, standing at the entrance to St. Louis Cathedral, welcomed the general and they entered the church to celebrate a solemn high mass. The festivities reached their peak during the evening when, at the Grand Ball, General Jackson led his round dumpling of a wife in a reel, to the tune of "Possum Up De Gum Tree."

The sight of the tall, thin general and the short, plump *Madame la Generale* jigging up and down together was too much for most of the Creoles. But the laughter was goodnatured for wasn't he their hero? And any Creole appreciated a woman who liked to eat, as Rachel Jackson obviously did.

If only the aftermath of the war could have ended on that happy note. But it was not to be. Jackson, who was not certain that the British wouldn't return, maintained martial law. He refused to discharge the men from the army, even after everyone had heard of the peace signed at Ghent between the United States and England. When state senator Louailler argued with Jackson, the senator was arrested and courtmartialed.

Federal Judge Hall protested this move and Jackson

clapped him in jail, too. Only when an order to pardon all military offenses came from Washington did Jackson relent and release the senator and judge, and send the soldiers home.

Judge Hall promptly retaliated by arresting Jackson for contempt of court. New Orleans divided, pro and con, but there was no doubt in any Baratarians' mind who was wrong. On March twenty-fourth, when Jackson appeared in Judge Hall's court in civilian dress, the room was full of them. Dominique You leaped to his feet.

"*Generale!*" he shouted. "Say the word and we'll pitch into the river the judge, the lawyers, and the courthouse itself!"

Jackson quelled the near riot that followed, stood before the judge, head bowed, and listened to Hall sentence him to a fine of one thousand dollars. Jackson paid the money, bowed to the judge, and left the court. The Baratarians lifted him onto their shoulders and carried him off to Maspero's Exchange to toast him far into the night.

Arguments still waxed hot over who'd been right, Jackson or Hall.

Guy shrugged, feeling it unimportant who was right or wrong. The bitter feelings that remained in the city after General Jackson's departure in April troubled him more.

A hero ought to depart in triumph.

He saved us from the British, Guy told himself, as he spurred his horse along the river road, eyeing the shell-shattered plantations to his left. New Orleans would look as bad if Jackson hadn't rallied us, and kept us together to fight. I'm proud to have been one of his soldiers.

He passed war-ravaged Chalmette, then Bienvenu, his dark mood deepening, though the sun sparkled on the brown water of the river. The sidewheeler *Enterprise*, captained by Henry Shreve, steamed upriver. Guy watched the boat, wondering if, now that the fighting was over and Jackson no longer was using Shreve's boat to ferry ammunition, the captain would be arrested—along with the owner of the boat, a man named French—for defying the

Fulton-Livingstone steamboat monopoly on the Mississippi.

The thought depressed him further.

Perhaps Madelaine was right and he should consider marrying. Annette-Louise would make a good wife. She was *agreeable,* certainly, and he loved little Gabe like a son. Annette-Louise could give him sons of his own. The war had thrust home to him man's fragile hold on life, and he felt an urgency to father a La Branche heir. He needed a son to carry on the name.

He rode past de la Ronde, La Coste Villere, seeing ahead the crumbling chimneys of La Belle. They were all that was left of the manor house. Guy slowed General to a walk as he looked at the shell-pocked fields and the splintered grinding mill.

Most of the giant oaks still stood, but three had been shattered by the cannonading, leaving gaps along the shaded avenue leading from the river. A lump came into Guy's throat as he gazed at what had once been one of the finest plantations in Louisiana.

He turned away, wheeling the black stallion, and galloped toward the city. Nothing was left for him here. There'd be a new home on the lake, a new beginning. He'd marry Annette-Louise and sire sons. Madelaine would marry, too, he'd make her see it was necessary.

The La Branche family would start afresh, grow and multiply stronger than ever.

Madelaine paced along the bayou, east of the city, her new rendezvous with Philippe. Empress was gone, taken by the British and her new mare, Dolly, snorted, twitching her ears before dropping her head to crop the grass near the water's edge.

What was keeping him? Madelaine rubbed her hand across her forehead, it seemed she always had a slight headache these days, always felt a bit nauseated. She lacked her usual energy.

Dolly lifted her head, and, a moment later, Madelaine heard a horse picking its way through the underbrush. She turned toward the sound. Philippe rode into the clearing and slid off his bay gelding.

"Sorry if I've kept you waiting, but I had some trouble finding what I needed," he said, holding out a small packet.

"What is it?"

"Vedette Rusert made it up for you. It's certain to work."

"You've brought me a voodoo potion? Why?"

"What other solution is there?" he asked.

Understanding left Madelaine momentarily speechless.

"You mix the potion with . . ." he went on.

"Philippe Roulleaux!" she cried, knocking his hand aside so that he dropped the packet.

"What's the matter?"

Tears came into her eyes. "How could you?" she asked. "How could you possibly go to that *voodooienne* and buy a potion from her to be rid of our baby?"

He tried to put his arms about her but she jerked away.

"I won't take anything to hurt our child," she said, laying her hands protectively over her stomach. "How could you think I would?"

"But Madelaine . . ."

"It's a sin!"

"Other women . . ."

"I won't!" Her voice rose. "You can't make me!"

Philippe took her into his arms. "No one is going to force you," he said soothingly.

She looked up at him. "You don't love me—or you wouldn't have asked me to attempt such a thing."

"I do love you. It seemed the best remedy."

"We'll run off together. Oh, Philippe, why don't we?"

He sighed. "I've explained why. Now is the worst possible time to leave Nicolas. The war . . ."

"Don't tell me how the war has hurt the planters, I'm tired of hearing it." She stepped back. "I won't take any potion to rid myself of the baby and you won't consider taking me away from New Orleans. What do you plan to do?" Her tone was cool.

Muscles bunched in his jaw. "I'll talk to your brother," he said. "That's all there's left for me to do."

Guy crossed the courtyard of the townhouse and climbed the steps, well-satisfied. He'd just returned from De Cheminee, the Davion plantation across the river, where Annette-Louise had listened to his proposal of marriage unsurprised, though not unmoved.

While she hadn't given him a definite yes, saying she must think what was best for Gabe's future, Guy felt certain she'd agree. There'd been something in her glance, a beckoning coyness that he'd never seen before, and she hadn't objected at all when he kissed her.

If he wasn't in love with her, still she was a most *agreeable* armful of woman.

"Madelaine," he called as he entered the house, "I have news for you, dear sister."

"Pardon, please, *Monsieur,*" old Louis said, intercepting him. "*Mademoiselle* say to tell you a gentleman be waiting in the salon." Louis eyed him nervously. "She be telling me to let him come in," he added.

Guy frowned. What was this all about? He strode along the corridor and into the salon. He stopped short, aghast.

Philippe Roulleaux stood in the salon, his image reflected in the gilt mirror so that, for a moment, Guy thought both the Roulleauxes awaited him.

"What are you doing in my house?" Guy demanded.

Philippe was very pale. "I've come to ask for your sister's hand," he said. "For your permission to marry her."

"Madelaine? You wish to marry Madelaine?" Guy's voice was incredulous. He stared at Philippe in disbelief.

"I do."

"*Nom de Dieu,* what arrogance, what nerve! You, a

Roulleaux, not even welcome in my house, to ask for my sister's hand. *Incroyable!*"

Philippe didn't move, standing stiffly before him. "Nevertheless, I am here. Madelaine loves me as I love her."

"Get out. Get out of my house, out of my sight. Your presumption angers me. Get out, I tell you. Immediately."

"Madelaine carries my child."

There was a silence. The room seemed to echo Philippe's words: *My child, my child.*

Guy stood frozen, his mind recalling recent happenings—Madelaine rushing from the table, coming back pale, with no appetite. Laying abed until noon, which was unlike her. *Dieu,* the man spoke the truth. His sister was very likely pregnant. By a Roulleaux.

Guy drew himself up. "You have insulted me," he said. "I challenge you to the death. What is your choice of weapons?"

Philippe swallowed. "I accept the challenge. Pistols."

"Pistols it will be. Second?"

"Marc de la Harpe. Yours?"

"Andre Lafreniere."

"I'll have Marc contact him to set the time," Philippe said. He turned and strode from the room. Guy waited a few moments, wanting him out of the house before he left the salon. He heard the murmur of voices, a woman's scream.

Guy rushed into the corridor, saw Madelaine by the staircase supported in Philippe's arms. Her head dangled backwards and he realized she'd fainted. Odalie came running down the stairs.

"The maid will see to her," Guy said. "Louis, show this man out."

Philippe, not looking at Guy, handed Madelaine over to Odalie and, back stiff, walked down the corridor not waiting for old Louis to precede him. He let himself out, closing the door behind him.

"Is she all right?" Guy asked Odalie.

"You know how it be with her?" Odalie said.

He nodded curtly.

"She be fainting a bit, likely she do it again."

"I'll carry her upstairs."

In Madelaine's room, he stood at the bedside looking down at his sister's colorless face. How could she? he asked himself. Was it possible Philippe had somehow taken advantage of her?

Her eyelids quivered, opened. She stared up at Guy.

"You're going to kill him," she whispered. "If he dies, I hope I die, too."

"Dr. Goodreau says he's getting too old for these affairs," Andre Lafreniere told Guy. "He's asked another doctor to attend us. "Is that satisfactory?"

Guy shrugged. "Any doctor he recommends is fine."

"Marc says Philippe offered no objection, so we may proceed," Andre said. "Everything's ready for dawn tomorrow."

That evening Guy checked his duelling pistols, then asked Louis to bring Odalie to the library.

"I want you to dose *Mademoiselle* with laudanum tonight," he told Odalie. "Put it in a drink so she doesn't know."

"I do what you say."

"Be certain you do. Otherwise she may be hurt trying to stop the duel. Once a bullet's fired it can't be called back to the gun. Make certain she sleeps through the duel."

"Oui."

When Odalie was gone, Guy lowered his head into his hands. He should be elated, full of eager excitement at the thought of facing a Roulleaux on the duelling field, but all he felt was a dark foreboding.

Whatever happened, the love and trust between him and Madelaine was lost, perhaps forever.

Chapter 18

EVEN at sunrise, the June morning was sultry. Guy rode along the Metarie Road with Andre toward the *Les Trois Capelines,* the three moss-draped oaks just the other side of Metarie Ridge, a common duelling spot, and the one Philippe had chosen.

Guy, with time to think about it, had lost his first flush of rage. I don't want to kill the bedamned fool, he told himself, even if he is a Roulleaux. Philippe once saved my life, it would be wrong to end his, no matter what his ancestry. On the other hand, neither do I want to die. Ah, well, he has first shot and I must take my chances.

"I love him!" Madelaine had cried the night before, standing in the entrance to the library, Odalie's black face at her shoulder. "Don't do this to me," she begged. "Don't kill the man I love—the father of the child I carry."

Already the pupils of her eyes were tiny from the dose of laudanum Odalie had given her, and her tongue thick from its effects. "Guy, I pray you won't harm Philippe." Madelaine staggered, clutching at the door frame. Odalie caught her.

"Come to bed, *pauvre 'tite,*" she murmured.

Guy helped Odalie support Madelaine as she climbed

the stairs. Once in bed, she fell asleep immediately, drugged by the opium mixture. He'd promised her nothing.

Back down from a duel? Such a thing wasn't done. He'd be scorned forever among his friends, labeled a coward. Still, he wished this duel didn't have to be fought. "To the death," he'd said, and so he'd have to at least wound Philippe.

The right arm would be best. Philippe might not attempt a shot at him with the second pistol and he could declare himself satisfied. He'd try to miss the bone to save the loss of the arm.

"I don't believe I asked you the name of the doctor," Guy said to Andre.

"Dr. Goodreau told me you knew him. An *Americain* who was with Jackson's army. John Kellogg is his name."

Guy stiffened, then relaxed. The red-haired *Americain* was competent, and Philippe would need a good doctor's services. Kellogg could be trusted to keep his mouth shut about the duel or Dr. Goodreau wouldn't have recommended him.

When the seconds finished pacing off the distance between the duellists, Guy took his position, facing Philippe. Andre handed him one of his pistols, primed and ready to fire. At the same time, Marc gave Philippe his pistol. Although his heart hammered against his ribs, Guy stood calmly, waiting for Philippe to shoot first.

May *le bon Dieu* have mercy on my soul, he prayed soundlessly.

He saw the flare of Philippe's pistol, heard the report, felt a blow to his head that knocked him off balance so that he staggered, confused for a moment. Andre hurried toward him, but Guy waved him back.

Philippe's bullet, he knew, had grazed his temple. He felt the trickle of blood down his cheek, but disdained to wipe it away as he brought up his pistol, carefully taking aim, fighting off a wave of dizziness.

In the forearm, he decided, for if I do smash the bone,

Philippe will lose only part of the arm. He pulled back the hammer to full cock and squeezed the trigger. To his horror, as the gun cracked, Philippe moved.

In a whirling kaliedoscope of motion Philippe stumbled back, fell, Marc ran to him, the red-haired *Americain* doctor ran to him. The trees to either side of Guy whirled, from behind him he heard a woman scream, the pistol dropped from his hand and everything went dark.

When Guy recovered consciousness, he was lying on his back under an oak with John Kellogg leaning over him. His head ached abominably. He tried to sit up but a violent vertigo forced him flat again.

"Concussion of the brain," Dr. Kellogg said. "You'll be all right in a day or two."

"Philippe?" Guy managed to ask.

"Dead. Shot through the heart."

I meant to hit his arm, Guy wanted to say. If only he hadn't moved. Pride prevented him from speaking.

"Your sister's condition is less favorable than yours," Dr. Kellogg went on, "but I believe she'll recover."

"Madelaine?" Again Guy struggled to sit up. The doctor helped him brace his back against the tree. "What happened? Where is she?"

"In my carriage." As she spoke, Annette-Louise stepped into view from behind the oak. Her dark eyes smoldered with anger. "I brought Madelaine here as she asked me to do. How could you do such a terrible thing?" she demanded. "And to your own sister!"

"Annette-Louise . . ." Guy began.

"Don't speak to me. I never want to see you again." She whirled and stalked away.

Guy turned to the doctor. "Please tell me what happened."

"Madame Davion's carriage drove up just as you fired," Dr. Kellogg said. "Your sister jumped out and ran toward *Monsieur* Roulleaux as he fell, mortally wounded. She fainted. When I saw I could do nothing for him, I went to her. She's extremely disturbed."

"Madelaine took—I ordered her maid to dose her with laudanum."

The doctor nodded. "Her maid told me. She's with your sister in the carriage. The opium may be contributing to her confusion." Guy saw the muscles bunch as Dr. Kellogg clenched his jaw.

"Would you ask my second to help me onto my horse?" Guy said. "I believe I can ride home."

The doctor stared at him for a moment, nodded curtly and strode away.

Guy closed his eyes. His ordeal wasn't over. He'd have to decide what should be done with Madelaine, what was best for her. She might well never forgive him.

As for Annette-Louise, she'd made it clear she'd never marry him. If she didn't change her mind, he'd lost Gabe, too.

John Kellogg sat by Madelaine's bed, watching her. She moaned and turned restlessly, but didn't open her eyes. Madame Davion had wanted to take her to De Cheminee, the Davion plantation, but he'd told her she couldn't, insisting that Madelaine would be best cared for at home.

How long had it been since he'd sat beside her bed at La Belle, afraid she was dying? Seven years. His heart still turned over at the sight of her, even though he knew from having examined her that she was pregnant with another man's child. It took no great power of deduction to see that the father was Philippe Roulleaux.

Madelaine's physical condition was good, although she was a trifle thin. Her mind—that was another matter. He hoped that when she woke from her drug-induced slumber she'd be rational, and the not the wild-eyed, incoherent creature who'd fought him as he forced more laudanum down her throat. He neither knew nor cared if Guy La Branche approved of him being in the house, for he intended to stay here until Madelaine recovered.

He'd tried to see her in December when his army unit

was sent to New Orleans to assist General Jackson. The war and the hideous aftermath of amputating limbs and treating suppurating wounds had kept him from her, and then his battalion had been transferred north to Baton Rouge. He'd come to New Orleans on leave, met Dr. Goodreau and offered to take his place at the duel.

"John?"

With a start he realized Madelaine's eyes were open and she was gazing at him, recognition and bewilderment in her expression.

He leaned over. "How do you feel, Madelaine?"

"Weak." She blinked, obviously trying to orient herself. "I don't still have yellow fever? I remember getting well . . ." Her words broke off and her face went stiff, despair and horror in her eyes.

"No," she breathed. "Oh no, John, tell me it didn't happen."

He took her hand in both of his.

"He's dead," she wailed. "Philippe's dead, isn't he?"

"Yes, Madelaine."

Tears filled her eyes and she began to sob. He sat on the bed, gathering her into his arms, holding her as she wept, doing nothing to try to stem her tears, for grief was best assuaged with tears.

At last she eased away from him. He handed her a handkerchief and helped her sit up among the pillows. He knelt beside the bed and took her hand.

"I know you'll have Philippe Roulleaux's baby," he said. "Marry me, Madelaine, and I'll accept the child as my own. The first year you'd be an army wife but then my enlistment time is finished and I'll set up a practice. In New Orleans, if you like, for I feel at home here."

Her eyes widened as she stared at him. Finally she drew her hand from his. He rose from his knees and stood looking down at her.

"My brother—Guy's not badly hurt, is he?"

"No. A mild concussion of the brain."

186

"I—I can't marry you, though it is most generous of you to offer."

"It's not from generosity—I . . ."

"No, wait until I finish. I can't marry you. How can I marry anyone now? And Guy . . ." Her eyes hardened. "I won't give him the chance to kill anyone else."

"Never mind your brother. This is between us."

She took a deep breath, let it out slowly. "My answer is no. It wouldn't be right. Philippe . . ." She closed her eyes and tears seeped from beneath her eyelids.

"It's no use, John, but thank you. I'll not forget you."

I've never forgotten you, he said silently. I never will.

"No," Estelle said. "I won't let you take my Anton. He's mine." Her dark eyes snapped with fury as she stood facing Guy in the main room of the cottage.

Guy glared down at her. "I have the right to him, he bears my name. Anton comes with Denis, as I've told you. Both the boys will sail with me to France."

"If Anton goes, I go."

Guy, taken aback, opened his mouth to tell her she wasn't giving the orders, then closed it without replying. Having Estelle along might be wise. Madelaine remained so listless he knew she'd be no help with the two boys. He'd planned to take Odalie but she made an uncomfortable companion with her silent hatred, blaming him, he knew, for everything that was wrong with Madelaine.

Estelle could easily manage the boys and look after Madelaine at the same time. In fact, it might do his sister good to get away from Odalie's overprotectiveness for awhile.

"You'll come, of course," he said. "But, mind, the boys will be left there and you'll come back with me. You'll not stay in France to interfere with their education."

She eyed him sullenly.

"You'll also see to my sister's needs on the journey. Naturally you'll be paid for this service."

Estelle blinked.

"Those are the conditions, Estelle."

"Very well. I'll care for the boys and your sister." The look in her eyes plainly said what she did not—that she had no intention of caring for him as well.

Madelaine accepted the idea of a voyage to France as she did everything since the duel, without argument, moving through the days as though she wasn't aware of anything around her.

By the time Guy had arranged for their passage, she was four months along, but so thin that no one in New Orleans knew she was with child except Odalie. Madelaine hadn't told Annette-Louise.

A week aboard ship made Madelaine's condition obvious to Estelle.

"You're taking her to France to have her baby," she said to Guy as they walked the deck. "I wondered why you were in such a hurry to leave."

"We won't discuss the matter," he warned.

Estelle smiled, but didn't bring it up again.

The ship dropped anchor off Le Havre and Guy hired a coach and headed for St. Ambrose, the boarding school in the wine country north of Paris, where his father had sent Francois. He left Estelle with Madelaine at a country inn on the outskirts of Paris, then went on with Denis and Anton to St. Ambrose.

"I have need of a convent where my sister can stay for her confinement," he told the abbe at the boarding school. "A place where the child might be cared for as an infant."

"The Sisters of the Blessed Miracle," the abbe replied. "The convent is some distance from here, but I can't think of any order better suited to your needs."

"Tell me their location, if you'll be so kind."

Later, Guy said goodbye to the boys, who he was leaving at the school.

"Denis, you're almost a man, ten years old, and you must console your little brother when he feels sad for his *maman*. He's only four, not yet big enough to hold back

188

tears. Learn what the good priests teach you as best you can."

Denis, his lip quivering, swallowed and looked at his father. Wordlessly, he nodded his head.

Anton still clung to Guy's hand and Guy gently disengaged his fingers, kneeling down to join his hand to Denis'.

"You be a good boy, Anton," he said. "You listen to Denis, he'll look after you and so will the priests. When papa comes back to see you you'll be almost grown and think how proud he'll be of you." He kissed the little boy, then embraced Denis.

Tears filled Denis' eyes and rolled down his cheeks but he struggled to be brave. Impulsively, Guy slid the ruby ring that had been his father's off his finger and put it in Denis' free hand. Then, with tears in his own eyes, he left hurriedly lest he break down himself. Little Anton cried, "Papa, papa," after him until the door closed and shut off the wails.

How well he recalled his own father leaving him at his French school; the despair, the homesickness. And he'd been eleven.

He wiped his eyes, knowing he had done what was best for the boys. There was no way to educate them in New Orleans and, besides, here in France their color wouldn't matter. If they chose to stay as adults they'd be accepted as equals, he knew. In Louisiana they'd always be black.

Why hadn't Francois stayed in France? He could have made a name for himself as a fencing master in Paris. Fencing masters were highly respected—what had driven him back to New Orleans and the humility of being an unrecognized La Branche? Guy shook his head. He'd never know.

Once Guy placed Madelaine with the Sisters of the Blessed Miracle, he felt somewhat at a loss. Madelaine's time was several months away, but he couldn't bear to have her travel with him any longer, her silence accusing

189

him. He certainly didn't want to sit around idly in the country, waiting for her to deliver the child.

It wasn't as though she'd miss him if he didn't stay, for she seemed content with the nuns and barely acknowledged his daily visits. He felt out of place when he went to see her in the convent, a man in the midst of a community of women. In the end he left Estelle with Madelaine and departed for Paris.

"I plan to visit the *marquis* de Lafayette," he told Madelaine, "and invite him to come to Louisiana. Ah, how honored we'd be."

She nodded vaguely.

"I'll come back in a month. The Sisters will take good care of you, and you'll have Estelle." It occurred to him his assurances to his sister were much the same as those he'd given the boys.

"All right," she said.

He took her hands. "Madelaine, look at me."

She focused her eyes on his face, but he had the feeling she wasn't really seeing him.

As the baby grew within her it seemed to Guy that her face became thinner. With her pale skin, dark hair and air of otherworldliness, she resembled Italian paintings of the Madonna. He felt a pang, a threat of loss. Some women died giving birth.

He caught her to him, embracing her. She submitted, not returning his kiss but not resisting. The child inside her, though, twisted so violently that he felt its kick.

Guy remembered Paris from his student days. Wonderful, glittering Paris. He decided to journey there first and then plan his visit to the *marquis*. Andre Lafreniere had a cousin who lived in the city, and had exhorted Guy to call on him.

"He's married, has a family. I haven't seen him in years—ten years, anyway. Tell him to come to New Orleans, to bring them all. I've not the stomach for the ocean, never did have."

The Georges Lafrenieres insisted that Guy stay with them in their elegant mansion on one of the islands in the Seine, the Ile St. Louis, in the center of Paris. He was just in time, they told him, to attend the masked ball scheduled for the following night.

With little time to plan his costume, Guy decided to dress as a Baratarian privateer, with a red sash about his waist and a black patch over one eye such as Pierre Lafitte wore. Since no one knew him but his host and hostess, the patch would be mask enough.

The Creole women were lovely, but the flair of the *Parisiennes* was not to be found in all of Louisiana. With an effort Guy kept himself from staring at the glittering costumes, the lavish display of jewelry, the elegant women. He wasn't an ignorant *Kaintock*, after all.

Madame Lafreniere introduced him to no one, for the object of a masquerade was anonymity. Guy singled out a ravishing white-robed angel, her wings and mask gleaming with brilliants, but before he'd crossed the floor to ask her to dance, a woman dressed as a French peasant girl caught his eye.

She wore a square-necked blouse cut so low that her breasts all but tumbled from the embroidered muslin. He found himself remembering Roxanne St. Luz, for never until this moment had he seen breasts to surpass hers.

He swaggered up to her, imitating a seaman's rolling walk. *"Mademoiselle,"* he said. "I have captured you and you're my prize. Shall we dance?"

She eyed him from behind her white velvet mask. He thought her eyes were green but he couldn't be certain. Her lips were painted, and she wore a black beauty mark on her cheek.

"Ah, *capitaine*, dare I trust myself to a wicked pirate?" Her voice mocked him.

"I fear you have no choice," he said.

"A woman always has a choice, even peasant maids. I

refuse to dance. You may take me onto the balcony while I decide whether or not I shall ever dance with you."

Excitement raced through Guy. Not mere desire but the thrill of the hunt. This was no quadroon to be bought by a display of wealth. Here was a woman who challenged him to conquer her.

192

Chapter 19

ON the way to the balcony, Guy, the pirate, and the beautiful peasant maiden found their path blocked by a Roman soldier, a centurion complete with shield and spear. Without a word he reached for Guy's companion who twisted smoothly away, flashed a mocking smile and slipped in among the crowd, eluding both men.

"Ah, that Fabrienne," the centurion said. "Always a tease." He plunged into the dancers after her.

Guy, seeing the angel he'd admired earlier on the arm of a harlequin, shrugged and went on to the balcony. He opened the glass door and stepped out. The night breeze carried a chill promise of the winter to come. He was the only masquerader to brave the November night.

The balcony, on the second floor of the Lafreniere Ile St. Louis townhouse, overlooked the Seine, and Guy could see the towers of the Conciergerie grim against the sky. Once a king's palace, the massive building was now the house of justice and had been the prison where Queen Marie Antoinette languished with other aristocrats until the guillotine ended their suffering. He grimaced.

He'd been in France during the revolution. Although he and the other Creole boys from Louisiana hadn't been threatened, some of the Frenchborn students at his school were taken away by armed *citoyens*. To their deaths? The abbe had sent the Creoles home to Louisiana as soon as he could get them aboard a ship, and Guy had never found out what had happened to those French classmates.

His *melancolie,* momentarily banished by the glittering masquerade, returned. The lights of Paris glimmered from the right bank of the Seine, and the lights of the buildings on Ile St. Louis reflected in the dark water of the river, but nothing lightened his spirit.

True, Louis XVIII once again ruled France jointly with the Chamber of Deputies, but the fate of Napoleon, exiled to St. Helena, made a man wish the great emperor had died a hero's death in battle.

"I thought pirates performed daring deeds," a woman's voice behind him said. "I thought they were ruthless and demanding."

Guy whirled. The woman in peasant costume, Fabrienne, stood on the balcony.

He wanted her. Guy saw the intricate dance of courtship stretch out before him—the pretended withdrawals, the coy advances, all the artifices of coquettery—and realized he didn't care to tread those measures.

Reaching for Fabrienne, he swept her into a close embrace and kissed her with all the pent-up passion and loneliness he'd kept stored these last four months.

She met his passion, but drew back before he was ready to let her go.

"Are you married?" he demanded before she could speak.

She blinked at him. "I'm a widow," she said.

"Then you're free to marry me."

Fabrienne's amazement dissolved into laughter. "*Monsieur Boucanior,* I don't even know your name."

"It doesn't matter. I've chosen you. Will you marry me?"

"Your speech is so strange—are you perhaps the *Americain* guest?"

194

"I'm a Creole," he said impatiently. "Tanguy La Branche from New Orleans. Now you know my name, but you still haven't answered my question."

"Ah, you chose the proper costume after all. You're indeed impetuous. How can I give you an answer so quick—*pouf!*" She tilted her head and looked at him. "Cannot we see one another a few times before you force me to make a choice?" She smiled and he saw a dimple in her cheek below the mask. "I might not want to marry a man with one eye. Or do you, perchance, have two?"

Guy lifted the eyepatch. "I assure you everything is intact," he said.

He put out a hand to her mask and her smile faded as she stepped beyond his reach.

"No. You've already accepted me, mask and all. Or have you?"

"Yes."

Fabrienne sighed and turned as if to go inside. He caught her hand.

"Your last name so I may call on you tomorrow."

"*Madame* Cordeaux," she said. "I'm visiting friends, the Vinaches." She gazed at him, the darkness and her mask making it impossible for him to guess her thoughts. "Be careful, *Americain,* for I may agree to your impulsive offer and you may regret making it." She took her hand from his, stepped to the door and slipped inside.

The next day, Guy found the Vinache townhouse. He caught his breath when Fabrienne Cordeaux came into the parlor where he awaited her. He'd thought it was possible that last night's mask concealed some slight blemish, but her beautiful face was unmarked. Her grey-green eyes gazed assessingly at him.

"Will you go with me to Notre Dame Cathedral?" he asked. "I recall the cathedral from my days here as a schoolboy, and I wanted to see if the rose windows in the ceilings are as magnificent as I remember."

"They awe me," Fabrienne told him. "I'd enjoy visiting

Notre Dame with you, and seeing the rose windows again."

When they stood in the cathedral beneath the intricately cut stained-glass—arranged like the petals of a flower, with the center showing the Virgin holding her Holy Babe—Guy agreed with Fabrienne's word.

Awe, mixed with pride that humans could fashion such a tribute to God. Fiery light blazed down from the flower windows as though God showered the nave with His special holiness.

But the rose windows also reminded him of Madelaine, and, as they left the church, he couldn't stop thinking of her, waiting at the convent to deliver her child. What would become of his poor sister?

"Have you come to Paris for a visit or do you intend to remain?" Fabrienne asked.

"I came to France to put my sons in school."

"Ah, then you're a widower."

He nodded. After they were married he'd explain New Orleans customs so she'd understand about Denis and Anton. As for Madelaine—she'd be explained later, too. He needed every moment to woo this fascinating woman.

Guy found Fabrienne as desirable in more conventional clothes as she'd been in peasant costume. He thought her eyes were almost the color of a Louisiana cypress.

"What is New Orleans like? Is it much like Paris?" she asked.

"Nothing is like Paris. But I prefer New Orleans, my heart is there. I wouldn't want to live anywhere else—not even in *la belle* France." He smiled at her. "You'd be surprised how sophisticated we Louisianians are, though we seem backwoods *cousines* to a *Parisienne*."

"I, myself, am from the country," she said.

In the days that followed, he saw Fabrienne as often as she'd consent to be with him. He told her of New Orleans, of the ruined La Belle, and of the mansion he was building on Lake Ponchartrain.

"All will be new, you'll help me choose the furnishings,

it will be your home in truth," he said as they stood in the parlor of the Venache townhouse.

She raised up on her toes and kissed him, a quick delicate brush of her lips as soft as the touch of a moth's wing.

"You tempt me very much, *mon ami,*" she said. "But you don't ask me what my life has been."

"It makes little difference."

She shook her head. "One should know such things. Do you understand I'm very poor? You say you need money, but you are very wealthy compared to me. I'll bring no *dot,* no marriage portion, to you."

"How many times must I tell you that it makes no difference? I've chosen you, as you are, for my wife."

She glanced quickly about, then up at him through her lashes. "My friends are in the country," she said softly. "The servants will know, of course, one can keep nothing from them, but it doesn't matter."

He stared at her, not quite certain of what she meant. Only when she took his hand to lead him from the room toward the staircase did his pulses leap in delighted anticipation.

Fabrienne's lovemaking was unashamed without being bold. She guided him without seeming to, heightened his pleasure with her hands, with her mouth, satisfying him completely while making him eager for more. What a wonderful wife she'd make.

"You're a marvelous lover," she told him as they lay side by side on her bed afterwards.

He smiled lovingly at her. "Is that what you had to find out before you agreed to marry me?"

Instead of answering she took his hand and held it to her cheek.

"Is it yes?" he demanded. "Tell me, my beautiful, my love."

"First, tell me about your sons. How old are they?"

"I have a confession to make." He rose on one elbow,

easing his hand from hers. "Denis and Anton are what we in New Orleans call Creoles of color."

"I don't understand."

"Their mothers were quadroons. Although I'm a widower, I have no legitimate heirs. Even though both boys bear my name, they can't inherit my property."

"Your wife—were you married to . . . ?"

"My wife was Spanish. No Creole marries a quadroon."

"Then you—you'd want children. Sons."

"Sons, daughters, yes, as many as possible." He saw her face change as he spoke, tighten. Her eyes shifted from his.

"No," she said.

"What do you mean?" A chill foreboding touched his heart.

"I can't marry you. I can never give you children. Not ever."

"But that's incredible." He sat up. "You're young, strong, healthy . . ."

"I had a child by my first husband." She gazed at the ceiling as she spoke. "Something went wrong while the baby grew, and he was so badly deformed that neither the midwife nor the doctor she called could get the baby out. He—the doctor—realized the child was dead and so he . . ." Her voice broke but she swallowed and went on. "He cut the baby in pieces and pulled him out a piece at a time. In doing so he damaged the place inside me where another child might grow. I almost died. Perhaps I should have."

She turned her head and stared at Guy. "I appear strong and healthy but inside, where it doesn't show, I'm deformed. The doctor told me no baby would ever be able to grow within me again. My husband wasn't a young man and I fear the shock of all this helped to kill him."

Guy wanted to tell her it didn't matter, that he loved her, but the words stayed locked inside him. After a moment she turned her back to him. He got up, hating himself, dressed and left her bedroom, left the house. A late

November wind swept icy rain along the city streets but, unheeding, he walked the two miles back to Ile St. Louis.

The next day Guy thanked the Lafrenieres, inviting them to visit him in New Orleans, and left the city. He traveled to the *marquis* de Lafayette's estate, La Grange, some thirty miles northeast of Paris.

The *marquis* limped badly, Guy saw, and looked old, though he couldn't be quite sixty. He greeted Guy with enthusiasm.

"*Americain* visitors are always welcome at La Grange," Lafayette told him.

"I came to invite you to visit the country you helped create," Guy said. "We Creoles of New Orleans would be honored to have you as our guest."

"Journey to America?" The *marquis* sighed. "Ah, that would be a pleasure—but my pleasure must wait until France is herself again. The King, the Chambers—everyone is nervous these days. As long as Napoleon lives I fear there'll be endless schemes to free him from St. Helena.

"If I can—yes, I'll come, and I promise to visit Louisiana. New Orleans. But tell me, Guy, can you not stay at my chateau for a few days more? Your talk of the United States has stimulated me, made me feel young again."

"If only I could," Guy said with regret. "It's a great honor to have seen you, *marquis,* but I must be going."

He left the chateau and rode hard for Paris. It wasn't too late, why had he been such a fool? All his life he'd wanted a woman like Fabrienne, and he'd let her pitiful story dissuade him. Wasn't Madelaine about to bear a child? Her son would be the heir. He would arrange to adopt him, and could claim that the boy was a French *cousine.*

He wanted Fabrienne, he needed her. With her at his side, the great plantation he was building on the lake would take on meaning, truly become a home. Their home, his and Fabrienne's.

When he arrived at the Venache townhouse he was taken aback to find her gone.

"But didn't Fabrienne tell you?" Auguste Venache asked. "She was visiting us to take time to decide whether she should agree to a marriage with a man who was a friend of her first husband's—one of the wine Fronchots, I believe. An excellent match for Fabrienne, though he's twice her age."

"Where is she now?"

"The wedding was yesterday, and she has left for the country with her husband."

"It won't be much longer, Madelaine," Sister Nativite said, "if you do as I tell you. Push down. Now—as hard as you can."

Madelaine gasped with effort, the pain so intense she thought she would surely die.

"Push," Sister said.

Madelaine screamed as the most violent pain of all took hold of her, lasting and lasting, making her feel she was being wrenched apart. She pushed, not because she was told to, but because she could do nothing else.

Suddenly the agony vanished. A strange, high wailing began.

"You have a lovely daughter," Sister said.

Minutes later, she handed Madelaine the baby, wrapped in a soft cloth. Madelaine examined her child with loving fascination. So tiny, so perfect. A girl, when she'd never thought to have anything but a son. A daughter. Her daughter. Hers and Philippe's.

I won't let anyone hurt her as I've been hurt, Madelaine vowed.

When Sister Nativite came to her the next day to inquire how the birth should be registered, Madelaine told her.

"Her name is Cecile Marie Roulleaux. Her father's name was Philippe Roulleaux and he is dead."

By the time Guy returned to the convent, Madelaine

was feeling strong enough to sit by the window to nurse her baby.

"A girl," he said, gazing down at the nursing Cecile. "She doesn't look like you. Or anyone."

"She's her own self," Madelaine said, smiling down at the baby.

"Mother Angelica tells me the child is entered in the parish register as Cecile Roulleaux. I wish you'd waited to ask me, Madelaine."

Madelaine turned toward him. Her eyes blazed. "Cecile is my business, my daughter. I'll do as I wish where she's concerned."

"Cecile stays in France when we sail." Guy spoke flatly.

"*No*, no, I won't leave her. Oh, Guy, you can't be so cruel."

"The Sisters will raise her and educate her as befits a young lady. When she's old enough for marriage I'll send for her and pass her off as a *cousine*."

Tears gathered in Madelaine's eyes and she hugged Cecile so tightly the baby squirmed and began to cry. Madelaine fussed over her until the child started sucking again.

"Listen to what I say, Madelaine. I want what's best for you *and* Cecile. Who in New Orleans would marry her if all were known? If you were to bring her home now? And you—you would be scorned. I won't have it!"

"She needs me. She's so little. And—she's all I have."

Guy got down on his knees beside Madelaine's chair. "I know you hate what I've done. I love you very much, dear sister, and I need you with me more than you can realize. You have me, if you can accept that."

"I—I don't want Cecile to be an outcast," Madelaine said.

"Of course you don't. Think—you aren't giving her up forever, just for a few years and you do this so that Cecile will benefit from your sacrifice."

"The Sisters are kind. But I'm her mother."

"What I say is best, Madelaine. Think about it."

"I could stay here with . . ."

"No. If you do, Cecile will know you're her mother. You'll be alone in France with a daughter who's not legitimate. All alone. My way is the only practical plan to assure Cecile's future. Think how easily she could be hurt when she discovers, as she's bound to if you say in France, that . . ."

"I won't have her hurt, I can't bear to have her hurt," Madelaine cried. "I'll do as you say, Guy, but I don't know how I'll stand it."

Aboard ship, Madelaine was as silent as she'd been during the crossing to France. She brooded in the cabin she shared with Estelle, coming onto the deck only when Guy insisted. She spent hours on her knees saying her rosary, and Guy was worried about her. He hadn't yet told her that, although Cecile was Roulleaux on the parish records, he'd instructed the nuns to call her Cecile La Branche. He would have told her, but her withdrawal from life frightened him, and he didn't want to upset her any more than she had already been.

"She'll come around," Estelle told Guy as she stood next to him at the rail the fifth day out. "She's grieving for her baby. I know how it is, I miss my Anton and Denis, too."

"But you don't talk of becoming a nun, of shutting yourself away from the world."

Estelle smiled. "Even if they'd have me, I'd make a poor nun."

His gaze fixed on her, saw the gleam in her eyes that he'd seen before, years ago, a glow that beckoned, lured a man into strange passions. His stab of lust startled him with its intensity. He felt like throwing her to the deck and taking her in full view of the sailors and other passengers.

As she watched him, her smile changed, grew mocking. "What makes you think I'm going to let you touch me?" she asked softly.

"What makes you think you're not going to?" he said.

He brought Estelle to his cabin and she came with no protest. But once the door was shut she began to fight, struggling against him as he tore off her clothes, biting and scratching him.

He ignored her writhing, aware she was working herself into an explosive passion that would find its fulfillment in his bed. He forced her down, rammed into her violently, hearing her gasp, feeling her clutch at him, feeling her uncontrollable response.

Whether she liked him or not, she wanted him desperately. This inflamed him, made him wild with desire for her.

"I'll come to you in the cottage when we're home, Estelle," he said into her ear. "You'll be mine and no one else's."

She gasped for breath, thrusting against him. "Perhaps," she moaned.

He laughed. "You can't deny what you feel for me."

"I hate it, hate it, hate it," she chanted, moving against him in rhythm to the words.

He could control his need no longer and thrust into her harder and faster until her shriek of completion drove him to release.

Chapter 20

ON his return to New Orleans in the spring of 1816, Guy threw himself into the building of Lac Belle, a new, more magnificent La Belle on the shores of the lake. He visited Estelle often in the cottage and each encounter was a repeat of those aboard ship—a violent, passionate struggle, with no love or tenderness between them.

Madelaine spent too much of her time at the cathedral or with the Ursuline Sisters, but she seemed content and Guy was too busy to fret over her.

Money. He needed more money. One April afternoon, reminiscing with Dominique You in Maspero's Exchange, an idea struck Guy.

"*Bigre,* those were the days," Dominique said. "With the *Carolina* hurling shells from the river and the general's men pounding the British into the ground at Chalmette. The great Napoleon couldn't have fought better than General Jackson. We haven't heard the last of Old Hickory."

"I agree," Guy said. "But Napoleon is another story, marooned on St. Helena."

Dominique smiled wisely. "Ah, but will Napoleon stay there? The stronghold doesn't exist that Dominique You can't storm. Have you not heard how Mayor Girod and others raise money for a schooner? I, Dominique You, will command this rescue ship and we will bring the great Napoleon to those who will honor him—to New Orleans!"

Guy had heard of the scheme, but he was thinking about what the Baratarian had said about buying a ship. He recalled Captain Shreve's little sidewheeler, churning up and down the river, carrying supplies and ammunition to Jackson's forces.

"What's happened to the *Enterprise?*" he asked. "The steamboat that helped us?"

"No one dares move against Captain Shreve since the defeat of the British. The *Americain* Livingstone says the captain can't sail on the river, but he does. Fulton's built another *New Orleans* since the first sank, but the *Enterprise* sails upstream quicker and farther."

"Why don't you captain a steamboat, Dominique?"

"*Sacre bleu,* that I should have to! No, I sail the ocean, not the muddy river, on a ship with sails, as is proper."

Soon after this, Captain Shreve steamed into New Orleans on a new sidewheeler, the *Washington.* It was an odd looking craft with such a low, flat bottom that the engines and boiler were on the first deck. The *Washington* sported an upper deck and a pilot house above that. Twin smokestacks thrust high into the air and she had no sails at all.

"She rides *on* the water, not *in* it like the *New Orleans* and the *Enterprise,*" Captain Shreve explained to Guy at the Hotel Marina, where Guy had invited him for coffee. "Those boats have deep hulls, mine is flat."

The captain sipped his *cafe noir,* his black coffee. "You Creoles know how to brew coffee," he said. "Strong enough to stain the cup."

"How long is the *Washington?*" Guy asked. "One hundred and thirty feet?"

"Close. One hundred and thirty-six. She's twenty-eight feet wide. Did I tell you that a boiler blew up below Marietta when I was sailing her down? Tossed me into the

Ohio." Shreve shook his head. "Killed some of the crew—scalded to death. I fixed the damn boiler and everything worked fine after that. She's just right for the Mississippi, like I knew she'd be when I built her."

"This one's your own boat, then, not French's?"

The captain nodded.

"If I can finance a fleet of steamboats, can you find men to captain them?" Guy asked Shreve.

The captain hesitated only a moment. "I think so. What's your proposition?"

"A partnership. You, myself and perhaps one other—someone with money to invest. You have the expertise, we contribute the money."

"Fulton's monopoly?"

"I talked to friends who are lawyers. They say the monopoly is illegal, and claim that the Supreme Court of the United States would back us up if we fought it. The legal business might take years, of course, but no one has challenged you since Jackson used the *Enterprise.* I'm betting they won't challenge the *Washington* or any other boats you build, either. Are you willing to take the risk?"

Shreve stared at Guy for a long moment. "Why not?" he said finally.

Guy approached Joubert Le Moyne, whose plantation, D'Argent, was on the right bank, upriver. He'd heard Joubert boast of getting all his sugar to market after the British were defeated, so he knew Joubert would have ready cash—and he knew the planter as a man who liked to risk all on the toss of the dice.

"Steamboats?" Joubert asked. "What do I know of such things?"

"You don't need to know how to build one or sail one," Guy assured him. "Captain Shreve is our expert. Surely you, as an intelligent observer, see the usefulness of a boat that can move almost as quickly upriver as it does down. Your money will return on these muddy waters tenfold."

Captain Shreve took Joubert and Guy aboard the *Wash-*

ington and steamed up the Mississippi to Le Moyne's plantation, where he brought the sidewheeler smartly to the tiny dock, blowing the whistle as they pulled up. Joubert, all smiles, prepared to disembark.

"Wait but a moment, Captain," he said, "while I bring my daughters to see your craft. Then we'll all go up to the house for refreshment."

Guy saw a pony trap coming down the drive from the manor house. "Joubert," he said, "I think your daughters anticipate you."

Guy remembered Yolande and Julienne as giggling small girls, and when they dismounted from the trap he was surprised to see they'd grown into lovely young ladies. He had trouble thinking of himself as thirty-one. Where had the time gone?

Yolande, the elder, was quietly attractive. He handed her aboard the steamboat, where she examined the engines with interest, asking intelligent questions. Julienne, pert and pretty, flirted with him and Captain Shreve, showing far more interest in *them* than in the boat.

"Papa has asked you to the house?" she asked, looking at Guy from under her lashes. At his nod she smiled demurely.

"Does that please you?" he asked.

She shrugged daintily. "Why would I ever go against papa's wishes?"

Several weeks later, the three-way partnership now a fact, Guy invited Joubert, his wife and daughters to an *intime* dinner at his townhouse. He thought Julienne charmingly saucy and thoroughly enjoyed the dinner. Madelaine, who'd been reserved but courteous during the evening, stopped by the library to say goodnight to him after the Le Moynes had left.

"The youngest daughter, Julienne—is she not fascinating?" he asked, smiling as he recalled her sidelong glances, her *moues* with pursed lips, lips begging to be kissed.

"I like Yolande," Madelaine said. "She's a bright girl."

He blinked. "I thought Julienne quite eclipsed her."

"A shallow little minx. She'll bring nothing but trouble to the man who marries her." Madelaine spoke more sharply than was her wont.

"Just because a girl likes to flirt . . ."

"Julienne has nothing in her head but the thought of attracting every male in sight. Perhaps she'll grow out of it, perhaps not."

Fabrienne came into his mind, though he'd disciplined himself not to think of her. Beside Fabrienne, Julienne paled to the silly girl Madelaine believed her to be. But Fabrienne was a lost memory, while Julienne lived only up the river. She was unmarried, and she attracted him.

"You know I must marry," he said. "I could certainly persuade Julienne to behave as a wife should."

Madelaine raised her eyebrows but made no further comment.

Andre Lafreniere called on Guy the next morning. Guy hadn't seen his old friend since his return from France. Andre's hair had thinned, and his scalp shone through, but he was as vigorous as ever.

"I hear you've convinced Joubert to go into the steamboat business," Andre said. "You, the man who harangued me about our duty to the Creoles, here you are, arranging to pile up riches while I fight the *Americains* in the Louisiana legislature because you shamed me into it."

"I meant to run for representative," Guy said.

"The opportunity is still there. Pierre Vivert isn't well, he won't be coming back next term. Your opponent will be Marc de la Harpe. No need to tell you who sponsors him."

Guy knew Nicolas had been elected when Andre was. Obviously Nicolas wanted his good friend, Marc, in the House of Representatives with him.

"There's been talk that the proceedings will be in English only, that French will be dropped from the legislature," Andre said. "You're a fighter, Tanguy, and you speak the *Americain* tongue better than any of us. We need you."

Guy held up his hand. "I'm convinced. I'll run."

The year passed in a blur of activity. Guy made speeches as a candidate for representative, he supervised the house going up at Lake Pontchartrain, he consulted with Joubert and Captain Shreve—and he courted Julienne Le Moyne.

Julienne exasperated him with her coy withdrawals whenever he seemed to be assured of her attentions. He was occasionally tempted to forget about her, but then she'd allow a snatched kiss, and the fever to possess her would compel him to continue the chase.

Every once in a while, guilt about his sister would overcome him, and he'd arrange to escort her to the theater or to visit friends—anything to try to get her to resume a social life. As far as he knew, Madelaine called only on Annette-Louise. Although Annette-Louise refused to set foot in Guy's home, much less see him, she was as fond of Madelaine as ever.

"We'll be going to the St. Philip Theatre this week," Guy told Madelaine. "They're offering *Une Folie* by Mehul."

"You might asked Julienne instead," Madelaine said.

"I prefer to take you. Don't argue."

The opera stimulated Madelaine. Her cheeks grew pink with excitement as she chattered to acquaintances at the intermission.

"What's this I hear about you helping the Ursuline Sisters?" Annette-Louise's mother, *Madame* Courchaine, stout and grey-haired, asked her.

"I don't do so much," Madelaine murmured.

"Not do much! Why, don't you go to their school every day? I fail to understand how you can bear it, actually teaching those youngsters."

"It's not so very different from when you taught your own children, *Madame*," Madelaine said.

"Well! I don't see how you can compare such things." *Madame* Courchaine, offended, turned her back and pushed her way through the crowd.

"What was she speaking of?" Guy asked. "I wasn't aware you went every day to some school."

"I teach the children of the free colored," Madelaine said. "I got the idea in France when Estelle asked me to teach her to read." She smiled at him. "It was so easy. But, of course, Estelle is very bright. She learned to write, as well, and do sums."

Guy was flabbergasted. Not only had he not known about Madelaine's teaching here in the city, but he'd had no idea that Estelle had learned to read. She'd never told him.

Why were women so damned secretive?

"I'm not sure I find it appropriate," he said at last.

"Pouf."

He frowned at her.

"I'll continue to teach the children no matter how you feel," Madelaine said calmly. "The nuns arranged the school for me. It's most proper and I enjoy what I do."

"But you ought to be . . ."

Her eyes narrowed. "Don't tell me what I ought to do, Tanguy La Branche. I *will* teach the children. The free colored must compete with *Americains* when they grow up, as well as with the Creoles. If I can help a little, well, that's what *le bon Dieu* intended for me. Not all of them have rich papas, like you, to send the boys to France for educations. And the girls—no one teaches them. Not every girl is pretty enough to be a *placee*." There was irony in her voice.

"Teaching quadroon children isn't a fitting occupation for a La Branche."

"I don't care." She crossed her arms and glared at him.

He could forbid her to continue, but what good would it do? Madelaine might defy him, in which case he'd either have to back down or try to force her to stop. And how, in the *nom de Dieu*? At least she wasn't inside the cathedral, praying all day.

It was such a waste, Guy thought, for Madelaine was a beautiful woman. Perhaps in time she'd tire of this teaching and begin to notice that men still glanced her way with admiration. A little encouragement and one of them might propose marriage. No one knew of little Cecile in the French convent, and so Madelaine had every chance to make a respectable marriage. If only she'd take an interest in a man.

As the election neared, Nicolas Roulleaux began campaigning actively for his friend, Marc. Andre supported Guy just as fervently. Wagers were laid daily in the coffee houses with the odds favoring one, then the other.

Guy, Joubert, and Captain Shreve received an official notice that they were violating the law with their steamboats, but no action followed, though Shreve reported mysterious fires at the boatyard near Baton Rouge where their new sidewheeler was being built.

"Think," he said, "two years ago there were only six steamboats on the entire river, counting the Fulton-Livingston boats and French's. Soon we'll have six boats of our own."

"If someone doesn't burn them before they're built," Joubert pointed out.

"I've set guards," Shreve said. "We won't have any more trouble. The guards I've hired are keelboaters, and not easy to get around."

The *Americains* had prohibited public masked balls in New Orleans in 1805, worrying about Spanish intrigues, but the public dances were still held and Guy fell into the habit of going regularly, bringing Julienne when she'd agree to go with him. Madelaine refused to attend, despite his urging.

Just before the election, Guy went alone to a dance, arriving rather late from a session with the dice in Tremoulet's. One of the first people he saw in the ballroom was *Madame* Le Moyne and he immediately looked about for Julienne. He couldn't find her, but Yolande was sitting beside her mother. Guy climbed the stairs and asked her to dance.

As they took their positions for the quadrille, Guy asked after Julienne.

"I don't know where she is," Yolande said. She was attractive enough, he supposed, if one hadn't seen Julienne.

"But is she here? At the dance?"

"I haven't seen her," Yolande said evasively.

The music began and he swung her through the figures of the quadrille automatically, his mind on her sister. Could Yolande be afraid to admit Julienne was with another man? He thought her a timid rabbit of a girl, despite her intelligence.

Julienne had made him no promises, but still his muscles tensed in anger as he thought of her with someone else. Who could the man be? One of the young sons of the upriver planters, boys that Julienne had grown up with?

He'd stay calm if this were the case. He wouldn't offer a challenge, for the young blades would have no chance against him. After a round of dances, he escorted Yolande to her mother, who sat talking to another matron.

". . . will be the death of me," *Madame* Le Moyne was saying as they came up. She didn't see them immediately.

"How two girls can be so different," *Madame* Le Moyne went on, "only *le bon Dieu* knows. I warned Julienne. I said, 'isn't it enough you have a *tres* eligible man courting you?' But, no, she must smile at Nicolas Roulleaux, too, and you know what trouble . . ."

"*Maman*, I'm back," Yolande said loudly.

Guy now clearly understood why she wouldn't tell him what her sister was doing. He bowed and left the Le Moynes. Scanning the dance floor, he found Julienne was nowhere to be seen. The private rooms near the rear of the hall? He strode to the back. All four doors were closed. He took up a position where he could watch. He waited there, his anger building.

Wasn't it enough that Nicolas had taken Roxanne from

under his very nose? Aimee. Senalda. Roxanne. Julienne. With each woman, Nicolas crossed his path like an evil shadow. Was he truly interested in Julienne, or did he mean to provoke Guy into a challenge?

"I didn't see you come in." Joubert Le Moyne was at his shoulder, smiling. An uneasy smile. "Won't you join me for a drink?"

Guy glanced at the doors, then back at Joubert. He noticed the glances cast his way and realized many knew why he stood waiting. They'd leave him no choice but to challenge Nicolas. But wasn't that why he stood here?

What would happen to Madelaine if he duelled with Philippe's brother? She'd begun to trust him again, letting him take her to the opera, playing backgammon with him in the evenings. Yet he couldn't compromise his manhood because of Madelaine.

He'd stand here until a door opened and Julienne came out with Nicolas. What was she doing in there with him? How dare he take her into a private room? What was her mother thinking of to let her go with him?

With an effort, Guy got hold of himself. Nothing much ever went on in those rooms, as he knew very well. A few kisses, an indiscreet caress—no girl of good family would allow more. If he left now he could pretend he didn't know the truth.

"We could walk over to Maspero's, perhaps," Joubert said, "you and I."

Guy wrenched his gaze away from the doors to look at Joubert, who was perspiring heavily. All at once Guy nodded at him, forcing himself to smile.

"Yes, I'd like a drink," he said. "Why don't we go?" He turned and walked deliberately away, conscious of the eyes following him.

Not yet, Nicolas, he said to himself. But I won't forget.

Guy drank more than usual, Joubert keeping pace with him so that when they left the coffee house, Joubert staggered, nearly falling. He shook off Guy's helping hand with immense dignity.

"Don't need assistance," he said, his voice slurred. "You go your way, I'll go mine."

Guy watched him walk along the *banquette* until he was satisfied that Joubert would find his way back to the dance without mishap. He headed for his townhouse, feeling the brandy he'd drunk make his own legs wobbly and maze his thoughts until they were as shapeless as cotton.

Get home. Go to Bed. Keep thinking that. Home. Bed. No use to bring Julienne to mind, she's with Nicolas. He hesitated, stopping. Bastard Nicolas. Challenge him. *Duel.* No. Go home.

Guy began walking again. Strangers passed. Acquaintances greeted him. He nodded. Carriages clopped past. Drays. Carts.

On the river a steamboat whistled. He smiled. Build hundreds of boats. Joubert was his friend. Henry Shreve was his friend. Partners. Two Creoles, one *Americain*. The right proportion. Keep control.

As he left the commercial district fewer people passed, then none. An occasional man on horseback trotted by. The fresh breeze hinted of frost.

Hooves clattered from behind him, a horse being ridden fast. Someone in a hurry. The horseman drew even with Guy, slowed. He turned his head too quickly and lost his precarious balance. Staggered. Heard a sharp crack. Something hit his left arm. He grabbed at the arm with his right hand and fell to one knee. The horseman spurred his mount and galloped away.

"Wore a mask," Guy said aloud.

He got to his feet and walked on. He let himself through the gate into the courtyard. Crossed it. Climbed the steps. Reached for the door. The lantern, gleaming yellow from its hook above the door, showed dried blood on his hand. Guy stared at it, uncomprehendingly. He let himself inside.

His left arm hurt like the devil when he tried to shrug off his coat. He touched his arm, saw fresh blood on his hand. The horseman. The mask. The crack.

214

A pistol?

Guy sank down in the nearest chair. *Dieu*, he'd been shot at.

Someone had tried to kill him!

Chapter 21

GUY's wound healed slowly, even though it wasn't a serious injury.

"I can't think why you persist in believing Nicolas Roulleaux shot at you," Madelaine said just before Christmas as they sat over coffee.

Guy shrugged. "He could have been the one."

"Over Julienne Le Moyne? He'd have challenged you, not shot from ambush. And thank *le bon Dieu* he didn't challenge you. For if you face Nicolas on the field, I'll leave your roof, Guy. Don't mistake my words, for I'm serious. I no longer worry over you duelling. Everyone knows you're the most skillful swordsman in the city. But you've killed one Roulleaux and I won't stand by and see you kill the other."

Guy spread his hands. "In one breath you say I can best any swordsman in the city, in the next you say Nicolas couldn't have been my cowardly assailant. What if he fears to face me?"

She shook her head. "I don't believe it."

"I won the election. He may have realized Marc would lose and decided to . . ."

"Ridiculous! What of those fires Captain Shreve mentioned at the Baton Rouge boatyard? Have you no other enemy but Nicolas Roulleaux?"

"I admit it's possible the Fulton monopoly might have hired a man to rid them of me. But why not shoot Captain Shreve and Joubert Le Moyne as well?"

"You haven't mentioned your *placee* at all. Estelle is much admired among the free blacks. What if. . . ?"

"Enough!" Guy exclaimed. "I won't discuss Estelle with you." Underneath his annoyance, a persistent tendril of doubt thrust. Could the masked assailant have actually been Estelle, dressed as a man? Sometimes he felt her hatred for him was greater than anyone else's.

"Very well, have it your way—though it's foolish to pretend I don't know she exists. Whoever the man was, I've said many novenas in gratitude that your life was spared." Madelaine held out her hand to Guy and he reached across the table to touch her fingers.

"Promise me you won't challenge Nicolas over the Le Moyne girl," she went on. "Julienne isn't worth anyone's life."

Guy scowled. "How can I make such a promise?"

"Will you at least try to keep your temper? Let Julienne choose." Madelaine shook her head. "That is, if she intends to. It strikes me that she enjoys playing one man against the other far more than she enjoys the idea of marriage."

"I'll keep my temper. Though you're wrong about Julienne. She's young, she'll change."

Madelaine's raised eyebrows told him she had her doubts, but he knew his sister would do all she could to help Julienne become a proper wife once he married the little minx.

"We'll be able to move into Lac Belle by February," he said to take Madelaine's mind off Julienne and Nicolas.

Guy roused from a doze. Beside him Estelle slept, arms and legs outflung. He eased one of her arms from his chest and rose to his feet. Despite the nap he felt exhausted, drained, as he always did after bedding Estelle.

After he wed Julienne he'd have no need for these savage encounters. He began to dress.

"People say you're going to marry," Estelle said.

He turned to look at her. She lay in the same position, her dark eyes fixed on him.

"I plan to."

"The younger of *Monsieur* Le Moyne's daughters."

"Yes."

"She's not going to marry you." There was no threat in Estelle's voice, she spoke as if stating a fact. Nevertheless, a *frisson* crept along Guy's spine.

"That's nonsense," he said.

"I danced. I asked *Zombi*. He told me, spoke in my head."

"I thought I told you to stay away from voodoo."

"You told me. I do what I must."

"Don't go near Julienne."

Estelle smiled slightly. "Why would I do that? You think I need you?"

"I know you do."

"Not forever. But you listen to what I say. You won't marry that girl."

The steamboats brought in money so rapidly that even with the expense of building additional boats, Guy's share was more than he needed to finish the manor house. It had been a favorable day when he spoke to Captain Shreve.

What if he built a place especially for Julienne? Not Lac Belle. Though she'd be mistress there when they married, Lac Belle was for Madelaine as well, for La Branche children to come, not just for Julienne.

Wouldn't she like a picnic house of her very own? Not a simple wooden structure such as the old summer house on the lake had been. He'd had that torn down.

He thought of the glittering splendor of Versailles. He could plan a palace in miniature for Julienne, a dreamland along the lake, complete with canals and tiny boats, sparkling fountains and flower gardens. A castle with furnishings fit for a princess. What could Nicolas offer to compete with that?

He began to prepare for Julienne's dreamland the next day, setting the slaves to dig the canals.

By the time he and Madelaine moved into the manor house, the little palace was beginning to take form. To his surprise, Madelaine approved.

"It's a lovely toy," she said. "Julienne will surely enjoy it and later your children will have a charming playhouse." She fell silent, staring pensively at the plantings between the canals.

Guy knew she was thinking of Cecile. A pang gripped his heart. How cruel it was to deprive a mother of her child. But what else could he have done?

When his fantasy was almost completed, he brought Julienne to Lac Belle.

"How beautiful," she said over and over as she walked throughout the manor house, admiring the crystal teardrops of the chandeliers, the carved plaster embellishing the ceilings, the white marble fireplaces, the graceful floating staircase, the brocade wallpaper from Paris.

When he handed her into the miniature carriage drawn by a pony, she clapped her hands in delight. He led the pony along a winding path of crushed oyster shells to her own domain, Belle Fantaisie, hidden from the manor house by tallow trees.

"This I had made for you alone," he told Julienne as he helped her from the carriage.

She looked around, her eyes wide.

There was an acre of intersecting canals with a scaled-down steamboat complete with a slave boy, whose feet on pedals furnished the power to turn the paddle wheels. Plantings of shrubs and flowers grew between the canals, and delicate drawbridges spanned the water. Songbirds in an aviary fluttered from branch to branch near the entrance to the nearly-completed palace.

"Mine?" Julienne breathed, incredulous.

"All yours. When they're through inside, you'll have three rooms downstairs and two upstairs, one with mirrors for walls."

"Oh, I can hardly wait to live in it! When will it be finished?"

"By July."

"That's a long time," Julienne pouted.

He put an arm about her. "By the time we finish all the preparations for the wedding, July will be here."

She drew back. "The wedding?"

"You know I want to marry you."

She shot him a sidelong glance. "Do I?"

He caught her to him, kissing her lips, and she allowed him a brief embrace before turning her face from his and pushing at his chest.

"Stop, that's enough."

He let her go.

She straightened her bonnet. "I haven't agreed to marry you."

"You can hardly live in your palace if you don't."

"You said it was mine!"

"But Julienne—it isn't proper for a young lady to accept a house from a man. I couldn't possibly . . ."

Julienne stamped her foot. "I hate you!" she cried. "You tell me this is all mine, and then you say that I must marry you or I can't have it."

He tried to take her hand, but she turned her back petulantly.

"Your papa would surely challenge me if I offered you Belle Fantaisie without offering marriage," he told her.

"Well, haven't you offered marriage? Why can't I have my palace without saying yes?"

"Julienne, it's not proper. Your papa . . ."

"Papa, always you say 'papa.' Don't you know I may do as I wish?" She tossed her head. "You may take me home. I don't wish to stay here any longer."

The next month Joubert Le Moyne held a party to celebrate Julienne's betrothal to Nicolas Roulleaux.

"She did it to spite you," Madelaine told him. "Watch, you'll see the engagement will be broken. Julienne isn't ready to marry any man."

"It was my own clumsiness," Guy said.

"*Pouf!* Julienne's a willful, spoiled young woman who wants her own way in all things. If you persist in wishing to marry a Le Moyne, Yolande is by far the better choice."

"Yolande bores me."

Joubert's invitation to Guy to attend the betrothal party included Madelaine. Guy understood that courtesy demanded he be asked since he was Joubert's partner, but realized that no one expected him to actually come to the dinner.

"I believe I'll attend this celebration," he told Madelaine.

"Why would you want to be at a dinner honoring Nicolas Roulleaux? I thought you avoided him whenever possible."

He shrugged. "Don't I have to be in the same room with him every day that I attend the legislature?"

"You'll cause trouble."

"No, certainly not. I wouldn't embarrass Joubert. He has no control over Julienne, I realize that."

"Guy, it's not a good idea."

"You don't have to come."

"If you intend to go, I shall certainly attend this party. Who'll keep an eye on you otherwise?"

D'Argent, the Le Moyne plantation, was brilliant with lights as the steamboat *Creole Folie* brought the guests upriver from New Orleans. Lanterns hung from ropes strung between high branches of the oaks that lined either side of the road from the river, and colored illuminations decorated trees about the house.

Inside, chandeliers blazed with hundreds of candles. There were flowers everywhere—reds and yellows and oranges, vivid colors that enhanced the dark beauty of the rosewood paneling. Guy escorted Madelaine into the double parlor. He thought she looked especially young and pretty tonight in a new Paris gown of deep rose, the high waist showing off her shapely breasts.

Odalie had coaxed Madelaine's hair into a new fashion, tiny curls about her face, the rest caught back with a star clasp of rose garnets. The style became her. She was more beautiful than any of the younger women, Guy thought—except, of course, for Julienne.

Guy tried to keep his eyes away from Julienne's glowing loveliness as she fluttered from one group to another, as fragile and dainty as a butterfly in her yellow and white dress. She touched the arm of a scowling young man, dancing away as he tried to catch her hand. Guy, watching, saw the man turn to glower at Nicolas, who glared back at him.

Guy smiled wryly. More than one disgruntled suitor in the party. Perhaps there'd be a challenge tonight, after all.

Servants carried trays of wines, liquors and lemonade. He took a glass of champagne for Madelaine, whom he found talking to Yolande.

". . . terribly upset," Yolande was saying. "I wish he hadn't come."

Guy handed Madelaine the glass. "Are you speaking of that sullen young man by the archway?" he asked Yolande.

She nodded. "He's Ignace Proulx—you know, the Proulxes have the next plantation to us. I do hope he doesn't make a scene and ruin Julienne's party. The Proulx family are very close friends, but Ignace is so—so uncontrollable."

Guy thought he saw a resemblance between Ignace and Antoine Proulx. Antoine, who had fought with Beale's Rifles, must be the young man's father, Guy decided.

"I'll watch Ignace," he offered.

Madelaine raised her eyebrows and he grinned. "That ought to keep *me* out of trouble," he whispered to her as he left.

As Guy mingled with the guests, he kept an eye on young Proulx. I don't want to challenge Nicolas over Julienne, he told himself. It would mean nothing, for she doesn't want me anyway. If I can keep Ignace from disrupting the festivities, that can be my wedding present to her.

When the fifty guests had been seated at the three long tables in the dining room, Joubert stood, raising a hand for silence. He pulled a long ribbon attached to a gilt cage suspended from the ceiling. A door opened in the cage and a white pigeon flew out, made a circle of the room and fluttered down to alight on the table directly in front of Julienne.

While the guests exclaimed, Julienne picked up the pigeon and took a rolled paper from a band on its leg. She unfolded the paper, scanned it, and blushed becomingly.

"Read it aloud," a girl called.

"Oh, I couldn't," she protested.

"Is it a love note from the bridegroom?" Ignace Proulx asked harshly.

She shook her head, handing the paper to Nicolas. "You read it aloud for me," she said.

Nicolas stood up. After a quelling glare at Ignace he began.

> *Oh, fair sister of mine*
> *Beautiful belle of Louisiana*
> *May your days be sunshine*
> *May your nights be moonlit*
> *Be happy forever*
> *Oh, sister, oh, lovely Julienne.*

"It's signed *Yolande*," Nicolas added.

Everyone clapped, craning their necks to look at

Yolande, who sat smiling at her sister. Julienne, Guy thought, looked almost petulant, as though she resented Yolande's brief moment of glory.

As Nicolas sat down, Joubert rose again. "It was all my elder daughter's idea—the bird, the poem. My wife and I are proud of both our girls, and we're thrilled and happy to announce Julienne's betrothal to Nicolas Roulleaux." He spread his hands. "I welcome you to D'Argent to join us in celebrating the happy occasion."

Sitting on the same side of the table as Ignace Proulx, though separated by four chairs, Guy watched the young man carefully. Ignace was on his seventh glass of champagne by Guy's count. With luck he'd drink himself under the table.

A parade of servants came in with tureens of soup—bouillabaisse made with redfish, red snapper, crabs and shrimp, and also a crayfish bisque. The soup was followed by *file* and okra gumbo made with both seafood and chicken, oysters on the half-shell, frog legs fried golden-brown, and three kinds of jambalaya. There were cuts of ham and roast beef on silver platters, baked squabs, peas and beans, plus assorted fruits in syrups, *pain patate*, sweet potato cakes, *calas tout chaud*, hot rice cakes fried and sprinkled with sugar, *batons amondes*, almond sticks, and pecan candies.

Ignace, who sat directly across from Nicolas, ate little, scarcely speaking to those on either side of him. Guy, on the other hand, found he had a good appetite for the tasty dishes, but he kept part of his attention on the brooding Ignace throughout the meal.

As the servants cleared the table, Ignace began fumbling with something under cover of the tablecloth, his hands out of sight. Guy tensed.

An immensely fat black woman wearing a blue *tignon* entered the dining room bearing a silver salver with two tiny stemmed glasses filled with layers of different colored liqueurs. She offered one glass to Julienne and the other to

Nicolas. They touched glasses, then drank. Everyone cheered.

Other servants brought in trays of liqueurs for everyone. Guy, watching Ignace, eased his chair back from the table, stood, then, as he saw the glint of metal, lunged at Ignace, catching his arm as the young man steadied a pistol on the table, its muzzle pointed at Nicolas.

A flash of flame, an explosive crack, a clang as the bullet struck the gilt cage suspended from the ceiling, the shatter of glass when the bullet ricocheted to smash a wall mirror.

Ignace struggled, cursing, in Guy's grasp. The pistol, muzzle smoking, lay on the table amid spilled creme de menthe. Men rushed at them, as many grabbing at Guy as at Ignace, for they weren't certain what had happened. Women screamed.

Finally, with Ignace held firmly by two men, Guy by two more, Nicolas shouted above the noise. "It was Ignace Proulx, not La Branche. Let Tanguy go."

Guy straightened his coat and shirt after he was turned loose, then strode to Ignace.

"You shot at me one night a few months back, didn't you?"

Ignace said nothing, giving him a look of hatred that momentarily silenced Guy. Why should this man hate him so? He grabbed Ignace's waistcoat in his fist.

"Only a coward shoots a man without challenging him. You've forfeited the right to ever fight a duel in Louisiana. Gentlemen don't duel with cowards. If it weren't for that you'd be a dead man, for I'd challenge you and kill you in a fair fight."

He released Ignace and turned from him in disgust. Behind him he heard Julienne's high, clear voice.

"Oh, Ignace, how could you do such a thing? You've ruined my party."

Guy glanced back.

Ignace stared across the table at Julienne. "I love you!"

he cried in a strangled voice. "These old men don't deserve you—you belong to *me!*"

Julienne brought her hands to her face, swayed, and, before Nicolas could catch her, fell face forward onto the table.

Chapter 22

BEFORE anyone else could reach Julienne, the fat Negress in the blue *tignon* had the girl clasped in her arms. Tears rolled down the black woman's face.

"My sweet child," she cried. "I don't be meaning to hurt you, no, never."

Madame Le Moyne, pale and trembling, leaned against her husband. Yolande was the one who, with Nicolas' help, managed to pry Julienne from the fat slave's arms.

"Stop that, Lulie," Yolande ordered. "Let *Monsieur* Roulleaux carry Julienne to her room."

With Lulie wailing after them, Nicolas bore Julienne from the dining room, Yolande leading the way. The guests milled about, shocked and upset and, in the confusion, Ignace Proulx broke loose from his captors and dashed from the house.

Guy started after him, then stopped. What use would it be to try to catch Ignace? Nothing would be done with the young man even if he did succeed in taking him prisoner.

The words Ignace had shouted at Julienne still rang in Guy's ears. The young pup thought of him and Nicolas as old men. Old! At thirty-three? Nicolas could be no more than thirty-four. The prime of a man's life!

He hurried back inside the house and sought Madelaine. "How is Julienne?" he asked. "Have you heard?"

"Perhaps it was no more than a faint," Madelaine said. "Such excitement for her—the engagement, the gun going off, the fighting. Oh, Guy, you were so brave. I can't tell you how proud I am of you. You saved their lives."

"Nicolas' at any rate."

"The boy must be very much in love with Julienne."

"She shouldn't have encouraged him," Guy said positively.

Madelaine said nothing.

After a moment Guy nodded. "All right. My eyes are opened at last. Yolande may not be the rabbit I thought she was. She took charge admirably. No doubt she'll make some man a much better wife than Julienne. Nevertheless, I don't wish to make Yolande *my* wife. Nor Julienne, for that matter." He glanced toward the stairs. "I hope Julienne isn't seriously ill. What was her old nurse carrying on about?"

"It made no sense. Something about not meaning to hurt her."

There was a stir among the guests and Guy saw Joubert on the stairs.

"I regret tonight's disaster," Joubert said. "Julienne is awake but she needs to rest. Please stay, if you wish. I had planned dancing to follow the meal."

No one felt like continuing the party. Madelaine and Guy were among the first to leave.

Joubert pressed Guy's hand. "I can't thank you enough for preventing a tragedy. Nicolas, who's waiting outside Julienne's door in case she wants to see him, asked me to express his gratitude. He is quite aware that you saved his life tonight."

"I told you *Mademoiselle* Le Moyne wouldn't be your wife," Estelle told Guy the next week. "Didn't I?"

Guy frowned. "I don't wish to discuss her."

"Shall I tell you something more? If *Monsieur* Roulleaux doesn't take care to sit by her side until she recovers, he won't marry her either."

Guy grasped her arm. "What do you mean?"

Estelle shrugged. "Everyone knows she's ill. Everyone knows what happened at the party. Why shouldn't I know?"

He resisted the urge to shake Estelle until her teeth rattled. Violence between them always led to bed, and he'd already taken her once.

"You haven't answered my question," he said.

"She may give her heart to another."

He shrugged, relieved. For a moment he'd thought Estelle had meant Julienne would die. Not that he believed in voodoo, but one couldn't deny that strange things sometimes occurred—that a *voodooienne* had some powers. And, after all, Estelle was Vedette's daughter.

In October, Guy walked with Andre from the legislative chambers, heading for Tremoulet's.

"Unless we can muster at least one more vote," Andre said, "all is lost. What's the matter with those *Americains*? Do we ask them to learn French, even though our language is certainly more specific as well as more melodious than English? Of course not! Why, then, do they try to force us to learn their barbarious language?"

"I agree, I agree," Guy told him. "Besides, think how we'd miss the fun of waiting for the translations if we all had to give speeches in English."

Andre grinned. "The look on Samuel Cannon's face today when he finally understood what I'd said about him was one I'll treasure for years."

Guy laughed. "There you were, waving your arms while you called him no better than a son of a dog, worse than the foulest pig that ever rooted in a gutter, and he looked you blandly in the eyes, not understanding one word. That is, until you finished and the interpreter translated what you said."

Andre's smile faded. "I didn't make the same mistake when he stood up and began raving at me in his uncouth tongue. I glared at him even before I understood what he said, for I know an angry man speaks abuse."

"I can't think how the interpreters keep a straight face," Guy said.

"One of an interpreter's qualifications must be having no sense of humor," Andre said. "You've managed to learn English, I've never understood how. Oh, I know the odd word, but as a language it makes little sense, unlike ours."

In the coffee house, they sat with another state representative, Leroy Carmelet from the German Coast.

"One more vote would save us," Leroy said. "Trouble is, we'll have to go after an *Americain* vote, for every Creole in the House is already with us."

"We never should have let them vote to eliminate Spanish," Andre said. "That was the camel's nose in the tent."

"Let me run down the list of *Americains* and see if either of you think any one of them is a possibility," Leroy said.

Guy listened. Some of the men he knew, others were almost strangers.

"Then there's Timothy O'Donnell from upriver," Leroy said, "and that's it."

"O'Donnell's been sick. He probably won't be in for the vote," Andre said. "He's been absent so much . . ."

"Is that the Timothy O'Donnell who was with Jackson at Chalmette?" Guy asked. "I haven't seen him in the House."

"I was just saying he'd been away more than he's been there," Andre said. "Yes, I believe Tim did fight in the war against the British."

"I know him. In fact, he might well do me a favor," Guy said.

Both the other men gazed at him.

"If you can persuade Tim to vote with the Creoles," Andre said, "I'll personally carry him into the House on my back if I have to."

Guy found that Timothy O'Donnell was living in Baton Rouge. He caught a ride up the Mississippi on the *Creole Folie*, captained by a man named Kendrick.

"I raced one of the Fulton boats coming downriver," the captain told Guy. "We were behind her, and as we pulled alongside they fired up her boilers. Even then we held even, then edged ahead. We've got a nice little boat here. I'll bet she can beat anything on the river."

As they steamed past D'Argent, Guy thought somewhat guiltily of Julienne. Strange how she'd gone out of his mind once he realized how shallow she was. Madelaine mentioned that she'd heard Julienne was still abed and, though her condition wasn't considered dangerous, she was refusing to see anyone but Lulie. Nicolas was said to be furious, and the wedding had been postponed indefinitely.

Was Estelle's prediction coming true? Guy shook his head at the notion. Nonsense.

Timothy O'Donnell sat in a rocking chair on the verandah of his riverside home. His skin had a yellowish tinge and he'd lost weight until he was little more than skin and bones. Guy saw that his arm had healed crooked.

"By God, 'tis all of four years since I've clapped eyes on ye, lad," he said to Guy.

"I'm in the House now. We're sorry not to see you there."

"I'll tell ye, 'tis this damned ague. Just when I get to thinking I'm over the thing, down I come with the chills again."

"Hasn't the quinine helped?"

"The what?"

"Doesn't your doctor prescribe quinine? In New Orleans I know that's how intermittent ague is treated."

"Damned if I know how he'd treat me. The bastard tried to clap leeches on me and I threw the man out of me house. Been doctoring meself since Mary passed on from the yellowjack."

Guy looked at him. "I came upriver to ask you a favor. I'll find quinine for you, but I'd certainly hate to cure you and find I'd collected another vote against the Creoles when the bill comes to the vote."

"What bill?"

"Samuel Cannon has a bill pending to suspend the French language in the General Assembly. The House votes on it next month. All speeches, bills, everything written or spoken would be in English instead of both languages."

"Seems a lot of fuss over a trifle."

"It's not a trifle to the Creoles!"

"Well, I don't owe Cannon any favors, and I'm certainly not afraid of the bastard. I owe you—damned if I don't. Tell ye what. Ye get some of that medicine for me; and, if it makes me well enough to go downriver, I'll come and vote against Cannon. Fair enough?"

Guy held out his hand. "Just tell me your doctor's name so I don't call on him by accident. I'll find out how much of the quinine you should take and bring it to you."

Tim held out his crooked right arm, offering Guy his hand. Guy could feel the scars as he shook it.

"Hell, lad, who'd ever think Guy La Branche would come sailing clear up to Baton Rouge to help old Tim again? We'll have a drink or two when ye get back and talk about the whipping we gave the damned British at Chalmette." His eyes twinkled. "I'll wager ye ain't heard what happened to General Pakenham."

"The general was killed in the battle," Guy said.

"I mean after that. Don't ye know his men gutted the corpse and preserved it in a keg of spirits? Some say brandy, some say 'twas rum. Whichever it was, they shipped the keg with the mortal remains of General Pakenham off to his dear wife in England." Tim winked at Guy. "He never got there, I hear."

"Why not?"

"There comes up a storm and the ship founders off the coast of the Carolinas. The keg, though, comes floating in to shore and a couple of men who look out for such things find the keg, tap it and drink off the spirits before they discovers what else is in the keg." Tim laughed until he choked, recovered, and added, "Oh, and wouldn't it have angered the dear general if he knew they drank his *esprit de corps?*"

Guy chuckled. "I'm thinking of those poor fellows who drank the brandy. Imagine how they felt!"

Guy found a doctor, got the quinine and brought it to Tim. "Here's the names of my steamboats," he said. "Tell the captain of any one of them I said you were to have the best accommodations."

"That's if I feel better, don't forget, Guy, me lad. But if I do, I'll not forget me promise. I'll send a message by your boats."

Guy brought the good news to Andre two weeks later when Captain Barton off the *Sugar Belle* brought him a letter from Baton Rouge.

"Tim O'Donnell's a new man. I haven't felt so good since Old Hickory led us into battle. I'll be there with bells on."

After the session the next day, Guy saw Nicolas Roulleaux coming his way. He expected Nicolas to nod quickly and go on as was his wont since Guy had been elected. Nicolas stopped in front of him.

"I've bad news," Nicolas said.

Guy said nothing, waiting.

"I've heard a rumor there's a group of *Kaintocks* hired by Cannon on their way upriver to prevent Timothy O'Donnell from coming to New Orleans for the vote. Somehow the word got out that he was our man."

"The *Kaintocks* are on their way?" Guy asked.

Nicolas nodded. "I heard it from one of the free blacks, a man who's done cabinet work for me. He says a friend of his overheard their plans."

"Can you trust the black?"

"I believe so. He's a man who served under Daquin at Chalmette and has never forgiven the *Americains* for the way they treated the free colored afterwards. Can you commandeer one of your steamboats?"

"The *Petite Joyau* is loading at the docks." Guy raised his fist. "I'll take her over. We'll catch them."

"They're an hour ahead."

"It doesn't matter. They must be on a Fulton boat because the *'Tite* is the only one of ours in New Orleans at the moment. We've beaten his steamboats before."

"I'd like to join you."

Guy hesitated for only an instant. "Come along," he said.

Captain Leonard of the *Petite Joyau* greeted Guy's plan with enthusiasm as they came aboard near sunset.

"Stop loading, boys," he called, "we're casting off."

The crew, like all those on Henry Shreve's boats, were former keelboat and barge men, brawny and aggressive, a match for any *Kaintock*. They all carried knives and both Guy and Nicolas brought pistols aboard.

"It's the *Yarmouth* we're going to catch," Captain Leonard told Guy. "She's got a good enough captain but she draws too much water. Going upriver, the *'Tite* can run circles around her. Wait and see."

Sparks and flame shot from the *'Tite*'s twin smoke stacks as the captain urged the boilermen to toss wood. The big wheels on either side of the flat-bottomed boat churned the brown river water into white foam.

Nicolas watched the shore for D'Argent, Guy noticed, and kept his eyes on the manor house until a turn in the river hid the plantation from view. Guy thought it best not to ask after Julienne's health. This was a precarious alliance between a La Branche and a Roulleaux that a feather might upset.

"If the boiler holds and we don't run into a sawyer or a boil, a chute or a snag, then we'll see the *Yarmouth*'s wake before dark," Captain Leonard said.

Seeing Nicolas' raised eyebrows, Guy translated. "The

captain means floating tree trunks, whirlpools, sand bars that come and go, and caved-in banks. The Mississippi changes daily as my partner, Shreve, has taught me."

Nicolas nodded in thanks. "I was beginning to believe I didn't know the language as well as I thought."

It was strange, Guy mused, that he and Nicolas spoke and understood English better than any other Creoles in the House. He shrugged. Nicolas was far from a friend but he'd never underestimated his abilities.

As dusk closed in, a crewman shouted, pointing ahead. The *Yarmouth* was in sight, churning around a bend perhaps a mile ahead. They came up on her quickly. Not until they were only some thirty yards away did anyone aboard the Fulton steamboat seem to realize they were being chased.

Flames flared from her smokestacks.

"He's going to try to outrun us," Captain Leonard said. "He can't, but he's going to make us prove it."

"A boil. Boil ahead," the pilot called. Bells jangled and the starboard wheel slowed, the boat turned in a loose curve.

"Wood's getting low," a boilerman shouted.

"Damn. Keep the wood flying all the same," the captain shouted back.

The *'Tite* lost a few yards skirting the whirlpool, now she bored straight ahead, making up the loss as the gap between the boats narrowed. Guy saw dark figures on the *Yarmouth*'s decks, outlined in the red glow from the stacks.

"Ahoy, the *Petite Joyau*," a voice called from the other vessel.

"I hear you," Captain Leonard replied.

"What's your hurry?"

"I am to beat you to Baton Rouge," the captain shouted.

"The hell you will!"

"You sure as hell ain't going to stop me!" As the captain spoke, the *'Tite*'s bow pulled even with the stern of the *Yarmouth*, passing to her larboard side.

Crack!

"That's a God-damned gun," Captain Leonard said.

Crack! Crack!

"Stop the starboard! Stop the larboard!" the captain ordered. "Set her back on both. The bastards are shooting at us."

Chapter 23

"We've got to pass that boat," Guy told Captain Leonard.

"They'll pick us off. Those were muskets, not pistols. I was willing to run a race but I ain't willing to get shot."

The *Yarmouth* pulled farther ahead, sparks shooting high into the darkness from her stacks. Suddenly a roaring explosion shattered the night, and the *Yarmouth* was hidden from sight in a dense cloud.

"She blew her boilers," Captain Leonard shouted. "Stand by to look for survivors."

As the steam cloud thinned, Guy saw the *Yarmouth* heading for the right bank, flames licking along the decks.

"He'll beach her if he can," Captain Leonard said.

The boat burned fiercely, lighting the faces of men struggling in the water.

"I'll try to pick up the poor bastards," the captain said, "but we have to steer clear of the fire."

The river current caught the men in the water and, though the crew from the *'Tite* threw lines, only one man was pulled aboard. The *'Tite* steamed past the burning *Yarmouth*, now aground. Men jumped from the flaming boat into the shallows and splashed ashore.

"They're lucky," the captain said as he looked down at

the scalded flesh of the man pulled aboard the *'Tite.* "He wasn't. Dead. Just as well he died right away. Lingering on to suffer for days is a hell of a way to die."

Tim O'Donnell grew increasingly angry as Guy told him of the attempted abduction.

"Jesus, Mary and Joseph!" he said, pounding his fist on the table. "Cannon and his friends are mad—the lot of them! Why shouldn't a man speak the language he was born with? Me own mother, God rest her soul, spoke Gaelic from the cradle. Her family lived in the hills of the old country. She never did get the hang of English."

O'Donnell not only voted with the Creoles, he swung five more votes their way with his tales of the race up the Mississippi and the bullies he claimed he had to fight off to get to New Orleans.

"Never say an Irishman won't fight," he'd finish. "Sure, and didn't the Spanish have to bring in an Irishman, Bloody O'Reilly, to do their dirty work in New Orleans away back when they took over? I don't say O'Reilly did right or wrong, but fight he surely did."

The temporary alliance between Guy and Nicolas didn't make them friends, but now Guy greeted him in the chambers of the House and even nodded if they happened to meet in the streets of the city. He was entirely unprepared to have Nicolas rush angrily toward him in Tremoulet's one December afternoon.

"You!" Nicolas shouted. "You planned it all. *Cachon!* I challenge you to the death."

Guy stepped back, completely confused. "I accept," he said automatically. What in the *nom de Dieu* had happened?

"Julienne might have died," Nicolas said. "No thanks to you she didn't. I hadn't thought even a La Branche could stoop so low as to use voodoo potions." He glared at Guy. "Second?" he snapped.

"Andre Lafreniere."

"Marc will contact him." Nicolas turned on his heel and strode off.

Guy had a terrible sense of *deja vu*. The duel with Philippe, the same seconds . . . But why was he being forced into this duel? Voodoo?

What was Nicolas talking about?

Voodoo. Estelle.

Guy pictured the fat slave, Lulie, crying over the unconscious Julienne as she cuddled her, saying she hadn't meant to hurt her. Was there a connection between Lulie and Estelle?

He flung himself out of the coffee house and pounded toward Estelle's cottage. He found her in the kitchen.

"What did you give Julienne Le Moyne?" he demanded, taking her by the shoulders. "What devilish brew?"

Estelle jerked away from him. "I told Lulie to put a love potion in her drink to make her marry Nicolas Roulleaux. Lulie was afraid her little darling would change her mind about the marriage."

"What you gave Lulie almost killed Julienne."

"No. It was merely a love potion."

"The girl's been ill for months. Ever since the night she drank your poison." He reached for her again but Estelle evaded him, slipping behind the table.

"I ought to whip you."

"You won't do that to me again. You won't do anything to me. I'm finished with you. Through. Take your cottage. I want nothing of yours."

He lunged at her, but Estelle grabbed a bread knife from the table and thrust at him with its sharp blade. He twisted away and, knowing her easily aroused fury, stepped far out of reach. Estelle was dangerous.

"I wanted that Le Moyne girl out of your way, married to Nicolas Roulleaux so you couldn't have her. I wish her no harm. I didn't give Lulie poison. The girl shouldn't have been sick so long." Estelle breathed hard, her eyes dark waters of hatred. "You're the one I want to suffer—like Aimee suffered."

Guy stared, shocked at her words of pure loathing. He was unable to speak. "The potion is strong. She had to go to bed, that's part of it. She's a foolish kind, no good for any man, but Nicolas Roulleaux also deserves punishment for what he did to Aimee. To marry Julienne Le Moyne is to be tied to trouble." Estelle shrugged. "Lulie says she won't see him, so I don't know what will happen, who the potion will force her to love. I don't care anymore."

"Estelle . . ."

"Don't you talk to me, I don't have to listen to you, don't have to have you touch me. You look like him, feel like him, like Francois, is why I let you. But no more. I'm *voodooienne* now, *maman* is sick, she makes me the queen. Don't need men except when I choose. Don't need you ever again. The Great *Zombi* is my only true lover."

There was nothing to be said. Guy backed away, unable to trust her not to knife him. When he reached the door to the main room, he turned and left the cottage with as much dignity as he could manage, his mind churning with foreboding.

At Lac Belle, he found Madelaine in her bedroom. Odalie was helping her pack.

"Odalie brought me the news of the duel," she said. "I don't want to hear any more."

Odalie looked from one to the other and scuttled from the room.

"I didn't tell Estelle to give Lulie the powder she put in Julienne's drink," Guy said. "I had no idea . . ."

"Be that as it may, you didn't decline to fight over it."

"What could I do? Be reasonable, Madelaine. Nicolas challenged me. Was I to brand myself a coward forever by refusing?"

"I told you I'd leave if you fought him. I'm doing just that. I don't wish to discuss it further."

"Well, of course you can stay in the townhouse but . . ."

"I want no part of your plantation, your townhouse. I want no part of you. I'm going to Annette-Louise. She's invited me to stay as long as I wish. Goodbye."

"Madelaine! Please listen to me."

"Why?" She turned to face him, hands on her hips. "You've never listened to me. Wasn't killing Philippe enough?"

"I didn't mean to kill him. I tried . . ."

"Don't talk to me!"

"What do you want of me? That I should let Nicolas kill me? Would that satisfy you?"

"You know what I want. I want no duel between the two of you. None ever again."

"If I back down I'll be the laughing-stock of New Orleans. No Creole would ever respect me again. How can you ask that of me?"

"You asked me to leave my baby daughter alone in another country. Did you think that was easy?"

"Madelaine . . ."

"Please leave me, Guy. I have nothing to say to you. I'm through with you, with everything you stand for. Goodbye." She turned from him and continued folding her clothes.

After dinner, alone with the servants, Guy sat in his library with a bottle of brandy. Damn all women, he thought. They cause most of the trouble on this earth. There was no way to satisfy any of them.

As the level of the brandy dropped he grew morose. He was friendless, deserted, accused of something he hadn't done, misunderstood on all sides.

Estelle blamed him for Aimee's death, had never forgiven him. Yet how could he have saved Aimee? Senalda was mad, had gone mad while he was away. How could he have predicted the actions of a mad woman?

He'd tried with Senalda, tried his best. Was a man expected to have eternal patience? She couldn't learn to accept a husband's love and he'd turned away from her because of it. How could it be his fault she lost her reason?

Then Annette-Louise. They might have had a good marriage, they were fond of one another, but, no, she had to reject him by siding with Madelaine over the duel with Philippe. *Dieu*, he'd never meant to kill Philippe.

Fabrienne was the one he regretted. She'd come the closest of any woman he'd ever met to understanding him. If only he hadn't reacted so quickly to her terrible revelation. Children. Yes, he wanted children—but was the desire for an heir worth losing Fabrienne?

Julienne had been a mistake from beginning to end, he knew that now. He'd been intrigued by her pretty face, captivated by her flirtatious manner. Madelaine had been right.

How empty the house would be without his sister. He couldn't remember how it had been without Madelaine. She'd been with him since he was four years old. He loved Madelaine.

He was alone. Andre and Rafe must have heard the news by now, yet neither of them had come to call, no one had. He'd been deserted by everyone. Perhaps Andre wouldn't even act as his second.

"I thought I did right," he said aloud. He buried his face in his hands and wept.

The next morning Andre came to Lac Belle.

"I've seen Marc," Andre said. "Have you decided on the weapon?"

Guy rubbed his forehead. *Dieu*, how his head ached. "Yes," he said. "Bowie knives."

Andre stared at him. "Have you lost your mind? Who fights with knives? Only *Kaintocks* and Indians."

"Bowie knives," Guy repeated.

"What kind of knife is that?"

"Fifteen-inch blade with a single cutting edge and a straight back that curves in to the point. You know Jim Bowie. He's been smuggling slaves with Jean Lafitte for the last couple of years. No doubt Dominique You can tell you where to get ahold of two Bowie knives."

"What will Nicolas say?"

"Neither Nicolas nor I are skilled with knives," Guy said. "Perhaps he'll think twice."

Andre shook his head. "He's determined to kill you."

"I won't make it easy."

Andre shrugged. "Do you wish to set the date?"

"Two days from now should leave us time to find the correct weapons. Tell Marc only a genuine Bowie knife will do. We'll meet under The Oaks at dawn."

On the morning of the duel, Guy turned to look at Lac Belle after he'd mounted the stallion he intended to ride to The Oaks. Would he ever return to his beautiful home again? How the white columns gleamed! If he was killed, there would be no one to carry on the La Branche name. It would die out before the seventh generation, exactly as the curse of that ancient Roulleaux had predicted.

He wouldn't die!

He'd ridden less than a mile when Andre met him, and they continued on together through the misty predawn.

"The duel is over nothing," Guy said, not explaining further.

"Most are," Andre said. "I asked Dr. Moudier to bring plenty of bandages." He shook his head. "Knives."

Nicolas and Marc were waiting.

The seconds discussed rules for knife fighting, but neither was certain of how to proceed. As Nicolas and Guy examined the wicked, curved blades of the knives they were handed, hooves clattered along the road.

Guy glanced in the direction of the sound. Not Madelaine again, he thought. I don't think I can bear to see her here.

"Ready?" Marc asked Andre.

As Andre said, "yes," a man shouted and a horse dashed toward them. Both Guy and Nicolas, who'd been facing one another, knives in hand, stepped back.

"Don't start! Wait!" Joubert Le Moyne cried as he flung himself off the horse. "She's run off, Julienne's run off with the Proulx boy. With Ignace Proulx." He took a deep breath. "I just found out she hasn't been ill all this time as we've thought."

243

Joubert looked from Guy to Nicolas. "I don't want you to duel over Julienne when she's been deceiving you as well as her mother and me. You know she'd have only old Lulie with her in her room. Apparently she's been feeding Lulie laudanum, then sneaking out to meet Ignace. For months! I can't think how it happened that no one discovered her deceit.

"I did let the boy in to see her once soon after the party. He came to me begging to apologize to Julienne and he looked so ill I hadn't the heart to refuse him the one visit." Joubert spread his hands. "They've been playmates since they were infants. Ignace's father and I are the best of friends. The man is heartsick."

"No one blames you," Nicolas said. "Or Antoine Proulx."

Guy thought Nicolas didn't seem as upset as one might think a man would be when he's lost his fiancee to another.

"I hope you won't challenge Ignace," Joubert said to Nicolas. "It's up to you, of course, but the boy truly went out of his head over Julienne. I should have suspected there was something between them that day I saw him kneel beside her bed. She looked into his eyes for a long, long time with none of her usual little ways. I thought it was because she was ill . . ."

Estelle would claim her love potion worked, Guy told himself.

"I have no intention of challenging Ignace Proulx," Nicolas said. "He forfeited all right to be challenged the night of the party."

Joubert again looked from Guy to Nicolas. "But now, you two. . . ?"

"We must fight," Nicolas said. He took a deep breath and, looking considerably more pained than he had over Julienne's defection, he said to Guy, "I'll amend my challenge to be satisfied with first blood. Is that satisfactory?"

"Completely satisfactory. Accepted," Guy told him.

Again they faced one another. Nicolas thrust out his knife and ran the point down the back of Guy's hand. Drops of blood beaded the scratch.

"First blood!" Marc's cry was echoed by Andre.

Nicolas threw down his knife. Guy did the same.

The beginning of January, 1820, was the coldest Guy could remember since the battle of Chalmette. In the middle of the month, a carriage pulled up at Lac Belle and Guy saw Ancin begin to unload boxes and bags under the direction of a bonneted woman.

Madelaine!

Guy ran out to the carriage, lifting her off her feet to hug her.

"I've missed you," he said.

"I've missed you, too. I know I said I've never come back, but . . ." She stopped, eyeing him nervously. "Have you heard about Annette-Louise?"

"What about her?"

She took a deep breath, let it out. "We'll go inside and I'll tell you."

Over coffee in the parlor, she chattered on about trivia until he grew impatient.

"I couldn't be happier to see you," he said. "I'm glad you're home. But what's all this about Annette-Louise?"

"I expect you to behave reasonably over this," Madelaine warned him. "No nonsense about challenges."

"*Bon Dieu*, tell me!"

"Annette-Louise and Nicolas Roulleaux are to be married."

His mouth dropped open. This was a match he'd never expected.

"I was surprised, too," Madelaine said. "She never said a word to me. Apparently he was seeing her while Julienne was ill. At first he went to see little Gabe, but then they fell in love."

245

"I can't believe it," Guy said.

"I know. She was terribly upset over the duel, but I thought it was because of me. She confessed later she'd have died if Nicolas had been killed."

"I can only hope she'll be happy with him."

"You don't still feel a little tenderness for her?"

Guy shook his head.

"So, you see, I had to come home. You couldn't expect me to stay in the home of a woman who was marrying a Roulleaux." She looked at him, only a trace of mockery in her smile, then got up and kissed him on the cheek. "Oh, Guy, I'm so happy you and Nicolas found a way to settle the duel without harm to either of you."

"No wonder he wasn't too upset by Joubert's news," Guy said.

But the next November, when Annette-Louise bore Nicolas' son, Guy found himself envious of Nicolas. Not for his wife, but for his son. His heir.

I must marry, he told himself.

The Creole girls were as pretty as ever. He was attracted first to one, then to another, but none kept his interest. How could he be expected to share his bed and his home with one of these light-headed creatures for the rest of his life?

"Why not court Yolande?" Madelaine asked.

"One entanglement with a daughter of Joubert Le Moyne was enough," Guy told her. "No, Yolande's a fine girl but there's no feeling between us. What I want in a wife is a woman who's lived long enough to know something of the ways of the world, who speaks with some intelligence. She must be pretty and desirable, but sensible, as well. We should feel a mutual attraction but also have a meeting of minds."

I know a woman who's all of those things, Guy told himself sadly. Who suited me as no one has before or since. I knew her and I could have had her.

"You've left out one thing," Madelaine said. "I'd have thought it was uppermost in your thoughts."

"What's that?"

"This wonderful paragon you describe must produce a La Branche heir."

He sighed. "No, I haven't forgotten."

Chapter 24

ON May 5, 1821, Napoleon died on St. Helena. Dominique You's group of Creoles, who were finally ready to sail to rescue him, wept when the word came. Indeed, all Creoles felt a sadness, for Napoleon had been much admired in New Orleans.

The next news from Europe to electrify the city came in 1824, when the *marquis* Marie-Joseph de Lafayette made his long-awaited visit to the United States, sailing from Le Havre on the American frigate *Cadmus* the day before Bastille Day, July thirteenth, and arriving in New York a month later. He journeyed to New Orleans the following year.

The *Natchez* brought Lafayette to the levee. The *marquis* was an old man who wasn't in the best of health, but he was a gallant and beloved hero all the same. An *arc de triomphe* was erected in the Place d'Armes and he was driven beneath it in a landau drawn by six matched greys, with a troop of cavalry as an honor guard.

One hundred Choctaw braves who'd camped outside the city for a month waiting to see "the great warrior, brother of the great white father, Washington," passed in review in full war-paint and feathers as Lafayette watched from the balcony of the Cabildo. The Indians were followed by the new militia company organized in honor of the visit, the Lafayette Guards.

"*Vive* Lafayette!" the crowds shouted. "*Viva la liberte!*"

The *marquis* stayed in rooms fitted for his living quarters in the Cabildo, but visited at the plantations, including Lac Belle.

"Why have you not been back to France?" he asked Guy. "Our visit there was so short, and I'd looked forward to your return."

"I plan to return someday, of course," Guy said.

"I think, sir, my brother will be sailing quite soon for *la belle* France," Madelaine put in.

Guy slanted a quick look her way.

"We have a *cousine* who longs to come to New Orleans," Madelaine went on. "As she's nearing marriageable age, we hope to help her meet an eligible Creole and settle here in Louisiana."

"Your country is what you proclaim it to be—the land of opportunity," the *marquis* said. "If I were a young man with no responsibilities to France, I would surely come to Louisiana and never leave." He looked at Guy. "When you arrive to escort your *cousine* to New Orleans, you must certainly visit me again."

"It would be an honor," Guy said.

After Lafayette left Lac Belle, Guy confronted Madelaine.

"What's all this about a *cousine*?"

"I've suggested more than once in the past year that you send for Cecile. She's almost ten and it's time she came to live with us." Madelaine shrugged. "You ignored me, so I spoke in front of the *marquis* to prod you. Don't forget what you promised me, Guy."

He sighed. "It was a promise, but I don't consider a girl of ten years to be marriageable. I'll sail when she has reached an appropriate age, no earlier."

"I want her with me, Guy." Tears glistened in Madelaine's eyes.

It was not until five years after Lafayette's visit that Guy finally set off for France. He left Madelaine behind at her request, surprised that she didn't want to go with him.

"My memories of France are unhappy," she said. "I've no wish to go there ever again. Bring Cecile home to me, that's all I ask."

Guy found the voyage crowded with his own memories of the past, particularly the bizarre and perverse attachment between himself and Estelle. Vedette was dead, Estelle had taken her mother's place as voodoo queen and Guy heard of her from time to time, for everyone in the city was aware of her power among the blacks, both slave and free. He hadn't seen her since the day in the cottage when she faced him with the knife.

And poor Madelaine. She'd been a tragic figure when he'd taken her to France to give birth to Cecile. She was now as beloved among the free blacks for her efforts to educate their children as Estelle was feared among them as a *voodooienne*. Still, he wished Madelaine had found a man she could love and marry. It was such a waste.

"You're a fine one to give such advice," she always told him when he brought it up. "I don't see *you* married."

Fabrienne was in France. He couldn't see her, of course, for her husband wouldn't appreciate a visit from a past lover. He thought of her often, the memory of the time they'd spent together living vividly in his mind. He could picture her grey-green eyes, relive the feel of her warm embrace. *Helas*, that it was only a memory now.

Once in France, Guy stopped first at the Paris academy where Anton was now being trained.

"He excels in fencing," the abbe at St. Ambrose had written Guy two years earlier, "and rides like he was born on a horse. As to being a scholar—it is not his *metier*."

With the abbe's help, Guy had arranged for Anton to transfer to a fencing academy.

The sight of Anton took Guy aback, for it might well have been a younger Francois standing before him; a slim, lithe lad, graceful, his warm brown skin glowing with health.

"I'm told you are the academy's star pupil," Guy said after they'd embraced.

"I try. It's what I like to do best in all the world." Anton spoke eagerly but with a trace of reserve.

"He'll one day be a fencing master," the director of the academy assured Guy.

Where was the little boy who'd sobbed when he'd left him at St. Ambrose? This nearly mature eighteen-year-old made Guy feel suddenly old.

Guy went next to see Denis. When Denis was ready to leave St. Ambrose, Georges Lafreniere had spoken to a banker friend and Denis now worked in one of the man's Paris banks.

"Yes, Papa, I'm quite satisfied," Denis told him as they sat over *apertifs* at a sidewalk cafe. "I'm certain to advance, as I've heard my work pleases those above me. I do sometimes think of returning to New Orleans."

"You're better off here," Guy said. "Things are viewed differently in Louisiana than France. There'd be no banking position for you in New Orleans."

"Yes, I've met Creoles—*gens de coleur libres*, free people of color, as you say—visiting Paris. They've told me of their problems. Have you read Hippolyte Castra's poem about the battle with the English? I believe that expresses something of what they feel."

"No, I don't know that poem."

"I can quote the last stanza from memory."

> *Arriving on the field of battle;*
> *I fought like a brave warrior*
> *Neither the bullets nor the shrapnel*
> *Could ever fill me with fear.*
> *I fought with great valor*
> *With the hope of serving my country,*
> *Not thinking that for recompense*
> *I would be an object of scorn.*

"It's true the free colored fought bravely," Guy said.

"Yet the great general, Jackson, didn't keep his promise to make them full citizens, *n'est ce pas?*"

"They're certainly not slaves!"

"But not, so I understand, considered equal to you or your friends, Papa."

Guy shrugged. "Things are as they are. I'm glad to see you doing so well here, Denis."

Denis was handsome. His well-groomed dark hair fell in ringlets, his cafe-au-lait skin was accented by a flashing white smile. He dressed elegantly and, Guy noticed with a stab of pride, wore the ruby ring.

"Have you a lady friend?" Guy asked.

Denis winked at his father. "Ah, Papa, you don't expect me to kiss and tell? Someday, I shall visit New Orleans and see the beautiful women I hear so much about. But I think I'll live in France, for I fear I wouldn't enjoy life in Louisiana."

Guy was glad and sorry at the same time, for he liked the man Denis had become.

Guy dined with Georges Lafreniere and his wife and several other guests at their home on the Ile St. Louis. During the soup course, Guy, who'd had the question on the tip of his tongue since entering the house, asked if they ever heard anything of Fabrienne Cordeaux.

"At least that was her name years ago. I understand she married a man named Fronchot."

"I've had no word of her since her marriage," Georges said. "We didn't know her well, you understand."

The next day Guy looked up the Venaches, Fabrienne's friends, but they'd sold their home and left Paris. No one seemed to know where they'd gone.

Guy was left with no more information than he'd come to France with: Fabrienne had married a man named Fronchot, who was somehow connected with wine. Perhaps Georges would be able to find out more about the man, but Guy was embarrassed to ask.

He was surprised himself at his persistence in trying to

track down Fabrienne. Hadn't he promised himself he wouldn't call on her? What was the point? Besides, her husband might be angry at the presumption.

After several futile attempts to discover the right Fronchot, Guy went to Denis.

"I met Fabrienne when I brought you and your brother to France," Guy told him. "I'd like to find her again."

"Fourteen years ago? She must have made quite an impression!"

"She's married," Guy said shortly. He gave Denis the scant facts he had.

"I'll do what I can," Denis assured him. "It may take a few days, maybe a week."

While Guy was waiting for whatever Denis could uncover, he left Paris for La Grange to visit the *marquis* de Lafayette, now ailing but still cordial and happy to see him.

"*Helas*, I shall never see your beautiful country again," the *marquis* said. "Tell me, is New Orleans still as merry and carefree?"

"It grows too fast," Guy said. "It's become a city of drays, sometimes there are block long tie-ups of traffic, and now there's talk of a railroad. I hardly recognize the city of my birth."

"That's the way of America—growth. I would that France had her vigor. I sometimes feel my country grows old along with me."

Back in Paris, Guy went immediately to Denis.

"I think I have the right Fronchot," Denis told him. "A man named Henri. He owns vineyards and a winery near Bordeaux."

I'll go there, Guy told himself. I'll say I was passing through and discovered by chance that her husband owned the winery.

In a small farming community near the winery, Henri Fronchot's chateau was pointed out to Guy. "You must pass *Monsieur* Jean Fronchot's holdings, they are first. Then *Monsieur* Henri's, they are next," Guy was told.

The chateau was impressively large, though not so vast as the one of grey stone he passed first, presumably Jean's. Fabrienne was surely content with her lot, for obviously Henri Fronchot could give her everything. Perhaps she had come to love him as well.

I should turn around and go back, Guy told himself. But he couldn't do it.

"*Monsieur* Fronchot is not at home," Guy was told by the manservant who opened the door.

"Perhaps *Madame* will see me," Guy said. "Tell her we met some years ago in Paris, if you please."

He was shown into a high-ceilinged room adjoining the foyer. Unable to relax enough to sit in one of the high-backed gilt chairs, he walked to a window to look out over a formal garden of topiary and statues.

What would she look like? She must be nearing forty.

"*Monsieur* La Branche?" a woman's voice asked.

Guy whirled about and found himself looking at a woman he'd never seen before. She was older than he, her grey hair immaculately arranged, her cheeks discreetly touched with rouge.

"You are—you're *Madame* Henri Fronchot?" he asked.

"*Oui.* But I fear I do not know you."

"I thought, that is, I've made a mistake. I had heard an old acquaintance of mine married Henri Fronchot. Obviously I heard wrong. A thousand pardons, *madame*, for inconveniencing you."

"I'm sorry you were misinformed," she said.

He bowed and was about to leave when he thought to ask one further question. "Is your husband related to the Jean Fronchot who lives near here?"

Her manner turned frosty. She drew herself up. "That name isn't mentioned in this house, *monsieur*."

Guy apologized and withdrew.

As his horse trotted back past the grey stone chateau, he checked him and, impulsively, turned in at the open gates. The Jean Fronchots could do no more than tell him to leave. He'd never be satisfied if he didn't stop. I won't ask for him, Guy decided, but for her.

"Madame does not receive strangers," the manservant told him.

"I'm not a stranger, though it's been years since we've seen one another. Please take her my name, as I've asked you to do." He stared the man in the eye, disliking his supercilious manner. No servant at Lac Belle would dare behave in such a way!

The man showed him, rather reluctantly, into a reception room that had no outside windows. Murals of nymphs bathing in woodland streams decorated the walls, and the ceiling was festooned with gilt cupids. He stood watching the door, determined not to be taken by surprise a second time.

He heard footsteps hurrying across the slate of the foyer, then *Madame* Jean Fronchot appeared in the doorway.

"Guy!" Fabrienne cried.

He strode toward her as she rushed forward, hands outstretched. He caught her hands in his, wishing he dared take her in his arms.

"I could hardly believe it when Jacques told me you were here," she said, smiling up at him.

"I thought perhaps you'd forgotten my name."

"Never!"

Fabrienne looked older, though her face was still beautiful. She'd kept the same delightful figure he recalled so well.

"I've thought of you more times than I care to tell you," he said.

She disengaged her hands. "Have you come to France often since those long ago days?"

She's affected by seeing me, he thought, noting her flushed face and quickened breathing. He wondered if she noticed his own excitement.

"This is my first visit since then."

"You've made this trip, perhaps, to bring sons to school again?"

"No."

Fabrienne raised her eyebrows. Her eyes were the green of the Atlantic at mid-ocean.

"You've had only daughters?" she asked.

"Fabrienne, I didn't marry."

She put her fingertips to her lips.

Though he hadn't meant to say it to her, to *Madame* Fronchot, so well married, Guy found himself pouring out what he felt.

"I was a fool to let you go. No one has suited me since, you've spoiled me for other women."

"But children? An heir?"

"I couldn't bring myself to marry for that alone."

"Oh, Guy . . ." Her eyes filled with tears.

He could stand it no longer and reached for her, taking her into his arms, holding her next to him. He put his lips to her hair, to her temple. She brought her hands up to his chest, pushing him away.

He stepped back. "I forgot myself," he said. "I beg your pardon."

"It's just that I can't yet believe you're actually here," she said. "That you've come to my house. Is this the reason you returned to France?"

"No. I came to bring a young *cousine* to live with my sister and me in New Orleans. But I knew I couldn't leave the country without seeing you again."

"I didn't realize you had a sister. You never mentioned her."

"Yes. Madelaine's a year or two older than you."

"I can't express how happy I am to see you," Fabrienne said. "Of course you'll stay for dinner, for the night."

"No."

The hurt in her face made him wince inwardly. He decided he must tell her the truth.

"I can't face meeting your husband. I still love you,

256

Fabrienne and I don't want to know anything about the man lucky enough to have you for a wife."

Her eyes grew round with surprise. "Did no one in the village tell you?"

"Tell me what? I've met only *Madame* Henri, for I thought she was you. She informed me *Monsieur* Jean's name was not to be said aloud in her house."

Fabrienne began to laugh. She laughed so hard she had to hold on to Guy to keep her balance. He put an arm about her.

"How upset she must have been," Fabrienne said when she could speak. "Her husband and mine fell out before I married Jean. A family feud—you know how unreasonable those are. I tried more than once to reconcile them but it was impossible." She leaned against his arm and smiled at him.

His grip tightened. "Fabrienne, I want very much to kiss you and never stop. I think I'd better make my . . ."

"What a wonderful idea," she said. "Why don't you kiss me?"

"But I—your husband. . . ?"

"I've been trying to tell you. Jean's been dead for two years. I'm a widow, as I was when we first met."

Fabrienne reached up and pulled his head down until his lips met hers, and Guy lost himself in the remembered wonder of her embrace.

Chapter 25

"MARDI Gras is coming, coming," little Ninette sang to a tune all her own. "Coming, coming, I can't wait for Mardi Gras."

"That's a nice song, Ninette, but it's not what the words on the page say," Madelaine told her.

Try as she might, Madelaine couldn't seem to teach Ninette to read. The quadroon girl was her first complete failure and she didn't know why. Certainly Ninette was bright enough, she'd learned ciphering as quickly as any of the children.

"*Mademoiselle* Madelaine, I like to sing better," Ninette told her. "Going to sing and dance at Mardi Gras. Sing about Layotte—you know about Layotte?" Ninette rose and began to pirouette.

Eh! pou' la belle Layotte	For the fair Layotte
Ma mourri 'nocent	I must crazy die
Oui 'nocent ma mourri . . .	Yes, I must crazy die . . .

Ninette raised her arms and twisted her body as though she heard drumbeats.

"I'll dance the Calinda," she chanted. "I'll dance the

bamboula, I'll dance voodoo, I'll dance and dance till the alligators crawl from the swamp, till Bras Coupe comes riding old alligator. Bras Coupe going to dance with me, going to dance . . ."

Madelaine stopped listening when the child mentioned Bras Coupe. He'd become a legend among the colored, still living in the swamp according to them, and appearing to dance voodoo sometimes.

But of course he was dead, had been dead for many years. I remember him, Madelaine thought. I remember how he danced with me, something strange and compelling in his eyes making me forget where I was, who I was. Something called to me and, though I feared that summons, at the same time I yearned to follow where it led. What lay between us was more than attraction between a man and a woman, though that was there, too. Something mysterious—perhaps evil—beckoned me, and I longed to go.

"*Boujoum, boujoum!*" Ninette sang, imitating the big African drums.

Madelaine took a deep breath. She was forty-two years old and still daydreamed of dancing voodoo, of her rendezvous with Philippe along the bayous. Living in the past. In a few months Guy would bring Cecile home to her, home from France, her fifteen-year-old daughter who wouldn't know her, who'd call her *cousine*, not *maman*. Perhaps seeing Cecile would make her feel as old as she was.

How was it possible to feel so young inside, forever eighteen?

"Will you dance in the Mardi Gras?" Ninette asked.

"I don't know," Madelaine said.

She'd never joined the street processions of costumed maskers, started four years ago by Creole youths just back from Paris. Mardi Gras had always been a Creole celebration, lasting from Twelfth Night to Mardi Gras, Shrove Tuesday, with balls, public and private. The *Americains* had frowned on masks in the early years of their takeover of Louisiana, and still issued edicts against them from time to time, but any true Creole loved to dress up and wear a mask.

Why not costume herself and parade unrecognized? Excitement flared in Madelaine.

"I have a costume with wings," Ninette said. "Pink and blue butterfly wings and my mask is pink and my slippers are blue and I'll maybe even fly." She leaped into the air, a graceful child as well as pretty. Did it matter she couldn't read? In a few years some Creole youth would undoubtedly ask her to be his *placee*.

Cecile would be no *placee*. Madelaine vowed her daughter would marry young, marry a man she loved.

What did Cecile look like? Madelaine had missed seeing her grow up, would never know her childish ways. A sense of loss dissipated her excitement. Philippe had been dead fifteen years and she'd been deprived of her child for almost as long.

Ninette's hands on her arm startled her.

"I wish you would wear a beautiful costume and be with me in the parade," Ninette said. "You look so sad, like you might cry. No one can be sad at Mardi Gras."

When she returned to Lac Belle, Madelaine couldn't dislodge the idea of a costume. At my age, she chided herself, I shouldn't be thinking of dancing in masked parades.

But why not? Who would know?

She stood up and examined herself in the pier glass. Her chin was still firm, she looked younger than she was, with scarcely any grey in her hair. As for her figure, her waist was slim, her breasts didn't sag. Masked, no one would guess she was Madelaine La Branche.

Shrove Tuesday, Fat Tuesday, Mardi Gras. A time to be merry, to celebrate, for penitence followed, days of sorrow.

Ninette's singing echoed in her mind. *"Dance, dance the Calinda! Boujoum, boujoum!"*

She'd stay in the townhouse, it would be easy to return

there after the celebrating. And she would wear—what? The fashion called for leg-of-mutton or puffed sleeves, waists that dipped to a vee and bell-shaped shirts held out with multiple petticoats.

If she went back to her own girlhood, though, she might dress as the Empress Josephine in the empire style with its high waist. A fur-trimmed short spencer, open in front to show decolletage, but long-sleeved against the coolness of the evening, could be made of velvet in a contrasting color to the gown. She had the sapphire and diamond tiara, Guy's gift from Paris, that she'd never worn. Now she would—to dance in the streets.

Madelaine smiled.

She woke early on Fat Tuesday, hearing a peddler calling in the streets.

> Oyster man! Oyster man!
> Get your fresh oysters from the oyster man
> Bring out your pitcher, bring out your can
> Get your nice fresh oysters from the oyster man.

Quite like the old days, staying in the townhouse, excited about Guy taking her to a public ball, she and Annette-Louise giggling over the glances of the young blades.

Annette-Louise was a plump matron now, Gabe was grown—old enough almost to be the father of his mother's younger children, Nicolas' son and daughter, Philippe and Lisette.

Gabe was a handsome and accomplished young man. She'd see that Cecile met him, no matter what Guy thought. After all, Gabe was a Davion, not a Roulleaux, even if his mother had married one.

Odalie was ailing, some days she couldn't rise from her bed, but she insisted she'd live long enough to meet Cecile, for of all the servants, only Odalie knew what had taken Madelaine to France.

"I be seeing that little girl, nobody putting me in no oven till I do see Cecile."

"You'll live long enough to see her married, Odalie," Madelaine assured the old woman. "And you're not going into an oven."

Odalie was referring to the double brick vaults in the cemeteries where poor people could rent an upper vault for the remains of their loved ones, then when the time ran out, the bones were removed and put into a common, lower vault and the upper again rented.

"You're going to have a vault all your own, like old Louis has," Madelaine went on. "Do you think I'd put you in an oven?"

"No, you be my own, I be raising you up, you don't do that to me."

Madelaine had taken Josefina with her to the town-house, since Odalie wasn't well enough to stand the short ride from the lake to the city. Josefina approved of Madelaine's notion to dance in the carnival parade, helping her dress and arranging the tiara in her hair with almost as much excitement as Madelaine felt.

When Madelaine fixed the blue velvet mask over her face, Josefina clapped her hands like a young girl.

"You don't look like anybody I knows," Josefina said. "All the gentlemen be wondering where the pretty woman come from."

"I don't intend to tell them," Madelaine said, buoyed by Josefina's enthusiasm. "I'll be like Cinderella and disappear at midnight."

But when she ventured out of the courtyard, she hesitated on the *banquette*, suddenly feeling very much alone and unprotected in the dusk. Should she have gone out into the parading earlier, while the sun still shone? That's when the children were out, she might have seen Ninette . . .

Madelaine almost laughed out loud at her fears. She wasn't dressed like the Empress Josephine to dance with the children, why not admit it? Maybe she was being foolish, but she wanted something to come of this escapade. Exactly what, she didn't allow herself to speculate over.

The flare of torchlight a street away lit the darkness, and singing and laughing drew her toward the revelry. As long as she was masked and costumed she'd at least take a look at the procession.

Madelaine found it impossible to be an observer. As she neared the undulating line of paraders hands reached out and pulled her into the procession.

"Who is she?" a man dressed as a court jester asked. "A queen, that's evident."

"The Queen of Beauty," another suggested, catching her about the waist and swinging her in an improvised dance in and out of the crowd.

"A toast to the Queen of Beauty," the first man said, lifting aloft a wine bottle.

Many of the revelers carried glasses, and now held them out to be filled. A man offered his full glass to Madelaine and, in the spirit of the celebration, she took it graciously and sipped before handing it back.

"Shouldn't beauty be for all?" a man dressed as an Indian asked. He swept Madelaine into his group, whirling her about before passing her on to the next man.

At first she laughed, intoxicated by the gaiety and singing, stimulated by the dancing and being able to act as she pleased without anybody knowing her name. Everyone was masked, and she didn't recognize a single person in the crowd. If a man's hand strayed to her breast it was easy to slip away to someone else. There was no need to wax indignant, for it was no insult to Madelaine La Branche, but a tribute to the Queen of Beauty.

But as the line, inching its way along, widened to fill the streets and spill up onto the *banquettes*, she found it harder to avoid unwelcome embraces, the press of so many bodies pinning her in place.

"A kiss, *Madame* Beauty," a bewhiskered, berobed king demanded, thrusting his bearded face at hers, his lips wet and soft.

She couldn't get away from him, all she could do was

shift her face so his mouth was against her cheek instead of her lips. He kissed her neck, slobbering against her bare flesh. She felt her stomach churn in disgust.

"Let me go!" she cried, her voice all but lost in the wild merriment.

He paid no attention, plunging his hand into the low bodice of her gown to fondle her bare breasts.

Madelaine screamed and he laughed. She struggled to free herself but he gripped her fast and the crowd hemmed her in.

Why had she ventured into this madhouse alone?

She beat at him with clenched fists, but he didn't seem to feel the blows as his breath came faster and he pressed her close to him, seeking her mouth again. She jerked her head away, catching sight of a cane held by the man next to her.

Desperately, Madelaine grabbed at the cane, jerking it away from its owner. She knew the cane for what it was because Guy had one—indeed, every Creole man had once carried such a cane.

A sword cane.

She felt for the release lever. A sword would be of no use in this mass of people except in one way. As she pressed the release lever, she raised the cane into the air, tip pointing at the ground, hearing the snick of the steel sliding out of the wood. She brought it straight down as hard as she could.

Madelaine felt the sharp sword point penetrate the leather of her tormentor's boot, into and through the flesh of the foot.

He shrieked with pain, releasing her to grab at the cane.

Madelaine dropped the cane and tunneled her way through the crowd, arriving disheveled and panting on the *banquette,* where the crush was less. She flattened herself against the front of a building, watching the torchlit scene with fear and apprehension.

Would he try to come after her?

Voices spoke to her, hands reached for her and she shrank away as much as she could, afraid each man who approached would be another like the one she'd stabbed in the foot.

"I want to go home," she whispered. "Please, I just want to go home."

"Your crown is falling," a voice said. She saw a Greek soldier. Automatically she reached up and settled the tiara more firmly in place.

"That's right," the man told her. "Come and dance now, empress."

"No," she said, "no!"

But his hands were insistent, pulling her relentlessly back into the mob of merry-makers. Up one street and down another they swept, laughing, shouting. Her head pounded. Her feet ached, and were bruised as men and women trampled on her fragile slippers. The Greek soldier had long since vanished, now other hands caught at her, and tried to swing her in dances made impossible by the crush of people.

She felt contaminated by so much handling, soiled as her gown was soiled by the dirt of the streets, and she made a concentrated effort to break through to the edge of the procession, angrily using her elbows on resisting backs.

Again she neared a *banquette*, stumbling up onto it. Next to her a woman tripped and fell face down onto the wood. Madelaine distinctly saw a man step on her.

"Wait, stop, someone's down!" she cried, but none paid heed.

She grabbed the woman's arm and, with effort, turned her onto her side. Blood smeared her face and mask. Madelaine wasn't sure she breathed.

"*Nom de Dieu!*" Madelaine called at the top of her voice. "A woman is hurt!"

No one came to help her though the crowd pressed close enough to jostle her as she stood over the fallen woman. Frantically, Madelaine bent and took hold of both the woman's wrists and pulled her to the wall of a building. There was an ugly gash across the unconscious victim's cheek.

"Help!" Madelaine cried. She put two fingers into her mouth and whistled piercingly.

Faces turned her way.

"I need a doctor," she cried. "Send a doctor. A woman's hurt."

Nobody offered a hand, though they couldn't miss seeing the helpless figure at her feet. How was it possible such a thing could happen? Weren't these her own people, Creoles? Why didn't anyone help her?"

Madelaine didn't know how long she crouched over the bleeding woman before she slipped into a numbed lethargy, rousing only now and then to call for help, for a doctor.

It seemed an eternity until, like a miracle, she saw the crowd parting before her like the Red Sea at Moses' command. A man on a horse rode through and stopped in front of her.

He slid from the saddle and knelt beside the unconscious woman. He wasn't in costume and wore a wide-brimmed hat.

"I'm a doctor," he said.

"Thank *le bon Dieu* someone sent you," she gasped.

"What happened?" he asked, his fingers gently examining the injury to the woman's face.

"I don't know. She fell down. I saw a man step on her."

He bent over the woman. Madelaine leaned back, easing her cramped muscles.

"I'm going to put her on the horse," he said, "for I've got to get her out of here." He spoke French with an accent, Madelaine noticed wearily.

"If you'll let me help you up first so you can hold her—I'm sorry about the saddle, I'm afraid you'll have to sit astride—I'll lead the horse."

Madelaine looked straight at him for the first time. She

lifted her mask to make certain of what she saw because she couldn't believe her eyes.

Beneath the hat was red hair tinged with grey. Blue eyes stared back at her.

"John Kellogg!" she cried.

Chapter 26

MADELAINE stared into her vanity mirror with dissatisfaction. Was it only yesterday she'd thought she looked youthful? Josefina, arranging Madelaine's hair, shook her head.

"I like to never seen such goings-on," she said. "That lady's husband and all."

"I'm glad she wasn't seriously hurt," Madelaine said.

"She be carrying a scar down her face, be reminding her for a long time. Fighting ain't worth getting scarred."

"It was the crowd," Madelaine said. "Most everyone was having a good time and so nobody noticed if one or two people were in trouble."

"I heard him say she be running off from him, that's what, because he don't be wanting to dance no more in Mardi Gras, cause he be wanting to go home."

"Well, she's safe now," Madelaine said, tired of the conversation.

John Kellogg had brought the woman she'd rescued to the La Branche townhouse. Once she'd roused enough to tell him her name, he'd summoned her husband, who'd taken his wife home.

"And the *American* doctor be back in New Orleans," Josefina went on. "Sure be strange, what can happen."

It hadn't seemed strange at all to see John once more. His auburn hair was streaked with grey and there were lines in his face that hadn't been there fifteen years ago, but he looked much the same. How very different she must look to him, Madelaine thought. She leaned forward and examined her face.

Josefina caught her eye. "Must be he coming here again, that doctor," she said.

Madelaine flushed, immediately angry at herself for doing so, annoyed that it mattered so much how she looked to John.

"Dr. Kellogg will be here for dinner," she said sharply.

This is ridiculous, Madelaine told herself in the early afternoon as she wandered from one room to another, making certain everything was perfect. You've been nervous and jumpy all day, like a young girl waiting for her first suitor. Didn't he hesitate before he said yes to your dinner invitation? He's coming out of courtesy, nothing more.

There'd been no time to exchange confidences last night. She only knew that John was in New Orleans. He could be married, his wife somewhere else, he could have a dozen children. She mustn't behave like a silly child.

John arrived after dusk, wearing a long broadcloth coat over a sapphire blue vest. She thought he looked handsome and distinguished. She'd changed her gown three times, finally settling for an off-the-shoulder gold satin with puffed sleeves and a beribboned belled skirt. Now she wondered if she should have dressed more simply.

"You haven't changed at all," John told her. "Still young, still beautiful." He smiled. "And just as willful. I can't think what your brother was about, letting you parade alone in the Mardi Gras."

"Guy's in France." Madelaine looked down at her hands, lowering her voice. "He's gone to bring back Cecile. She—she's almost fifteen."

"Cecile?"

Madelaine raised her head to meet his glance. "My daughter. She's been raised there. Guy and I will present her in New Orleans as—as our *cousine*."

It was a relief to get the words out, to be able to say the truth to someone.

He nodded. "You've never married?"

"No."

"Nor have I."

"Will you be staying long in New Orleans?" she asked, hoping he couldn't see the pulse throbbing so rapidly in her neck.

"I've settled in Louisiana." He paused while Leroy entered with a decanter of wine and glasses, setting them down on a low table.

Madelaine nodded and Leroy left as silently as he'd come.

"Shall I?" John asked, tilting his head toward the wine.

"Please."

John poured a glass for Madelaine, then one for himself.

"Now that I'm finally retired from the army, I've begun a practice in Baton Rouge," he said. "I came to New Orleans to see old Dr. Goodreau—he's confined to bed these days. I was just down the street when word came that a lady in the parade needed help."

She leaned forward. "I couldn't believe it was you. It's been so long. I never dreamed I'd see you again."

"And how do you feel?"

Madelaine blinked. "I'm quite recovered from last night. Only a few bruises . . ."

"No. How do you feel about seeing me after all these years?" His gaze was intent. She'd forgotten how very blue his eyes were.

"I—I . . ." She touched her face, knowing the blood was rising to her cheeks. "I'm happy."

John stood, crossed to her and reached out. She put her hands in his and he pulled her to her feet.

"I've never stopped loving you," he said. "You drew me

back to New Orleans, even though I promised myself I'd stay away."

Her breathing quickened. "John," she said. "Oh, John . . ."

His lips were warm against hers, his arms held her close and an almost forgotten desire flooded through her body. After a few moments he eased away enough to look down at her and she saw her own need reflected in his eyes. There was nothing in the world for her but John Kellogg.

Taking his hand, she led him up the stairs to her bedroom. When she bent to turn out the lamp on the night table, he stopped her.

"I want to see you. I've waited a long time, Madelaine."

With her gaze fixed on him, she unfastened the back of her gown, stepped out of it, removed her petticoats, stockings and slippers. She saw him catch his breath, and suddenly she felt beautiful and desirable. She slipped under the bed covers as he undressed.

His body was firm and muscular—a young man's body. He got into the bed next to her and took her into his arms, and she sighed as his bare flesh warmed hers.

It had been so many years since John had held her, thought it had never been like this. She trembled with the urgency of her desire for him.

He was gentle but insistent, caressing her into eager passion, controlling himself until she was wild with the need for him, until she arched to him, calling his name. Then he thrust within her, his abandon releasing her rapture. She clung to him, sobbing in fulfillment.

"Madelaine," he said later, "why do you weep?"

Tears in her eyes, she said, "I've never been so happy. Oh my love, my love . . ."

"But you're crying."

"Because I love you. I loved you before, but I was too proud to let myself realize how much I needed you. You offered, but I—I couldn't go to you. I didn't understand then that a woman could love more than once." She touched his face. "What a silly girl I was. So much time we could have spent together has been wasted."

"We'll waste no more." He held her to him again. "We'll marry as soon as possible. Why not tomorrow?"

Madelaine began to laugh at his impulsiveness, then sobered, remembering her brother.

"We must wait until Guy returns from France," she said.

John held her away. "Why?"

"Because he's my brother—the head of the family—and you must ask him for . . ."

"Madelaine! We aren't children, we're both over forty."

She bit her lip. "But I've never married, John. It's considered proper. Besides, I—I couldn't have the wedding without my brother here. Guy and I have been through so much together. Please understand."

"I don't understand." He sat up. "I can't understand. In one breath you tell me you've loved me for years and in the next you say you can't marry me unless Guy approves."

"It's only a matter of months before he'll be in New Orleans. We've waited all this time—surely we can wait a little longer. Besides—" she lowered her lashes—"isn't it possible to meet like this in the meantime?"

John got to his feet and began to pull on his clothes. "I asked you to be my wife, Madelaine, not my *placee*. A wife is what I want, what I need. Will you marry me and come with me to Baton Rouge or not?"

She sat up, clutching the bedclothes about her, chilled to the soul by his anger. "I—I can't until Guy . . ."

"Damn Guy!"

"John, please . . ."

He grabbed his coat and turned toward the door. As he opened it he looked back, hesitating a moment.

"I won't be visiting New Orleans again," he said. "Goodbye, Madelaine." Then he was gone.

She stared at the closed door, unbelievingly. "No," she whispered, tears rolling down her cheeks.

John Kellogg didn't call on her again.

Spring passed, and summer. Then fall. The cane harvest was in before Guy arrived at Lac Belle with Cecile.

And with *Madame* Tanguy La Branche, his wife.

Madelaine was stunned.

"You're very welcome," she told Fabrienne, "but I had no idea my brother intended—that is, I didn't realize . . ." she broke off, staring at the elegant French woman, marvelously dressed in what Madelaine knew must be the very latest Paris fashions. She felt dowdy by comparison.

She resented her attention being taken by this astounding development for she wished to concentrate on her daughter, standing wide-eyed beside Fabrienne, her quiet beauty eclipsed by the older woman.

"You're Cecile," Madelaine said.

Cecile's hazel eyes examined her. "I'm pleased to meet you, *Cousine* Madelaine," she said politely.

Did she look like Philippe? Madelaine couldn't see the resemblance except for the hazel eyes. Cecile did show a certain likeness to the little daughter of Annette-Louise and Nicolas. A Roulleaux look?

"Cecile is a La Branche through and through," Guy said heartily. "Aren't you, *'tite?*"

Cecile flashed him a shy smile. "If you say so, *Cousine* Guy."

Guy patted her cheek, then put his arm about Fabrienne. "Here's my prize, Madelaine. I know you'll love her as I do."

"Of course," Madelaine murmured, not at all certain she'd manage such a thing.

"I shall put myself into your hands completely," Fabrienne told her, "as I learn to run Lac Belle properly. Vineyards I'm used to, but sugar cane I know nothing whatsoever about. Nor Negro slaves."

She means to become the mistress here in fact, Madelaine realized, taken aback. Senalda had never really managed the plantation house at La Belle, but this wife was different. Very much so.

"But all that can wait until I'm rested from the journey," Fabrienne went on. "Perhaps we can begin the day after tomorrow?"

Madelaine nodded. "I'm sorry to keep you standing about like this. It's the surprise." She led the way up the stairs, wondering how she'd tolerate another woman as mistress of Lac Belle, the house that had been hers ever since it was built.

As the weeks passed, Fabrienne took over more and more. As she has a right to do, Madelaine reminded herself. She spent as much time as she could with Cecile, but the girl was reserved and shy with her, despite all of Madelaine's efforts to become better acquainted.

Fabrienne called Madelaine into the morning room late in January of 1833. "Please sit down," she said. "I think we must have a talk."

Madelaine did as she was asked.

"You should try not to overwhelm Cecile with attention as you do," Fabrienne told her. "I know how you must feel, but the child thinks of you as a stranger. And, I must remind you, as a *cousine*."

Madelaine stared at her. Guy's told her, then, she thought, a tightness in her chest. I mustn't think of it as a betrayal, she's his wife, she has a right to know, I suppose.

"I didn't realize I was upsetting Cecile," she said.

"It's only natural for her to confide in me," Fabrienne said. "Cecile and I had a chance to become close aboard ship and, too, we're both French. She's a lovely girl—a tribute to the nuns who raised her."

Resentment knifed through Madelaine. I wanted to keep my daughter with me, she thought. Fabrienne makes it sound as though I abandoned her.

She lifted her chin and looked Fabrienne in the eye. "I imagine you've come to think of Cecile as your daughter," she said, "since you've never had children of your own. Perhaps that will change when you and Guy . . ."

"We will have no children," Fabrienne snapped, interrupting Madelaine.

She can't be more than forty, Madelaine thought. How is she so certain? "Be that as it may," she said, "everything at Lac Belle belongs to you by right of marriage. Everything except Cecile. If, as you say, she still feels insecure in New Orleans, I shan't push her."

"That's all I ask," Fabrienne said.

Madelaine didn't believe her, but murmured a polite leavetaking and left the morning room. She has Guy, she has Lac Belle and now she wants Cecile too, Madelaine thought angrily.

"Looks like that little girl be a sweet child," Odalie said to Madelaine. "She come visit me, she be bringing sugar candy for me and talk so nice. You take care she don't do like you, be unhappy."

"Cecile isn't much like me," Madelaine said.

"All women be pretty much the same when it do come to men. You see she be happy."

"That's all I want for her."

"All I wanted for you," Odalie said, "Didn't do no good. It be true, just the same, I be dying happy now I know the child."

"You're going to live to see her married, just as I told you."

But Odalie did not. She died before Mardi Gras and Madelaine wept as she watched the black woman, who'd been a mother to her, laid to rest in her own vault. Now she had no one.

Madelaine tried to tell herself she didn't expect to see John again, but ever since Guy's return she'd hoped she was wrong, that John would come calling. After she buried Odalie she buried that hope as well. A leaden weight rested in her chest when she thought about him. Seeing Cecile's obvious preference for Fabrienne only increased her distress.

As the year passed, Madelaine grew more and more despondent. She tried to busy herself with the quadroon children she taught, but her pleasure in their accomplishments dwindled.

At Cecile's coming-out ball in December, Madelaine had no choice but to let Fabrienne take the credit, for her brother's wife had arranged everything—even choosing Cecile's gown at the girl's request.

I'm nothing to anyone, Madelaine thought. Not even to myself.

John Kellogg had never come back to New Orleans. Even though he was in Baton Rouge, there might as well be an ocean between them as the few miles of the Mississippi that separated them.

She'd never felt so alone in her life.

Cecile had looked forward to her coming-out ball, but at the same time she feared it. She smiled up at her partner, her lips stiff from polite smiling. So many strange young men, so many hands touching her, whirling her about in the waltz.

She didn't like being handled by men she barely knew, even in the formal patterns of a dance.

Cousine Fabrienne had gone to much trouble to arrange this ball. Cecile adored Fabrienne and *Cousine* Guy, too. She tried to like *Cousine* Madelaine, but it seemed Madelaine always wanted to hug her, to touch her in some way.

The Sisters in France had been kind, had loved her, but they didn't show fondness by hugs and embraces. She still wasn't used to these open displays of affection. Fabrienne understood, but Madelaine didn't seem to.

Yet none of them, neither the Sisters nor her New Orleans *cousines*, ever answered her questions about her parents, always putting her off.

Who was she?

"You're the most charming girl in the room," her waltz partner said.

Cecile blinked, coming back to where she was.

"Thank you," she murmured.

He was handsome enough, this dark-eyed man who

276

twirled her about the floor so expertly. Why couldn't she respond to him?

Cecile glanced swiftly about the room yet one more time, although she was quite certain the only man who counted wasn't here.

"Is there anyone you'd like to invite who I've forgotten?" Fabrienne had asked her before the ball.

Cecile had shaken her head. How could she tell Fabrienne that, unknown to any of her *cousines*, she'd met a man with eyes the color of sable, a man whose touch she welcomed? Whose kiss she longed for? How could she tell them that the man lived at En Dela—and that his stepfather was *Cousine* Guy's bitter enemy?

Gabriel Davion hadn't been invited to Cecile's coming-out ball.

Chapter 27

On November 13, 1833, Guy sat in his library looking out at the setting sun. He'd been sick with worry that Fabrienne or Cecile, as newcomers to Louisiana, would be visited by Bronze John when, in September, New Orleans was decimated by yellow fever deaths. This epidemic on top of those hundreds struck down since June of the dreaded cholera.

He'd kept everyone at Lac Belle, avoiding the city. Indescribable horrors went on in the town when the epidemic was at its peak: Bodies were thrown into the river, bricks tied to their feet to weigh them down; loved ones were buried within the courtyards; interments took place at the cemeteries continuously throughout the day and on into the dark by candlelight. There were so many deaths that the corpses were stacked like wood—not even in coffins—and in deserted hospitals the wards were filled with putrifying bodies, the doctors and nurses dead beside their patients.

A dark, thick cloud from the constantly burning tar and pitch fouled the city, making breathing difficult. The cannon, fired along the streets in the hope the gunpowder would purify the air, caused numerous fires. New Orleans had taken on all the aspects of Hell.

Only two days earlier, a terrible rain storm had roared in from the northwest with violent winds and lightnings, sweeping away the deadly miasma, washing the streets clean, and ridding the city of not only Bronze John but the cholera as well.

Just the same, he'd forego use of the townhouse this year, Guy decided. Lac Belle was safer. Thank *le bon Dieu* his beloved Fabrienne had been spared. Cecile, too, of course, but Fabrienne was his first concern.

The wisest thing he'd ever done was to marry Fabrienne. She managed Lac Belle with a flair that all the Creole women tried to copy. She'd taken Cecile to her heart and guided the girl suitably, while at the same time encouraging her to come out of her shell of shyness. And she loved him in every way a woman should love a man.

If only he could be as happy about New Orleans. It seemed to him that, while he'd been in France, the city had puffed up like a poisonous toadstool, expanding up and down river and all the way to Lake Pontchartrain. The railroad from the city to the lake was finished, some four and a half miles of track.

"We have the first railroad in the entire south, the first one west of the Allegheny Mountains," Rafe had said proudly. "Think of it!"

Guy hated to. He hated the puffing engine, nicknamed "Smoky Mary" because of the black smoke that choked the countryside every time it passed. He disliked the crowds who rode the cars to the lake of a Sunday. No longer was Lac Belle isolated and peaceful. The epidemic had stopped the excursions for a time, but they'd resume. He was certain of that.

So many steamboats crowded the levee that at night their lights made it seem as if a *faubourg*, a suburb, had sprung up atop the water. He'd sold his interest in the boats, finding them no longer either amusing or a source of pleasure.

279

Ocean-going ships, their grey sails furled, mingled with the white steamboats on the river. The waterway both up and downriver from the city was as clogged and busy as the streets.

And the attitude in the city was changing. Never before had the Creoles despised the free blacks. They'd viewed them with some wariness since, after all, one knew who they'd side with if a slave rebellion erupted, but there was no hatred. If a free man of color didn't have the right to vote, he did have many other privileges equal to any Creole.

Now restrictions and curtailments were enacted monthly, it seemed. The new laws changed Creoles' attitudes toward the free coloreds, even though the laws were initiated by *Americains*.

Damn the *Americains* for their increasing control of everything. It was ruining his city.

He hadn't yet spoken to Madelaine about giving up her teaching of the free black children. She'd stopped during the epidemics and he was determined she wouldn't start again, for he'd been warned that his sister wasn't safe with those "nigger brats."

He sighed. She was safe enough with the blacks. It was the whites who threatened. She'd been so despondent lately he'd put off the task, but he must tell her soon. Order her, for she had no choice.

He'd do it right now, this moment. Guy rose and crossed the room, only to be interrupted by Leroy's appearance in the doorway.

"A man say he want to see you, *Monsieur*."

Guy sighed. He'd heard the knocker but assumed the visitors were ladies for Fabrienne. "Who is it?"

"He say he be *Docteur* Kellogg."

Guy's eyes widened. "Bring him here," he said.

He greeted John warmly, offering him brandy.

"No, thank you. I try not to drink when I'm working."

"Perhaps coffee?"

"Yes, I'd like coffee."

"Did the army send doctors in to assist during the epidemics?" Guy asked.

John shook his head. "I'm no longer in the army. I did come down from Baton Rouge to help out. I've set up a practice there. Thank God the worst is over. There hasn't been a new case of yellowjack or cholera since the storm."

"You'll be returning, then, to Baton Rouge?"

"Yes. I've done quite well since I've been there. I have no worries about money."

"I see." Guy was puzzled. Why did Kellogg tell him how well he fared financially? It seemed unlike the man. "Well, the best of luck for the future," he added.

"Thanks." John took a deep breath and sat straighter in the chair. "Since I'm quite securely established," he said, "I've come to ask you for your sister's hand in marriage."

Guy couldn't speak, so shocked was he at this request.

"Madelaine thought it best that I speak to you first," John said, eyeing Guy levelly.

Rage gathered Guy's wits together. "You marry Madelaine?" he cried. "An *Americain* marry my sister? Never! Never while I live!"

Guy glared at John Kellogg. *Dieu*, he'd challenge this presuming *Americain*. They all wanted to take over. The city. The Creoles. His very family. This one, at least, wouldn't get what he wanted.

"*Docteur* Kellogg," he began stiffly, "I . . ."

The door flew open and Fabrienne rushed in. She ran to Guy and grasped his arm. "You must come immediately," she cried. "Hurry!"

Guy, who'd been about to order her from the room, stared in alarm.

"What's the matter?"

"Don't ask questions, come quickly!" she demanded, tugging at his arm.

Guy allowed himself to be led toward the door. He'd never seen his wife so distraught. What could be wrong? Was Cecile ill? An accident?

Fabrienne shut the door firmly behind them and took

Guy to the foot of the stairs, where she stopped and faced him.

"Don't you dare to challenge that man to a duel," she said. "He wants to marry your sister—in the *nom de Dieu*, let him! I understand he's perfectly respectable, a doctor. What's the matter with you that you. . . ?"

"Enough!" Guy roared. "How dare you interfere in my affairs?"

"*Pouf,*" she said. "They're my affairs, too. Madelaine is terribly unhappy at Lac Belle, for I've taken her place in the house and she has nothing to do. Would you deprive her of the only man who's likely to offer for a forty-five year old spinster? Don't be a selfish fool."

"Fabrienne . . ."

"I shall be very angry with you if you don't listen to me," she said. "Being a man you'll do what you wish, but I warn you—a challenge is not in any of our best interests. I'd like to be friends with Madelaine, but how can I when she resents me so? If she marries the feeling between us will improve."

"A wife doesn't interfere in these matters," Guy repeated, shaken more than he liked to admit by what Fabrienne had said. Was it true?

"You'll destroy Madelaine if you persist in your wrongheadedness," Fabrienne insisted.

"She can't be seriously interested in marrying this—this *Americain*," Guy sputtered. "It's true that Kellogg has mooned after my sister in years past but she—never!"

"I love him!" As she spoke, Madelaine hurried down the stairs toward them and Guy realized she'd been waiting on the landing above. "I love John Kellogg and I'll marry him if he wants me. I saw him come to the door. Did he ask you?"

"I was barely in time to stop the challenge," Fabrienne put in. "If you hadn't told me who he was, Madelaine, then we'd be facing a duel. As it is . . ."

"A duel?" Madelaine put her hands on her hips, glaring at her brother. "Tanguy La Branche, how could you? I'm through with you and your ridiculous adherence to the past. I'll leave this house immediately and I *will* marry John, whatever you say."

Guy looked from one to the other of the women, over-whelmed. What were things coming to when women spoke so to the head of the household?

Madelaine, starting for the library, turned again to her brother. "Furthermore, it's cruel of you to deprive Cecile of the truth about her birth. I can see she's unhappy not knowing. It's wrong to lie to her. As for me—John knows, has known from the beginning about Cecile and he loves me anyway. What do I care how others feel?" She whirled and ran from Guy.

Fabrienne shrugged as if to say—you see?

Guy, anger and frustration roiling inside him, strode to the front door and, banging it behind him, flung himself down the front steps and into the evening.

Louisiana wasn't what it had been, nor was the world. Everything he could see as he stomped along the road toward the city spoke of growth, of the cursed *Americain* drive for progress, no matter who or what got trampled in the process.

Like the Creoles were being trampled.

He'd fought to have the French language retained in the legislature and had won. Now he foresaw a day when there'd be no battle because everyone would speak English and the reason for allowing the French to be spoken would disappear.

How well he remembered the census of 1810 when he and his friends were amazed to realize that 76,556 people lived in Louisiana. What had the count been in 1830? Nearly 216,000, as he recalled. New Orleans had suffered the most from this influx. Not only *Americains*, but Irish, Italians, everyone came to the city, changing its ways.

No longer could he stroll along the old streets, Royal, Orleans, Esplanade and recognize everyone he met. Strangers sat in the coffee houses and thronged to the French Market.

The trouble with the *Americains* was that they saw no need to take the time to enjoy life, to meet with friends over a brandy, to talk of nothing in particular. They hustled about their business, always in a hurry. Why couldn't they see that business should be transacted leisurely, by friends, in a coffee house? Why didn't they see that it should be a part of a man's life, but not his reason for living?

Guy walked on through the city, coming at last to the levee, where he stood staring at the double-stacked steamboats gleaming white against the dark water. Thousands of them came to port here in a year's time. Thousands. He could remember when there was only one steamboat on the Mississippi. Fulton's *New Orleans*.

Still, he couldn't really complain about the boats. The side-wheelers had done well for him, and he'd helped proliferate them. His profits had climbed, too, from the increased population, more shipping, the need for more sugar. If the war with the British had almost destroyed him, the *Americains* must be given the credit for making him many times as wealthy a man as his father had been.

But the quality of life suffered. He watched the bustle of men loading boats on the wharves. Once he'd have thought the port crowded if three ships were at anchor at the same time. Now they were so busy they loaded day and night.

A light flashed across the dark sky and disappeared above the southern horizon. Like one of the rockets we waited for that night at Chalmette, he thought. So many of us, all trusting Jackson to lead us to victory.

The great General Jackson—he was President Jackson now, yet he never forgot a man who once fought with him.

Why do I complain? he asked himself. Hasn't my life been good, all in all? I have a loving wife, even if she does try to manage me as well as Lac Belle. The plantation is greater than the old one at La Belle, certainly more profitable.

In France, Denis is a son to be proud of, as Anton will be, in his way. My niece, Cecile, is all I could have wanted in a daughter. I only regret that I didn't listen to Madelaine and bring her to live with us sooner.

Madelaine. Did I destroy my sister's life? Poor Philippe—I never intended to kill him. What did I intend with John Kellogg? To rid myself of all *Americains* by running a rapier through one of them?

I must try to put a good face on this marriage, whether I approve or not. I don't want to lose my sister. Fabrienne is right, Madelaine needs to have a husband. If she loves Kellogg, why not let her be happy? Yes, I can agree to the marriage.

Cecile is another matter. I can't agree she be told of her birth. My sister calls my respect for the past ridiculous. She can't see that a man must be faithful to his roots, to what has gone before. Cecile will remain a La Branche. She must never know she bears the hated name of Roulleaux.

His thoughts broke off as another meteor arced overhead, closely followed by two more, then a dozen others, so many of them after a time that he stood watching in wonder as the entire night sky blazed with shooting stars. The heavens became a mass of coruscating brilliance.

"The stars do be falling clean out of the sky!" a black shouted from the wharf.

Other voices echoed his, cries of fear, of awe.

Guy stood transfixed. *"Dieu,"* he whispered reverently.

He'd learned about meteors at school in France, but as he stared at the flaming skies he felt as the Negro lader did. *The stars were falling.*

Le bon Dieu had given him a sign that he, too, must change as his world was changing. The time had come to forget what was outmoded and hold only to the true.

He turned and started back to Lac Belle, the heavenly display still flashing above him. Every Creole must become my brother, he told himself. Together we can hold our place in New Orleans, only together can we enjoy the benefits the *Americains* have brought, while we try to keep from being swallowed up by them.

They're like the Mississippi, the *Americains*, sweeping everything along in a swift current. But we Creoles can be an island in that river, can remain ourselves if we join together as one. Be *Americains* and yet Creoles, too.

Guy stopped to borrow a horse to gallop home. It was late, but not too late, if he hurried. He rushed into the house.

"Cecile," he called. "Cecile! Come to me, immediately."

Madelaine ran into the foyer, Fabrienne behind her.

"Marry him," Guy said to his sister. "Marry your *Americain* with my blessings." He embraced her, then let her go to turn to his wife.

"Where's Cecile?" he asked.

"Here I am, *Cousine* Guy," Cecile said, appearing at the curve of the stairs. "I was about to retire."

"No," he said. "Fetch your cloak and bonnet and come with me."

All three women stared at him as if he'd lost his mind.

"My eyes have been opened," Guy said. "The stars have fallen from the skies to show the last of the La Branches his way. *My* way. Tonight I'm bringing Cecile with me to learn of her origins. Hurry, now, and get ready, Cecile. I am taking you to meet your uncle—your Uncle Nicolas Roulleaux."

THE DONNER PEOPLE

by Lee Davis Willoughby

From the moment in 1846 when the Donner-Reed wagon train set out from Springfield, Illinois, the men, women and children of the party suffered from a plague of bad luck. There was illness, inept leadership and bitter feuding.

By the time they reached a certain storm-battered pass in the high Sierras, all the ingredients of horrifying tragedy were in place. There were heroes, such as the patriarch, George Donner, and the bold young mountain man, Thornbird. There were heroines, such as tiny, spirited Tamsen Donner, and the bewitching Liza Williams.

But there was also among them a madman, a murderer—and those accursed ones who, when disaster, starvation and death struck, would break the last human taboo.